BRASS NECK

**BOOK THREE OF THE SADDLEWORTH
VAMPIRE SERIES**

Brass Neck by Angela Blythe

Book 3 of the Saddleworth Vampire Series.

First Edition.

Please contact me for details of future books at
http://www.angelablythe.com

Published by Willow Publishers.

Other books in the Saddleworth Vampire Series

Sticky Valves

Silver Banned

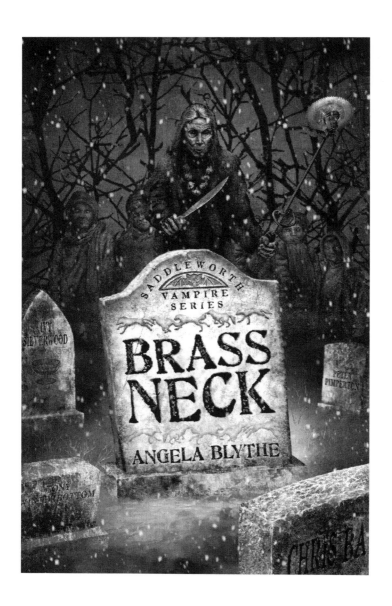

Table of Contents

Brass Neck

1 – Church

It was mid-morning – this was now the time that they went to bed. It had been a long night, and they stunk of petrol, and fire and death. Joe added another couple of marks on the wall in marker pen, another seven lines to the five bar gates he was making. Now there were six groups of five exactly. It was Craig's house. He had told him it was okay. Exhausted but content, they drifted off, either going over the previous night's triumphs or planning tonight's escapades.

Rick was pleased with how it had gone down. About 8 pm the previous night, he had spied the two vampires entering the cold and lonely home. They suspected that it was vampire footprints that they had spotted, not human. Fresh footsteps made at night after a snowfall. The four of them had listed the houses, and now it was time to check this one out. The two creatures dragged a dead old man behind them. An actual old man. This was their nest, they weren't up for sharing with the others. It was too late to save him. That was clear. In fact, they could be saving him from a fate worse than death. Maybe they would be turning him. Making some kind of unholy trio.

Rick trained his binoculars on the creatures. They needed no light as they entered the house. He wondered if it had been one of their homes. It was clear they had been using it for a while.

He put down his binoculars and rubbed his eyes. This was normality. Life was a day to day slaughter of the undead. Until they were gone, Rick would carry on.

'Right Joe, we're up. There's two of them, just gone in. With a victim.'

'Whole?'

'Yeah, so we need to check him out. I think there's a possibility we could have to slay three of them.'

Joe moved Darren's foot with his boot.

'Lazy arse, get up and bring your lighter,' Joe said. Craig was already awake. He watched the street below, whilst Rick had been on his binoculars. It wouldn't do for them to be spotted up here.

They put their coats on and picked up the weapons. Opening the door, Joe looked both ways before coming out and beckoning the others. This was always the most dangerous part. There could be any number of them walking about. This was the time they were the most active – after their long sleep. The men couldn't wait for them to get sleepy just before dawn, however. That would mean they could only sort one nest at a time. At the rate they multiplied, that would never work.

The road was clear – they quickly crossed it and went over to the shelter of the garden opposite. The house they needed to get to was the other side of this, and there was no way through the gardens. The four of them would have to be out in the open for between five and ten minutes. Walk down the street, on the pavement, round the corner and back up the other street. Vulnerable but it had to be done.

As quickly as possible, they moved along the road, single file, against the hedges, on full alert. Before they knew it, they were there. Success.

Banging and moaning could be heard inside. These days, the suckers didn't have to hide. Being silent wasn't as much fun. They weren't checking the windows, they never did. Why should they when they were the top of the food chain?

The four men moved up the path. Joe used a series of hand movements now that they had devised. He told Darren to stay by the front door outside. They would try to run, these creatures always did. They weren't set up for battle. Usually caught unawares they had done their fighting for the night, got their meal and were now absorbed in their work.

These creatures were in the back of the house. Rick had seen them. Joe hoped to pick at least one off before they got to the front and the prospect of the human roadblock that was Darren.

Joe held his axe ready, Craig had a pickaxe. Rick opened the door, and they rushed inside. He followed with two knives. The two creatures were in the kitchen above their prey. One knelt and fed from one arm of their victim, the limb lifted for easy eating. The other knelt too, but he was leaning forward, his head buried in the old man's stomach. He was chewing on something gristly in there, and it made a squeaking noise. His head was facing away from the door as he had turned it to use his back teeth on the tough old man. The burrowing vampire didn't see them, but the limb eater did.

He gave an almighty scream and leapt up. The other vampire, in a feeding frenzy of orgasmic proportions, didn't move. Joe buried his axe in the limb eater's chest, and he ran forward. Craig caught him in the skull with the pickaxe, his eyes rolled towards the strange object that now stuck out of his head at the side. Craig's pickaxe was stuck. It was far better to swing than Joe's axe, but it nearly always got wedged in somewhere. Rick stepped forward with the two huge knives. He crossed his arms, then drew the blades sharply across the vampire's throat, the soft flesh yielding effortlessly. The monster was now three-quarters decapitated. Craig pulled his pickaxe back and twisted, swinging it out. This successfully ripped off the head and removed it from the pickaxe. The vampires head flew in the corner, the teeth gnashing for the briefest moment.

Now the burrowing, gnawing vampire finally noticed and jumped up to a squatting position. There seemed to be an area in the corner where the vampires had been urinating, and this is where the limb eaters head had landed. In a massive pile of black vampire piss. The burrower scuttled across to the corner, with its friend's head, it screamed and clicked its tongue. It was calling for help.

In two strides Joe was upon him, the axe coming down once, expertly and finally. The squatting body relaxed. The legs languidly sliding forward on the pool of black filth. Darren ran into the back. He could tell by the noises that two of them had been slaughtered.

'How are we doing?' He asked.

'Two down. They weren't turning this one. Poor bastard.' Craig said.

Darren looked down. Entrails were pulled up over the man's face where the burrower had discarded them. It looked like he was ashamed to be found in this state of disarray. Hiding his eyes behind his intestines.

'Torch it, Darren. The whole lot. Before they come,' Joe said solemnly. Darren was in charge of that part, he knew the best places to put the petrol. The curtains, the bed, the sofa. That was all he had to do. He set them off one by one, joining the other three outside.

'Where's the next one?' Craig asked.

'There's one near the bottom of Springmeadow Lane. That's an obvious one. We'll do that next. I've got a spy hole,' Rick said.

'Eyes peeled on the way,' Joe said.

Lisa wished she had a dog. Yes, it might draw their attention to her, if it barked, but it would also bark if their attention had already been attracted to her. As it was, she had a whole tank of tropical fish and cat, who was always out. Not much good.

She was holding out. Help would come. It had to. What other options did she have? She hadn't seen anyone living for a couple of weeks. There had to be other people. She just knew there were. Living exactly like her. Dividing their food up. Keeping their lights off at night. She had braved a local delicatessen twice. Gone out through the back garden, jumped over a couple of low fences, pushed through someone else's hedge, then out on another street. Hopefully, that was enough to put them off her scent or not track her footprints in the snow. And they hadn't. She had brought back as much as she could. The cold meats were all off now, but there were copious amounts of olives, which luckily, she liked. There was chocolate and luscious ground coffee in bags.

Tonight, it looked like her luck had run out. Either they had tracked her back to here, or just by chance, they had found her. In the dark, she had been watching through the upstairs window. What else was there to do? She never made noise. The television or radio would never go on at night, she didn't to attract them by sound. She didn't even flush the toilet at night.

Lisa didn't really know what attracted them, was it noise, or smell? Or both. Could they even smell or hear? Maybe they just hunted by sight or heat from a house. Every day was a blessing. A day nearer to a rescue.

The lone vampire came up her path and sniffed the air. So, they could smell. He purposely moved forward. His head raised ever so slowly. He pointed upwards at her, then removed his backpack. It wriggled. Opening it quickly so she could see, he shut it again and smiled a humourless smile and shook the backpack. Lisa's cat howled inside it. He beckoned with one finger. She came.

When she woke up, she was in a dark room. Lisa was quite sure that she wasn't a vampire. She was breathing and was desperate to use the loo. She moved her hands, to raise herself. They were tied to a bed. Her wrists and her feet. A needle and clear pipe came from her inside elbow. There was no-else in the room. Lisa relieved her bladder. She had no choice.

As Wee Renee's group, the remainder of Friarmere Band, walked up to the church, they squinted against the sun that had risen behind the building and was now blinding them. The trees twinkled, ice-kissed. The sun shone through the crystals, a rainbow of tiny lights across the virgin snow. The footprints still undoubtedly led to this place.

After the silence of Friarmere, they could now hear the distant sound of children's voices. The friends were tired and would be glad to be inside. Terry was the first to see faces looking out of the stained-glass windows. Adult faces, that he did not recognise. They continued for a few more steps towards the building before they observed some movement and heard noise from inside the church. The large iron hasps began to turn, and the massive church doors swung open. Standing in the entrance, champing at the bit to get out were their old friends. Sue, Liz and Laura ran out to the group to help them with their luggage. Andy and Danny stood at the door grinning.

'What are you doing here so soon?' Sue asked as she hugged them all.

'That's for telling over a pot of tea,' Pat said. 'Let me get in and rest my trotters.' The whole party went inside, dragging the sledges with their contents up the icy stone steps. Andy and Danny came behind them, shutting the cold and danger outside.

'We're so pleased to see everyone's safe,' Wee Renee said breathily. The warmth of the church immediately flushed her cheeks. All of a sudden, they felt hot and began to disrobe. None of the new group had noticed that Carl and Gary were missing. The church smelled slightly of furniture polish, wood and strongly of wet children and old hymn books.

As well as everyone they knew, there were the children, twenty-four to be exact, and four other people inside. One of these was St. Dominic's Vicar, Father Philip. Terry asked where he should put the sledges and Our Doris said she needed somewhere she could put Haggis's bed, food bowl and water. Father Philip told her to lay it all underneath the font, which was currently adorned with an evergreen arrangement for the festive season. Our Doris got to work instantly and began to take Haggis's coat off. Bob came to help her as he had missed Haggis. Haggis for his part was quite confused but immediately recognised Bob, so became excited and very licky. The new group looked weary. Laura could tell something terrible had happened to her friends after leaving them in Melden.

'Not to be rude, but I could murder a cup of tea,' Pat said.

'Oh, and me,' Kathy added.

'I'm sorry, we can't offer you tea. We've run out. But we have coffee,' Tina said.

'I'll have a mug of that then, please.' Pat said sniffing.

'Coffee for everyone?' Tina asked cheerfully. They all nodded to her saying, *yes, please*. 'And a biscuit?'

'Have you got anything a bit more hearty?' Wee Renee asked. Tina looked down.

'We have run out of everything but biscuits, just this morning. I was going to try and go on a shop run in a bit,' Liz said. Then in a lower voice, she said, 'kids can't half get through some stuff.'

'We've bought some food from the shop. We couldn't fit loads on though because the sledges were pretty full already,' Kathy advised Liz.

Tina put the kettle on, and the new guests sat down. Our Doris instantly had to tell some children not to start chasing Haggis round the church, which upset them.

'He'll widdle everywhere if you do that!' Our Doris shouted. Pat laughed, but Tina flared her nostrils over the coffee cups as she filled them. Her lips were very tight, and she had angry spots on her face. Laura noticed this and gave a wry grin. It didn't look like Tina was impressed with Our Doris at all. She seemed to have taken offence to the word *widdle,* although there were worse words for it.

The other ladies from the church and Father Philip decided to try and occupy the children again after the excitement of the new arrivals and the dog. They got crayons, paper and glitter out of some drawers and began to tell the story of the journey to Bethlehem.

All the travellers sat as comfortably as they could on church pews and were given their drink and a rich tea biscuit. It was quite warm inside the church, and after taking off their coats, they now had to take off their cardigans and sweaters.

Kathy and Sally were happy to see each other and wouldn't leave each other's side. Kathy had wound herself up all the way about something happening to her sister, so there was a general outpouring of tears and emotion from her. Sally was fussing around Terry, asking how he felt, if he was tired and how the antibiotics were working.

'Oh, we've had a horrible time,' Kathy told her sister. 'But I will let you hear the whole story. Looking back, I don't know how we got through it,' Kathy said, her eyes full of tears.

Sally had been worried about her sister and father in Melden. She thought now, they had experienced even worse than she had imagined. Wee Renee congratulated Sue on her choice of sanctuary, which she felt was safe, warm and well away from the road. An excellent decision! Sue felt unexpectedly touched to have been praised by Wee Renee.

'I always knew Bob, got his brains from your side, Sue,' Wee Renee said. Excitedly and without being asked, Bob began to tell the new additions about the confrontation with Adam and how he was no longer human.

'We are surprised that he is even *that*. We were told by a certain person after you left, that Adam and all the other children had been eaten up by the old band!' Wee Renee informed them.

'You were told that he was dead? By Anne? No, he's definitely a bloodsucker. Either she was lying, or Norman had lied to her,' Andy said.

'Aye, she said they were all pushing up the daisies,' Wee Renee said.

'Where was the bugger?' Pat asked.

'Sitting on the stage in the school, in the dark. Adam was so white he was nearly luminous,' Bob replied. 'He's become quite cocky.'

'I bet he has!' Our Doris said. '*Cocky* seems to be one of the personality traits of these suckers!' She was currently putting her cowboy boots upside down on the radiator to dry out.

'I'll knock that out of him!' Pat commented.

'I think it's all talk though,' Bob said, who continued to tell them how he had asked the children if Adam had bitten them or any of the others. From what the school children in their care had told him, Adam was strictly forbidden to bite them. He had to look after them in fact, and keep them away from the blood-drinking vampires. Bob admitted he was quite proud of Adam for that, no matter what else he was up to.

'In the whole scheme of things then, he's a good egg,' Wee Renee concluded.

'Tell us then, why have you come back so soon? What happened?' Sue asked.

'I'll have a swig of my coffee first then you'll hear the whole tale,' Wee Renee said. She took a sip, stopped, raised her eyebrows and quickly took the cup away from her lips, placing it back down beside her.

'Have you got any squash?' She asked. Our Doris frowned and took a sip.

'It's bloody Camp Coffee!' Our Doris exclaimed.

'Of all the dirty tricks!' Pat said.

'And all the biscuits have gone. We're on dry Butter Puffs now. Beggars can't be chooser's,' Tina said.

'I'm not begging. Better off outside, taking our chances with dishy Norman, than drinking Camp Coffee and eating dry Butter Puffs!' Pat exclaimed. 'That barrel of eyes is getting more and more inviting!'

'Aye,' Wee Renee said sadly.

'A barrel of eyes!' Bob exclaimed.

'Human, complete with tendrils. In a liquor,' Terry advised them, shaking his head.

'Awesome!' Bob said, eyes wide with astonishment.

'Still better than this dishwater!' Our Doris said tapping the coffee mug the clasp of Haggis's lead.

'Well!' Tina said. She had been to get coffee and had actively chosen that brand. She loved it. Luckily, Father Philip was showing some of the children the Nativity Scene, so didn't hear the conversation.

'We'll nip out soon, for some more stuff. We know where there's some,' Wee Renee said.

Wee Renee started to tell them the story of her friend, Carol and why she hadn't come with them on their journey. Pat told them of the happenings the following night. The admission by Anne that the message was false and their friends were in a trap. About Anne's vampires, everything that had happened in the house, including the gruesome murders of Rose and Natalie. Terry also had to inform Sally that her Uncle Malcolm had also been revealed as one of Anne's monsters, and Kathy had killed him after seeing the full and surprising transformation that he had embraced. Pat also told them about the poisoning of the wolves and the final disposal of them.

Our Doris assured Beverly that her mother, Jennifer was okay, but Anne's favourite wolf, Sophia, had bitten Uncle Freddie. The rest of the group were very concerned at this, as they all loved Freddie without exception. Terry described how mangled Freddie's hand was but that he had supplied him with copious amounts of antibiotics and painkillers. However, given the circumstances and timing of their immediate departure, Freddie was still in shock and too weak to make the journey. Brenda and Jennifer had stayed behind to look after him, in the safest place in Melden, Jennifer's walled and gated house.

Liz and Andy told the arrivals from Melden, whilst hysterically laughing, about their encounter with Michael Thompson. They thought they had left him with a lot to explain to Norman. Everyone from Friarmere Band found this humiliation of their dishonoured ex-bandmate, hilarious.

It was at that point that Wee Renee noticed that Gary was missing. Sue regretfully told them about the bargain that Gary had made with Norman and that Carl had gone voluntarily to sort his wife Kate out.

'You mean Gary sacrificed himself, so the children could go free? And to release him, Norman Morgan wants me and Pat?' Wee Renee asked.

'That proves it, Rene,' Pat said.

'What?'

'I knew he had the hots for us two. I suppose he wants some kind of sexy orgy with us,' Pat said. She licked her lips. 'I will have to advise him that mine has had an *out of order* sign on it for years!'

'Pat, he doesn't want that kind of penetration!' Wee Renee said harshly to her best friend.

'Oh,' Pat said. All her ideas of being Norman's dream girl vanished into the ether.

'Don't you get it. Norman wants us to be one of his beasts!'

'Does he now? The cheeky swine! He can forget that!' Pat exclaimed. After explaining to Pat, what Norman expected of her, Wee Renee reflected on Gary's situation. She was shocked and quite upset about their friends being isolated and vulnerable to *The Beast*. Pat thought long and hard about it too.

'Drat, and I had saved Carl all the foil off my chocolate teacakes, poor lad,' Pat said.

'Yeah, keep it for him, Pat. We are getting them pair back soon. I'm telling you,' Danny said determinedly.

'Count me in,' Pat sniffed.

'Oh aye, and me. I've not seen gizzards for at least twenty-four hours,' Wee Renee said.

'Decapitation sounds in order,' Our Doris said, who was applying some cyclamen pink lipstick.

'How's your toe problem, Terry?' Liz asked winking. 'Shall we have a chat about it? Me, you and Our Doris?' This was a signal to have a little get-together about how they felt being on the antibiotics. It also informed the rest of the party that the six people from St. Dominic's were unaware that they were infected. Since their arrival, no one had thought it right to tell them of Liz's condition. The three of them wandered off to the Lady Chapel, where it was quieter, and they could have a full and frank discussion about symptoms, dreams, increased energy and the colouring of Our Doris's water.

Michael was back in The Grange after his trip to the shop earlier. Thinking about yesterday, in hindsight, he had been fortunate with Liz and Andy. They could have knifed him or anything. They certainly had enough reason to. Yes, he was a little bit thankful for that. Maybe they still had the teeniest soft spot for him.

Tonight, he was in for another night of repairing vampires. This seemed to be one of his jobs now. It was definitely one he liked to *beef* about too. Why should he have to patch them up? He didn't know a thing about vampire husbandry. Plus, that green powder that was inside them certainly got in your pores. Michael had cleaned motor oil out of his fingers better than he could remove this. It wasn't even sticky. It was like a dark green dye, and it smelled of them. Mouldy.

He had asked The Master for some Marigold gloves. Not only did The Master not know what he was on about, but he also denied his request. Michael said he wanted them for hygiene purposes. So that he didn't infect them. Like a surgeon. He couldn't tell him the real reason. The Master wasn't buying it, however, as he said it gave an ill vampire comfort to feel warm flesh moving inside them. This made Michael feel weird, and he wanted to do this even less now.

Tonight's delight was a vampire that had got caught on some barbed wire fencing. The flap of skin started at her armpit and came down in a diagonal direction to her hip at the other side. A perfect triangle that flapped over her hips, just about eighteen inches long. What was he supposed to do with that? They didn't heal. Their flesh was too weak to hold stitches. He was thinking of taping her up somehow. They certainly gave him a challenge every night. Maybe, when Michael told The Master his news, about seeing Wee Renee and Pat, his plans would change. He was sure they would do. Then he thought about dealing with the flap of skin at a later date. It would be dryer, deader and greener then. Yes, probably better for Michael that he dealt with that tonight. He would tell The Master after.

Michael was also getting a little bit sick of eating mutton. He could go to the shops and get the odd tin of beans every so often, but it was not very exciting. Fresh food was getting scarcer.

Norman surprised him with what he thought would be a fantastic treat for any human. A whole wheel of Gruyere, Swiss cheese. While Michael enjoyed this gift, after the third day of cheese, he was extremely thirsty and also very constipated.

He had gone into the shop to see about getting some cereal, but it had disappeared. Where, oh where was some roughage? He had ended up getting a bag of frozen sprouts. They were gently cooking in Norman's kitchen. The whole Grange smelled of them. Well, he had to do *something,* didn't he? This condition was unfortunate enough to have for the short term. If it got serious, he couldn't visit the doctor. For some reason that he couldn't work out himself, The Master had many boxes of Weetabix that were under guard. When he had asked for an explanation, The Master pulled him to one side and whispered what he used them for. Apparently, he mixed the wheat biscuits with blood and meaty bits, then dried them. From what Michael gathered, this ended up as a cross between a black pudding, a cereal bar and human jerky. Great for long journeys. He mustn't be needing his human trail mix today, as hadn't asked Michael to bring him any of these along with the scoop of imported Eastern European eyes.

The new additions to the church dished out what they had taken from the shops off the two sledges. This mainly consisted of individual boxes of cereal, longlife milk, biscuits, angel cake, strawberry jam and tortillas. Kathy said this was as good as bread, which the shop had none of.

Father Philip blessed it all and the food was gratefully received by both children and adults. Laura had had the idea of raiding people's houses after the incident with Mary. After all, they didn't need the food, and once the house was safe, they could see what was in their freezer and cupboards. There would be more food in all the houses in Friarmere than there would be in a couple of shops. They might even find some survivors. The rest of the group thought this was a brilliant idea, although Father Philip and Tina said that they still considered it stealing, even if it was from the dead. The raiders should write a note in each house, list what they had taken, and why. Giving thanks and a future promise of repayment.

Pat nodded at them. There was no way she was writing notes. Father Philip and Tina hadn't been on the front line. They needed to *wake up and smell the coffee*. And fast!

Wee Renee brought up the question about the fires. What did they mean? No one had any idea, even the people that had remained in Friarmere. The ones that had been in the church had gone there almost immediately after this group had travelled to Melden. Everything had deteriorated very rapidly after the Civic Hall Concert and groups of vampires walked around the village continuously throughout the night. They had seen them.

In the daytime, they knew that some vampires were lying in wait at the back of shops in the dark. Some of the women from the church had tried to visit the grocery shop and had seen the sleeping vampires. Of course, the most recent additions to the group knew this was a fact. They were too scared to get food. Instead, they had raided their own food cupboards, and their own neighbour's houses that they knew were away. The churchgoers had done the best for themselves.

Tina and another lady named Joy wanted to know everything about the vampires and the creatures in Melden. They said they had only seen them from a distance, so wanted all the details. It appeared that Tina, in particular, was extremely religious and when they told her about the more horrific details, she kept saying, *'just give it up to the Lord'*. In the space of ten minutes, Pat and Our Doris had heard her say it about thirty times. They were already sick to the back teeth of it. Even though she had to keep saying this, to get through the worst parts, it didn't stop her from constantly being nosy and asking for more. When Wee Renee told her, most sensitively about a succubus being in the village, Tina closed her eyes and breathed deeply.

'I think I need to meet her. I could bring her back if anyone can,' Tina said, fully confident. 'Then I could give the couple counselling. A way to move forward, for *Carl* is it?' Tina said this and looked upwards.

'Aye, I think you haven't been listening to a word we have said,' Wee Renee said. 'She is one of his Beasts!'

'Then it will be a bigger triumph for me, won't it?' Tina said, in an arrogant way. Pat took an immediate dislike to her and loudly sniffed.

Our Doris stopped rubbing her bunions and looked up at them all. A big smile spread across her face.

'I think you should, love,' she said, taking a swig of Malibu from her hip flask. 'Go for it!'

2 – Tripe

The group decided that a trip to the shops was in order and began to make a list of what was needed. Some children had colds, so medicines were required. Also, the stress of the situation meant that quite a few of the survivors had headaches off and on.

They needed food and lots of it. Food that needed little or no preparation and heating. Our Doris wanted to stack up on Haggis's dog food. Necessities were required. Coffee, milk, toilet rolls and more squash. Also snacks and sugary items, to keep people going, so crisps, chocolate and biscuits. That giant list would do for today. A few of them wanted to get out, escape the confines of the stuffy church and take in the minty air.

Our Doris, Haggis and a lot of the others who had just got there, needed to relax and declined unless they were really required. Our Doris's bunions were throbbing. Wee Renee who was still full of vigour, said she wanted to go out again and show them where to get in and to stretch her legs. Of course, this meant Pat went too.

With all the shopping required they would need to take three sledges. Our Doris's large metal one was still packed high with items from Melden. They thought that time wasn't on their side, so left it at the church.

Liz wanted to go and visit Ian in his shop and see what had been going on with him. Although some of the others did not want to see anything like that, she said that she had to go and see about getting him down, and away from his current final resting place. This, Liz felt was still *saving* him, especially as she hadn't had the chance when he really needed to be saved. It was something she had to do, and Liz felt her mind wouldn't rest until she did it. Danny said that he thought it would be better to burn Ian's body instead of letting him be a regular meal for something.

'I'll add,' Pat said, 'that to leave Ian like that, is like treating him like dog muck that your own dog has left in the street. You see to your responsibilities. No matter how distasteful they may be.' Some of them didn't' really get what Pat was on about, but generally, her word was final. So that was that.

They dressed warmly and set off to the shop. They had just over three hours before dark so could not hang around too much. Tina went with them, which Our Doris was relieved about, but Pat wasn't because she felt she couldn't speak freely with Tina about.

Wee Renee asked Tina who she thought had been setting the fires that they all had witnessed. Did she think it was the vampires or remaining humans?

'Well, to destroy property, or even the countryside is evil. We never had fires before. Only on Bonfire Night that is, and when the farmers set fire to their own land, of course. So, I would say, it is the vampires.'

'Aye, I see what you are saying, but fire can also be cleansing. Or a signal. I cannae make my mind up Tina. If it is humans, well, it means so much. There is life left in Friarmere.'

'*We* were life in Friarmere, and we weren't setting fires. Even if it isn't humans, it doesn't mean there isn't life. I say *just give it up to the Lord*. We will find out in time.'

'Aye, in time we will,' Wee Renee replied. Liz spoke to Pat about what food they could make for the kids. Pat didn't like to spend a lot of time preparing food and thus had become very inventive in her food combinations. These wouldn't be to everyone's tastes, however. Sue, Tony, and Bob were giving marks out of ten for each of her suggestions. A lot of them involved brown sauce and treacle. Bob thought he would try the spam marinated in black treacle, but leave the pilchards mashed with brown sauce. Danny hoped it didn't snow again – ever. Andy said he could murder a hot bath and a night watching the football. It was a beautiful bright day. It wouldn't snow today. The sky was azure and cloudless. Birds sang and in another time, in another year, this day would be perfect.

Terry had remained back at the church. He felt burdened with the conversation of Wee Renee and the single midge. Or faerie, as she called it. He confided in Our Doris, Sally, and Kathy. What did they think?

'I don't have any doubt that she was talking to one,' Our Doris said. 'How can you go through the last few weeks and not realise there is more in heaven and earth than we know.'

'She is as honest as the day is long,' Kathy said.

'And she doesn't have a crazy bone in her body. She is just more attuned to it all than us,' Sally added.

'If you are right, then there is hope for us. But I wish I was still living in ignorance. If destiny is known. *Our* destiny. What we will do, and the results.' He paused. 'Known by *supernatural* beings. I don't know what to think. Probably I am saying I feel like a puppet, dancing to their tune. No free will of my own. I don't like it.'

Tony, Sue, and Pat looked in at the Pub windows and were delighted to see that the fire was lit, and that the barmaid was sitting in front of it, looking bored but alive. Danny tried the door, but it didn't open. Wee Renee knocked on the window, which made her jump, she waved at her and pointed to the door. A smile instantly lit up her face, and she rushed to the door.

'Come in, come in,' she said.

'Just for a minute, we are on a mission,' Liz said.

They trooped inside, the familiarity instant and welcoming. Tina, tight-lipped said she would wait outside for them. Pat heard her say the word *immoral* under her breath. She apparently had issues with public houses.

'Fair enough. Hope you don't freeze,' Pat said with a sniff. Andy shut the door behind them to keep the warmth in, and they stood in a semi-circle looking at their new survivor.

'Time for a quick one?' The barmaid asked.

'No love, thanks. The clock is ticking towards darkness, always,' Wee Renee replied.

'How've you been?' She asked.

'Shit.' Pat said grimly. 'But we've been to Melden and got back at least.'

'And solved the mystery of the wolves, you will be glad to hear,' Wee Renee said with a smile. They gave her an abridged version of events in Melden. Her eyes were wild and terrified. She did not utter a sound during the five minutes they took to tell their story.

'What's gone on here, while we've been there?' Pat asked.

The barmaid told them everything she knew. Which wasn't much more than they knew already. The vampires roamed the streets at night. They were the only beings out. She hoped for survivors, but Wee Renee and the group had been the first she had seen since the day after the Civic Hall Concert. Wee Renee asked her opinion on the fires, which the barmaid was not aware of. Although she said, she hadn't seen the vampires with any fire, to torch buildings. So, she had to think it was humans.

'If you survived, and the people in the church, there could be pockets of people everywhere. We could trace the footprints to each house, but there isn't enough time,' Laura said.

'That's the next step,' Bob said. 'Check out each house. If a bloodsucker is in there, we stake them and prop the door open. We have already started that campaign. If humans are in there, they join us.'

'What about you? Do you want to come with us?' Laura asked the barmaid.

'What about keeping the pub open?' She asked them.

'Open for who? You have had no one in here for days. You are lonely and if they choose to get in here at night, they can. They can just smash the windows and be in. Gobble you up,' Pat said.

She looked around at all their faces. They waited for her reply. She couldn't argue with their reasoning. Vulnerable and lonely, she was keeping this pub open in the daytime for nothing. It was time to call it a day.

'Ok, I will. I need to get some stuff, though.'

'No problem. We have got a couple of errands to run. Lock the door again, get your stuff and we'll be back,' Andy said.

Once outside the pub, they happily told the news to Tina.

'Oh, er, we should have probably discussed it with Father Philip and the church committee, before inviting her. I don't know about this.'

'That's a fine attitude,' Pat said. 'Tell you what, kiss my arse!'

Tina's lips got even tighter. The compulsion to have a go back at Pat was powerful, but she managed to keep it in. They all stormed off, without another word. She trailed behind them all furious.

When they arrived at the grocery shop, they found that someone had been in since they had been there only a short while ago. It looked different already. Some of the food had been thrown on the floor. Who could this be? Sue thought it could be more villagers, survivors and was heartened. Liz was sure it was Michael Thompson. She said the disregard of the food generally told her it was someone who thought they were above everyone else. Someone who only cared about themselves.

Against Sue's best judgement, Bob was taken in to see the bucket of eyes. As only Wee Renee had seen them previously, some of the others wanted to see the spectacle too. Bob poked his long knife sharpener in the bucket and stirred it around. He had the idea that eyes might be a top layer to some other horror's underneath, like a trifle. But only more eyes bobbed up to see them. Sad and sightless.

Quickly loading the sledge's up with various items in bags, they were soon ready to go. They had no cooking facilities at the church, so everything had to be able to be eaten cold. The only kitchen equipment they had was a kettle, so they had put lots of packs of noodle snacks, on the sledge. Hopefully, this would be a little bit of warm food for the children.

Liz had picked up a box of instant hot chocolate sachets for the children to warm them up.

'Oh no. Not them. Put them back,' Tina said.

'Why?' Liz asked.

'They will make a right mess of the church cups. I'm sick of washing them as it is.'

'Put them in!' Pat growled. And as if to add fuel to the fire, she picked another box up, waggling it at Tina, before saying 'keep your nose out!' She put it in the bag with Liz's first box.

There was a bag full of cold remedies, tissues, ibuprofen, and paracetamol. Pat was hopeful that the chip shop was still opening at some point in the day, but the others knew it wouldn't' be. She had put in a bottle of malt vinegar on the sledge along with the other food.

The chip shop was indeed closed, and they moved on to Ian's butcher's shop. From a distance, they could see the door was ajar. Liz sighed at the thought of them just helping themselves to him. They prepared themselves for what they would see. On finding Ian again at the back of his shop, they could see a lot of footprints that looked like the same shoes coming in and out. They were mostly dirty ones, but occasionally they had stepped into the blood.

Most of Ian's stomach was missing. The flesh was gone from both arms and legs. The bare bones were meaty red. Disturbing. Most of the feet and hands remained, which made the stick arms and legs more horrific. His head was intact but now bloated and misshapen. Ian was in the most dreadful state a human being could be in. A couple of them tried to get him down. This wasn't easy as he was hanging above them, and even with parts missing, he was very heavy.

In the end, Pat held him around the waist and Danny, and Andy managed to unhook him, the hook retaining a triangle of flesh. As he flopped forward over Pat, his head lazily fell over her shoulder. Fluid began to drip onto her coat, from the shoulder to the hem. Tina's eyes widened behind her. The group had found large packs of carrier bags in the back and a roll of bin bags which they had opened out. Legs akimbo, and with the help of Tony, Danny, and Nigel. Pat laid Ian on the bags and covered him up. For the moment they had nowhere to keep him and no way to transport him. Their sledges were for provisions. Our Doris's metal sledge was large enough to carry him on, however. They would call again tomorrow, put him on the sledge and maybe burn him. At least he was not hanging up there any longer.

'Ian has dripped down the back of your coat, Pat,' Sue said gravely.

'I thought he might,' Pat shrugged. 'It had to be done. It'll wipe down. I'll get some toilet paper later.' Tina wrinkled her nose in disgust. Wee Renee took it all in and looked across at Laura and Liz, who was already looking at her. This was a volatile situation with Tina. Unless everyone trod on eggshells, it was going to *bully off* with Tina. And very soon.

Adrian was still on the floor, mainly just an uneven pile of powder in the rough shape of a human. Inside his clothes, he had deteriorated rapidly. The dust that was once Adrian had been trodden in too. Smeared across Ian's white tiled floor.

Tina was horrified at the sight of Ian. She had not really wanted to see him but needed to see it for herself, to believe it. They had been protected from this kind of sight inside the church, but this was the reality, instead of what she thought was happening. Tina closed her eyes finally and said. *Give it up to the Lord.* Wee Renee nodded, but Pat flared her nostrils. On their way out. Pat noticed that in one of his refrigerated cabinets, Ian had a large tray of tripe. Pat was very fond of tripe. Wee Renee liked a small piece but not as much as Pat. She took a bag from behind Ian's counter and emptied the lot into it.

'This has cheered me up no end. I knew there was a reason, I picked up that malt vinegar!'

Tony looked at his watch and said they had just over an hour to get back to the church, before darkness. They had considered breaking into the chemist's next door, but now that would be out of the question.

They called at the pub, and their new addition joined them, wearing a large hiking backpack.

'Hi, I'm Lauren,' she said, holding her hand out to Tina. She was the only person Lauren didn't know. Tina grunted back at her and walked off, leaving Lauren still holding her hand out. Sue linked her by one arm and Liz the other, smiling.

'Looks like you've encountered our resident dickhead,' Pat thundered, as she stomped in front of the three women.

'What's that down the back of Pat's coat?' Lauren asked.

'Don't ask,' Wee Renee said as she followed Pat. 'Just don't go dipping your bread in it!'

'Interesting,' Lauren replied. Wee Renee said she wanted the others to quicken their pace, as it would be nice to feed the children before it got dark. Of course, this wasn't the real reason. They made their way through the streets talking about the best way to dispose of Ian. As the ground was so frozen, the only possibility was burning. If they hid him, the vampires might sniff him out, as his flesh was open and reeking. On the way, Sue told Lauren about Gary and Carl. Danny was frantically thinking of a plan but said if he didn't have one soon, he would just do it. Whatever *it* was.

'Go off half-cocked? I don't think so,' Wee Renee said. 'Then we will have to rescue you as well. Slowly, slowly catch ye monkey.'

'Ok. But I hope I have inspiration pretty quickly. After we get them, where do we go from here? Do we stay in the church? Gathering survivors, killing vampires, going from house to house. Do we go somewhere else?'

'All will become clear. I think we may have to travel a bit further, that is all I know. Remember, the snow can't last forever. Once the rest of the country can get in, our problems are over,' Wee Renee said.

'Unless the rest of the country are worse than us,' Andy commented.

'Don't say that. That can't be true,' Liz said sadly.

They made their way back quickly, noticing that no-one else was on the streets. Laura looked back and realised that they were beating an obvious track to the church for Norman and his people to find them tonight.

When they got back with all the provisions, there was an awful lot of excitement about what was on the sledges. The other church ladies pulled Tina aside and wanted to know everything that she had seen.

At one point the others could tell that she was complaining that Pat had told her to *kiss my arse*. They all went very quiet and looked over at Pat in unison. Pat was eating three segments of a chocolate orange at once, so wasn't bothered. She drew herself up to her full height and stared back at them, waiting for the challenge, but there was none.

'Take no notice of them, Pat,' Wee Renee said.

'Bloody sanctimonious harpies,' Pat replied. Lauren introduced herself to all those who did not know her. Sally and Kathy made her very welcome and said she could sleep near them if she liked, as there were quite a few snorers in the group. It was now a noisy place with so many adults and children there, and it was hot. Bob was given the duty of walking round to every adult in the church and telling them that there would be a meeting later when the children were asleep. There was a quieter area in the Lady Chapel. It would be held there. Although the church was warm and safe, still the only seating was wooden church pew's, which were quite uncomfortable. Father Philip had walked around counting when they were out, and Our Doris suspected he was *losing it*. He now solved this mystery by announcing that there were enough prayer cushions for everyone, so at least they could use them as pillows.

Wee Renee thought that Father Philip should be trusted with the knowledge of Liz's, Terry's and Our Doris's condition. He was horrified that they had been violated in this way and very sensitive to their situation. When Terry explained the *miracle cure* that he had stumbled on, he was so pleased for them, and it gave him hope for the future of any further unfortunates that got in Norman's way.

3 - Little Michael

A few of the children seemed quiet and withdrawn. Kathy, Sally and a couple of others were trying to cheer them up but were having no luck. Sally couldn't imagine what must be going through their heads after being ripped away from their parents, kept captive in the dark for a few days, and the constant threat of what they would think of as *monsters*. When all the food was unpacked, the ladies spread it out on one of the tables. There were lots of instant noodle pots, tins with ring-pull tops, instant mashed potato, snacks and dried fruit. One boy, who seemed to have some influence over the group, was excited by the noodle pots and once he chose one of them, every other child followed suit.

'Put the kettle on,' Our Doris laughed, 'and be prepared to boil it about twenty times.' Not only was boiling water required for the noodle pots, but the adults were desperate for a drink too. The group that had returned from the shopping expedition were cold, tired and badly in need of refreshment and warmth.

Soon, all the noodle pots were filled and the drinks made. They had found some longlife cake in the shop and taken about ten of them. Some of the children had a piece with their orange squash, the adults with tea or coffee. Everyone was quite content. Bob had enjoyed an evening meal of cold stewed steak and instant mashed potato. The steak, he shared with Haggis, who sat beside him, his dark brown eyes enormous, his tongue occasionally licking his lips, begging for the tasty treat. Wee Renee told the adults to be on their guard about what would happen tonight. They knew they were not in the clear even in this sanctuary. It wasn't clear what the vampires could do, as they were surrounded by the consecrated ground. One thing was for sure, Wee Renee knew that they would come and their recent trip to the shops would have laid fresh tracks and a recent scent all the way to that church door. It was agreed that at least one person was to be on watch at all times.

The best place for this was where the original occupants had first seen them. Standing on a pew and looking out of the stained-glass windows. The windows were quite high in the church, and even on a pew, there was only perhaps a head and shoulders visible from outside.

Tina took first watch. She seemed to think that as she had discovered this method, she should do it first. Even though the others objected and pointed out that she had only just got in from a mission, she would not listen.

For a short while, there was nothing different in the cold crisp night outside. Her breath misted on the chilled glass, and she continuously wiped it down with a tissue.

Then there came a sound weird and unexpected. It was the sound of a handbell, which rang out cold and lonely in the winter night. Someone was walking through the village, ringing a bell. As there was only room for one person to see out of the window that faced the road, and Tina was there, they all rushed forward to see what fresh terrors this brought.

'Who is it?' Terry asked. Tina did not answer, her eyes scanned left to right outside frantically.

'Who is ringing the bell? What are they doing out there?' Father Philip added.

'It's a man carrying a crate. He is out at night, so obviously must be one of them. He certainly looks pale.' She said as he walked into the light from the street lamp.

'Could I have a wee look instead of you, please Tina. I might recognise him,' Wee Renee asked. Tina made a disapproving sound but got off the pew. Wee Renee quickly jumped up there, but the man had passed behind some laurel bushes then and was moving away from them. They could still hear him ringing his bell, but there wasn't a possibility that they would see him now unless he returned, so they were none-the-wiser.

'How long has this been going on? Why didn't you tell us?' Our Doris asked.

Father Philip said that this was the first time that he had heard the bell and the others agreed. The group that had been there the previous night had not heard it either.

'The village is seeing more changes, then. We need to find out about the bell ringing man,' Wee Renee said, in a curious voice.

Keith had important snippets to impart to Michael. Always the sadist, Keith would enjoy this. He still tormented Michael as much in death, as he had done in life. Whenever he saw him wandering around the school, Keith took that as a golden opportunity to pounce. Michael had been forbidden to look in on the two humans that the vampires had imprisoned in the classroom. Norman thought he might feel sorry for them. Or they would persuade him to let them out, as Michael was the only one about in the daytime. The Master thought they could manipulate him as he described Michael to the others as *soft-brained*.

Being a semi-undead suited Michael, he had upped his style. He had found a blue blazer from a house they had raided, which now, never left his back. After rummaging around the Headmaster's desk, he had come across an expensive silver pen, and pencil set – a recent Christmas gift from a thankful parent and these were displayed in his breast pocket. He brushed his hair back now, as Norman did. It had not gone unnoticed.

Keith saw Michael walking towards him *peacocking*. Keith had a plan to twist the knife today. Luckily for him, Michael brought up the exact subject that Keith wanted to talk about.

'Have you seen Kate, Keith?' Michael asked. 'I thought we could have a bit of the date tonight I'm feeling quite, you know, full of energy.'

'You make me sick,' Keith snarled at him.

'Very nice, that is. I must say!' Michael replied. 'What about – Hello Michael, what a wonderful day!' Keith curled his lip at this comment from Michael.

'Do you know who one of the hostages is?' Keith asked.

'No,' said Michael, 'tell me. You know I love gossip.'

'Well I shouldn't really tell you,' Keith said, 'and you haven't heard it from me remember?'

'Yes, of course. I am the soul of discretion.' Michael replied quietly, moving closer to Keith.

'Promise me,' Keith said

'I won't tell, I promise,' he replied. Pushing his glasses up his nose to look at Keith.

'It is a bloke from Melden, named Carl.'

'So?' Michael said, 'That means nothing to me.'

'Oh, doesn't it? I think you will be interested to know that he is married to a certain beauty that you are looking for right now.'

'Are you referring to Kate?' Michael asked in hushed tones, gesturing behind him with his thumb as if she was there.

'Yes, who else? It is Kate's husband coming to save her. What do you think about that?'

Michael thought for the moment, his mouth wide open. He didn't know what to think.

'She never told me she was wed!' He said breathily, shaking his head in disbelief.

'You are surprised she had secrets?' Keith asked. 'She is a vampire. We are by nature, duplicitous.' Michael took no notice of Keith's statement. His mind was elsewhere.

'I thought it was going somewhere, you know. What about *Little Michael* too?'

'Who?' Keith asked.

'*Little Michael*, you know,' he said, pointing to his groin region. Keith sighed. 'She will have to make a choice, and quick.'

'I wouldn't put an ultimatum on it. I have seen Kate's husband. She will pick him,' Keith said flatly, before walking away. As he moved down the corridor, a smile of immense satisfaction spread across his face.

Michael stood for a moment. Hmm….. maybe telling Kate to choose between them, was the wrong thing to do. Until she found out, they might still date. After that, all bets were off, and there probably would be no fun for *Little Michael* after that. Not with Kate anyway.

Carl and Gary sat in the classroom it was early evening and very dark. In there, the lightbulbs had been taken out for some reason. Gary knew that artificial light did not affect them or candlelight. He had seen them in artificial light in the Civic Hall. Adam had lit the school hall by candlelight. Maybe it was for their benefit. In a negative way, however. Keeping them sitting in the dark all night added to the horror. Either way, it had been done before they got there, so maybe this room had held some kids previously. Along with everything else, Gary thought this was just pure spite. The kids couldn't give them anything. They were a currency to Norman.

After spending the previous night stumbling around looking for some sort of illumination, they had put this matter at the top of their list for the next day. Hearing them drifting around the corridors last night, was very unnerving. Not knowing whether they would enter or not. Not even knowing if they had already quietly come into their room. The night was so long. Any form of light was better than nothing.

Tonight, they were equipped with candles. Not many. The two men had searched high and low and found some on a box placed on a top shelf, with other craft items. They would have to illuminate one at a time, which wouldn't give much light. Not knowing how many days they would be here, they would limit themselves to only certain times in the night. They had decided that ten o'clock, would be illumination time and they would blow it out at five am. With the candles, they found a small box of matches. Gary had a lighter too.

It would be several hours before ten o'clock. Early evening wasn't so bad. It had been recently light, and the worst atmosphere was when it was very late, cold, and the vampires were at their most active. They seemed to just potter about a bit after they had come out of their sleep every evening, if that is what you could call it.

The two men sat for a while, breathing in the now familiar smells of chalk, wood, new carpet and poster paint. To keep from them both from thinking about their current situation too much, Gary asked Carl to tell him about his life before with Kate. He had not heard most of the details that Carl had said in Melden. Firstly, in the Pub, and then later at the Dentist. He had had enough on his mind at that time, so when Sue told him, Kate was a wrong 'un, he took that as enough information.

Now they needed to talk. But especially Carl, after finding out that she was a succubus who had been turned by Norman, needed to sort this out. To lay all facts on the table, and to move forward. The two men sat with their bags against the wall, the windows above them, bringing in the briefest of lights. Carl's knees were bent, his hands hugging his legs. It was a defensive position. Gary sat upright, his legs stretched forward, ankles crossed.

Carl had met her at school. They had been in the same class from the beginning, but as with boys and girls they had moved in different circles, played different games in the schoolyard until High School. Once they were there and began to grow up, Carl noticed how beautiful she was. The only problem was that everyone else had noticed too. Kate, at first surprised at the attention, began to be flattered, then it was like a drug she was hooked on.

She needed the attention. For young men to tell her how fabulous she was. Even though she consented to be Carl's girlfriend as he had become an attractive young man, it was never enough. She couldn't resist a man's attention, and if Carl wasn't there, she would take it.

At first, she said she wouldn't do it again. That she was sorry. He believed in second chances so gave her one. Then a third chance. And a fourth. Pretty soon they both knew he would take her back, whatever she did. So, they fell into this kind of pattern. Sometimes it had been too serious to forgive, and they had split up. Like when all his family knew she was throwing herself at his Dad one Christmas. He had been back with her by New Year's Eve. His family hated her. Another time she had to admit that she had given him a disease. They had broken up that time too.

He had had a few friends that he could confide in. Beverly was one of them. They tried to fix him up with decent girls during the times he was not with her, but it was unsuccessful. She was hooked on men. He was infatuated with her.

All the time Gary listened, he rubbed his finger over the rough cog of the wheel on his lighter. Every so often he did it sharply so that it ignited. He looked into the flame and considered Carl's words.

'I can't be bothered with women. Honestly, I can't. I have had some experiences like yours. I've often been hurt. And I admit, I have hurt others. I am too old now and too stuck in my ways to start something new. They are way too much trouble for me. I can't handle it,' Gary said.

'I am coming around to that conclusion myself, Gary,' Carl replied honestly.

'Right mate. But the question is, what are your plans when you see her?' Gary asked. Carl sighed and took a minute to answer. Gary gave him all the time he needed.

'The more I see of these people, the more I realise that she will be a lost cause. Especially if what I have been hearing is the truth and she has been going around seducing everyone. Wee Renee says they have constant sex here, there and everywhere. Just for Norman's purposes. I don't know how many of them vampires she has done it with, and how many times she has done it with him, the head honcho. It makes me sick to think of her doing it with someone dead.'

'Yeah but she is dead too, let's be honest. It's probably not a bad thing to her,' Gary added frankly. Carl digested this thought, his eyes closed for a while.

'So, I am thinking that the only way to save her, is to kill her. I can't ever have what I thought I had and even that wasn't true. I look at the past now, and the hurt is starting to turn to anger.' He turned to look at Gary as Gary continued to flick his lighter on and off. 'I hope I'm just strong enough to do it. I think I am. I think my resolve gets stronger every hour.'

'Don't look in her eyes, mate,' Gary said, 'that will be your undoing if you do. They can hypnotise people, and you will just end up walking around like one of them, trying to bite down on me the night after. I don't think that is what you want.'

'I would rather kill myself that do that. If that happens, and I get taken over, you have my permission to deal with me harshly. If Kate turns me, please kill me,' Carl asked. Gary replied with a brief nod. 'I'm so glad that I have met you. If I had found this out on my own. If I had had to go through all this and not known you - Wee Renee, Pat, all the others, I don't know how I would have done it. If you hadn't given me the resolve to fight, then I probably would have just let her have me, as I had no understanding of all these matters before. What I have now, is hope and fight for the future. I am getting through it believe it or not. I can see the light at the end of the tunnel. I'm seeing her finally as the monster she was, even before she was dead. But I know to fully move forward, I have to do this. To end her existence. I cannot move on until she is sorted.'

'I understand,' Gary said, 'I really do.' He put the lighter down and smiled at Carl. 'Now let's see if we can find ourselves some food in here. There must be the odd packet of cheesy puffs, or something that some kid has left, that we could share.

They did find a couple of things. An apple which was just about on the turn, a KitKat, two yoghurt pouches which were unrefrigerated and went into the bin and what looked like an early Christmas present for the teacher inside her desk. A large Panettone cake in a box, with a ribbon handle. They thought about sharing it out over a few days, but Gary was sure that his friends would have a plan. Or that the vampires would bring them something to eat and drink at some point. Gary undid the box, saving the ribbon, as it could prove useful. They sat back down and began to eat the Panettone. Peeling it off in long fruity strips. It was very satisfying. They gazed upwards at the paper snowflakes that the children had mounted on cotton and stuck to the ceiling with blue-tack. They watched them twirl in silence. As they happily occupied themselves with their food, the vampires stirred in the distance. Would they be disturbed tonight? Would Kate find Carl? Would tonight be the day of reckoning?

4 - Parents

Len was thinking about Anne. Why did every family have to have one? The old saying was true, you could pick your friends but not your family, and he had chosen well. He had the best and most faithful friends that a vampire, or anyone, could ever have. They had been friends for so many years. They would be old friends to other people but to him, thirty or forty years was a short time.

Anne was trouble. Always was, always would be. Why did he have to threaten her all the time to keep her in line? As the older sibling, she considered Norman as her junior, a younger brother who was not capable of telling her what was what. So, it was left to him, and he really did not want the job. He couldn't be bothered much longer.

Why should he have to come out of a lovely evening, with his Marcel to sort her out? It would only be a week later and he would have to do it again.

Len had the idea that he only knew the tip of the iceberg too. She really was a basket case. He knew she hated him, but their upbringing and vampire law meant that she had to listen to him and she hated that.

Marcel entered and sat on Len's knee. Len stroked his leg. He loved Marcel. It had taken him so long, but he had found the perfect life. Here in this village. He loved the people, and all his special vampires were around him. No, he thought, Anne wasn't going to spoil this. It had taken too long to come together. He would have to take steps towards reining her in for good soon. Maybe in the New Year. He was having far too good a time to stop now. Let her carry on with her silliness for a little longer.

What harm could it do?

After they had all eaten, Kathy and Sally were trying to occupy the children by playing games with them. At first, they played I Spy and then musical statues. Kathy had her back to the children and would sing and then stop, spin around to them suddenly, and they had to freeze. It was hard occupying so many little children who needed their parents and had been living in terror for several days. They could tell that the children were distracted with each new occupation for five minutes, then the darkness would envelop them again, and they would lose interest.

The church had plenty of crayons and paper, which were used for Sunday school. Some of the others that did not want to play, and had been going within themselves, coloured and drew pictures quietly with Laura. She sat with them, talking but getting no reply. Laura sketched a large green Christmas tree, with lots of presents and spoke about the festive season to encourage their drawing. When she looked at their pictures, it saddened her immensely. Some drew pictures of their parents, or their house, or their favourite teddy waiting for them in their beds. Some drew pictures of Adam in the dark.

Our Doris wandered over to look at the pictures. She intended to sit with Laura and draw a picture of Haggis. When she saw what they had been doing, she went across to the table, which held their food and brought over a large tin of chocolates. Without a word, she took the tape off them, opened the lid and put them in the middle of the colouring table. A couple of the kids immediately took one. She didn't know what else to do.

Our Doris wandered sadly back to the others in the Lady Chapel. She was about to tell them about the children's pictures when Tina decided to say her piece.

'You will have them chasing after your dog again, and you won't like that!' Tina snapped.

'Mind your own business,' Our Doris replied.

'Children shouldn't have sugar at this time of night! Stupid woman.' Tina said, wagging her finger at Our Doris, very close to her forehead, as she was considerably taller than her.

'No, they should have their parents and warm beds. But we can't have everything we want, can we?' Our Doris said. The volume of their voices was increasing, and even some of the children looked over.

'You don't know anything about children! We will have to deal with it later. Just meddle yourself in your own business. Keep fluffing up your hair, *Doris!*'

'One more word out of you and you really will get it hot and heavy from me, lady. I promise you that!'

'Yes, shut your rip!' Pat shouted over to Tina.

Tina flared her nostrils and went back over to her small group. Our Doris heard the word *glamorous* said and laughed. She walked back to the food area, took another tin of chocolates and walked over to the children who were playing games with Sally and Kathy. She slowly unwrapped the tin. Keeping her eyes on Tina all the time. She loudly sang *Hound Dog*, doing a fair impression of Elvis as she did it.

The tension started to mount quite clearly when the darkness began to fall. As the shadows lengthened, some of the children got on the pews and pulled their knees close to them. They did not feel safe in the building. Father Philip tried to reassure them that they had been fine for several days and that nothing could get the children there. Wee Renee and Pat whispered in the corner. They thought that the kids probably had a good instinct about what was going on. After all, the footprints would lead right to their door. Even though Sue had needed a sanctuary for the children. What they had actually done, was jeopardise the people's safety that were already staying in the church.

As it became dark, a few of the occupants were on watch looking out for the vampires. There was no noise or movement outside, so as it looked like the vampires had not come straight to the church. As it could be a long night, the adults decided to have their food and drink. They took it in turns - eating, watching and changing positions.

Some of the older boys flocked around Bob. They saw him as someone that was just a little older than them and had been through the wars in Friarmere and Melden. He had fought in The Civic Hall, made a great journey over to the lady with the wolves and then back over here. The schoolchildren aspired to be him. They thought that some of his bravery would rub off on them. And if The Master retook them they could defend themselves or the others. The boys had meekly trailed around after Bob, hoping to absorb his heroism. One of the braver ones asked him to tell them everything so that they would be prepared. As Bob began, Tina rushed over to tell him off.

'You may think you are the golden child, and nothing can touch you, but you have just got lucky. These boys can't learn anything from you. Just because you have had to suffer it, and lose your innocence, do you think you can manage to try and keep the other boys pure and not infect them with your dark tales,' Tina hissed at Bob, who instantly looked upset about it all. Our Doris stomped up to the group in her cowboy boots, furious.

'Keep them in ignorance, you mean. That ship sailed long ago. You do realise where these children have been for the last couple of weeks, don't you? Living in a dark room, with vampires stalking the corridors. Hardly any food. No change of clothes. The reek of the monsters – and they do reek, to high heaven as well! No parents, no light, no hope. Where's the innocence there? I pity you, *Lady*!' Our Doris said.

'I've just about had enough of *you*, with your eyeshadow and your cowboy boots and your dog. You are guests here and will act as such. We control what goes on here.' She pointed her finger again at Our Doris, stabbing it towards her.

'Guests! Oh yes, it feels like it. You are one snooty bitch. I'm an adult, this place isn't Army controlled, as far as I'm aware. So I won't be told what to do by you or anyone else. And neither will he!' Our Doris pointed to Bob. 'Finally, don't ever, ever say anything about my dog. You aren't fit to wipe his arse.'

Tina started to wag her finger at Our Doris again. She wasn't licked yet.

Some of the children were starting to get uncomfortable with this. They liked both the ladies for various reasons. Two of the children, a sister and brother, left the group and climbed up to play with the nativity scene near the top of the church. Here there were animals made out of plastic. The other nativity figures and baby Jesus had yet to be placed in the Nativity tableau.

'I wouldn't do that to Our Doris, would you?' Andy asked Nigel from their seats in the corner.

'No. I think she could bring down the fires of hell!' Nigel replied, watching the argument with interest.

'Listen lady muck,' Our Doris said, squaring her shoulders to Tina. 'These are unusual times. You seem to want to keep your head in the sand, which will undoubtedly be your downfall! You go over there with your church gang and leave me, Bob and the kids alone. They are safer with us than you. We got them out of his clutches, not you. All you can offer them is Camp Coffee and a dry Butter Puff! It is our lot that are putting themselves in danger to feed everyone else here!'

The two children who were playing farmyard with the animal figures, climbed up onto the large Altar table with them. This was underneath a window near to the top of the church, and the little boy just happened to look out of it. He whispered something to his sister, and she left what she was doing, and joined him at the window.

'I'm not having it, you can shout as much as you like, you little tyrant. I have hidden all the weapons too. Those are dangerous to have near children. They will end up listening to that boy, picking up one of the weapons and play fighting. Then we will have a load of injured children on our hands. So yes, they are all hidden away from you all, hahaha,' Tina informed them gleefully.

'You stupid pious bitch,' Our Doris said. Pat stood up from where she was sitting. Putting down the tin of corned beef she had been eating, she looked at Tina gimlet-eyed and began to walk towards her, rolling up her sleeves.

'Do you remember that story I told you about, Rene. The one where I had a fight in a Fried Chicken Shop? Well, it's about to happen again,' Pat said slowly. Wee Renee made an O with her mouth. She wouldn't like to be standing in between Pat and Tina. When Pat was in full flight, she was like a Tsunami. Tina started to retreat to the safety of Father Philip and her friends.

'The problem is with your plan, Tina love, that you didn't get *all* the weapons.' Pat reached into her cleavage and took out her flick knife. She sniffed before saying. 'Get those weapons, NOW!'

Outside, just on the edge of the road, beyond the boundary of the church grounds and at an angle to the windows, where the adults watched, stood the two parents. Their skin was as white as snow, but no frosty breath came out of their mouths. Mum and dad together blinked at the two children. Mummy still wore her Christmas apron, fresh from baking cookies. Daddy looked at them under his eyebrows. Their Mummy beckoned towards them, to come outside. The children froze in fear. The father tried to catch a pair of eyes. Either would do. Then he could manipulate the children. It was The Master's orders. The two parents smiled at them, their eyes flat, cold and dead.

'I'm sad. Come home with Mummy and Daddy,' their mother said so quietly. But they heard every word. There were no other vampires with them. Not a creature was in sight. The children would be safe. They could go home with their parents and forget all this horror. Be safe and warm in their beds. Eat cornflakes and tangerines. Stay at home with their Mummy and Daddy. Wait for Father Christmas.

Surely their parents could not be the same as the people at the school. They had not seen them since they had been taken at the school concert. Their parents just hadn't known where they were or else they would have rescued them from the school.

The mother put her fingers to work. She mimed what they should do. She walked her fingers across her hand. They should walk to the door, open the hasp, run out to them. She smiled at them, to tell them that everyone would be happy if they did that. Then she and her husband eyes burrowed deep into the children's subconscious from the road.

The children looked around at the adults. All were very occupied with either looking after other children, keeping watch, or getting involved in current events. The two women had finished arguing, but each seemed to be gathering up a gang of followers for their next confrontation. Nigel was massaging Pat's shoulders as if he was her second in the ring. She was cracking her knuckles, her gaze was set on Tina.

'You've got one minute left, Stalin,' Pat shouted across to Tina. Wee Renee held the flick knife away from Pat. Over in the other corner, the church ladies seemed to be telling Tina she was in the wrong for hiding the weapons and Father Philip was insisting that she gave up her hiding place. Stubborn as ever, she refused to answer them and stared back at Pat. No one was watching them.

The children walked towards the doors. At this point, Tina realised that the whole church was against her. She gave in and told Father Philip where the weapons were, which he started to retrieve. Tina had stacked the hymnbooks on some pews earlier and had stashed them inside the hymnbook chest. Father Philip bent over the chest muttering 'blessed are the peacemakers', as he pulled out the weapons one by one so that he didn't cut himself.

Very quickly and in unison, the two children turned the iron hasps of the old door. They swung it open wide and ran out, shouting Mummy, Daddy! The cold rushed in with the danger. The older children looked up like a Gang of Meerkats, all turning in one direction. Mummies and Daddies were outside! This was the end of their nightmare; their Mummies and Daddies were here to save them and take them away from it all. They stood up and ran to the door.

The children were closer to the door than the adults were. Once they saw what was happening, they began to grab hold of the children, but some were already outside, barefooted, no coats, no protection. Father Philip ran full speed out into the church grounds after the children, his hands clutching his hair. He had to protect his flock.

5 - Doomed

By the time that Father Philip was outside, the two children were being held by their parents. The parent pulled their arms high, growling. One side of the child, slightly suspended off the ground. The foot up off the cold icy earth. They cried with the pain as their parent pinched the skin. The sister and brother now realised they had been tricked. Monster's lived inside their parent's bodies. This was the end for them. The other children were milling around outside looking for their own parents. Some were there but were no longer the loving people they had once known.

Other vampires came out from their hiding places underneath bushes just beyond the view of the church and rushed forward. They congregated just outside the church boundaries. Tonight, the snow was crunchy and the air very cold. Frosted gravestones stood amongst the inches of snow. Markers in the graveyard between them and the horde, which stood outside the gate and behind the bushes. Stephen had already grabbed an arm of a child smiling. Danny noticed the burn that he had witnessed being inflicted by Shaun. It was black, mottled, dry and ashy up the side of Stephen's face. It certainly did not look like it was healing.

Kate also had a child in her arms, and she was starting to walk away with him. The Master began to make his clicking sounds with his tongue, sensing the air. He began to laugh, as did the other vampires.

'I feel like the Pied Piper of Friarmere!' Norman shouted. Sue immediately ran out. Hers had been the first item that Father Philip had taken out of the hymnbook chest. They frantically tried to take their weapons out when they had seen the children running. Sue had a large knife that she held before her with both hands. It was one that Nigel had given her from his kebab shop.

She ran towards Kate, out of the church boundaries and into the street, trying to hack at her neck with the knife, the opposite side to the child that Kate held. Kate only had one hand free as the other was holding the child. She fiercely dodged Sue's blows. Managing to grab Sue on occasion who pulled away fast. Kate switched hands. Now holding the child by the hair. A trickle of spit dripped down her face.

Danny went to attack Stephen who had crossed one arm around his child so he could not run away. He would not be allowing his evening meal to escape so easily. Nigel saw that Stephen looked formidable and went to Danny's aid. He had his trusty skewer and a knife to attack the powerful vampire.

Sally ran down towards Sue and Kate. Of course, she knew who and what Kate was, and had vengeance on her mind, for Carl. She had packed her backpack with *interesting things* before she had left Melden. A lot of these were items from around the home that you could use as weapons. She held a candle lighter and a can of hairspray. When she got three feet away from the two fighting women and wriggling child, she stopped suddenly, ignited the candle lighter, with its trigger and held up the hairspray.

'Let him go!' she screamed.

She held up the two items as a warning to Kate, Sue looked around and saw what Sally was about to do. Kate either didn't remember what the two things would do together, didn't know what they did, or didn't care. She frowned at Sally, utterly bemused with her statement. Then smirked and began to lower her head to the boy.

'Sue. Move!' Sally shouted, and Sue stopped trying to fight Kate and let Sally take over. The boy was on the opposite side to where Sally stood, and she pressed the button on the golden can of hairspray. With a loud whoosh, the candle lighters flame ignited. The graveyard was illuminated, and everyone looked towards the improvised flamethrower. Kate ran – fast, into the night. The child stood alone, untethered and safe from his attacker. Sue grabbed him to take him back.

Norman looked around at the panic, the chaos. He loved it. This was so much fun. He just knew he was going to get what he had come for. This was going to be an excellent night.

Stephen was fighting a good fight. He was ducking and leaping out of the way of two attackers. Danny and Nigel, both powerful men, were attacking him with their weapons. Sometimes they would feel their knives catch on something. A part of Stephen or his clothes, but they were making no impression. The problem was that they were in the darkest area outside. Furthest away from the streetlamp, no moonlight and dark bushes surrounded them. He was dodging every blow and still managing to keep hold of the child. For one brief second, Danny and Nigel both attacked his head with their weapons. He dropped quickly, and their weapons clashed together, like an enormous set of cymbals, the sound rang through the graveyard. The vibrations coursing down both men's arms. Stephen threw his head back and laughed.

Tina and Father Philip were still trying to round up screaming children that were running around the graveyard. Some were just outside the church gates, looking for their parents. As they caught them, they shoved each one into the church grounds, where a few of the others still were. Tina kept shouting *we are all doomed*, which at least was a change from *give it up to the Lord*. Pat thought whatever Tina said was never very constructive, so looked in her direction and sniffed.

Diane went for Wee Renee who had come out of the church boundary. She had her machete, the cheese knife still lay at the bottom of the hymnbook chest in the corner. Our Doris ran out. Her sword was nowhere to be seen. It wasn't in the hymnbook chest. Tina had hidden it somewhere else, and how she needed it now. She was outside, trying to fight and had no weapon. What on earth could she use? She bent over and took her boots off. The cowboy boots with the very hard heels. These had been wonderful when she used to go line dancing, and now they were going to be used for a very unorthodox purpose. She held one in each hand, by the top of each boot. Running towards Wee Renee and Diane's fight outside, she lifted both arms up and out wide. Wee Renee was trying to cut the vampire, but Diane was undoubtedly springy. She jumped and twirled and bent unnaturally backwards, evading Wee Renee's machete as it whistled through the night. Our Doris ran behind her. Diane was concentrating on Wee Renee and how talented she was. Diane did not see Our Doris come behind her with each boot swinging. With all her strength, Our Doris clonked one and then the next boot around the side of Diane's head. She managed to strike her five times, black blood flowed thickly out of one of Diane's ears. Wee Renee lunged suddenly and brought the knife down.

'Aye, ye bastard!' Wee Renee shouted.

The damage would have been worse, but Diane was so dizzy with the clouts from Our Doris's cowboy boots, that her vision was blurred, and she felt herself tipping back. Wee Renee's machete came down straight, splitting Diane's nose centrally in two. Now Diane had two small noses, each with its own single nostril. If she hadn't tipped back, Wee Renee would have split her skull in two. Norman was over to her in a split second. He growled at the two elderly women.

'I'm coming for you. And now you, too,' Norman hissed firstly at Wee Renee and then Our Doris. Very quickly he smelled his sister's mark on this new small woman with the big fluffed up blonde hair. Interesting. He took Diane around the waist as she fell, and disappeared with her behind a bush.

'Let's get another one,' Wee Renee said.

'Get in the safety of the churchyard, Wee Renee,' Our Doris said. 'I need to put these boots back on and find a proper weapon. At least I can't feel my bunions, but I'll end up with hypothermia and then where will we be?'

They both ran back into the churchyard, Our Doris continuing into the church. The two women were now no longer under attack. It was clear that the Vampires still could not enter. At least the heroes had *that* in their favour.

In the darkness, in the polar snow of the churchyard, some of the children seemed to not know what direction to run to. There was an awful amount of shrill screaming from them. Some children were running close to the bushes to see if their parents were with the others. A few of them had worked out what was going on and had run back into the church themselves. Most were screaming.

Father Philip was disheartened to see that the initial brother and sister were still trapped by their parents. They were some distance away from him, and there were many vampires in between them. He also didn't have one thing to defend himself with. The churchyard and the surrounding areas were very dark. The moon was behind dense clouds, which threatened snow again. Only one weak streetlamp illuminated the monsters. They could see quite well in the dark. It wasn't a good place to be.

Father Philip saw one child running pell-mell down the path towards the entrance. Their father was outside, beckoning them mechanically while trying his best to look as normal as possible. Andy tried to grab the child, but he had already caught one with his other hand that he was trying to take back to the church. He grabbed frantically for the child who was just two inches away from his free hand. Father Philip ran as fast as he could but was about six feet behind the child. The child ran out and straight into the arms of Keith.

'Aha!' Keith shouted in triumph. Father Philip got to them both and tried to drag the child back by his coat. Keith immediately pulled the child round to the front him and grabbed Father Philip around the throat drawing him towards him. This squashed the child in between the two men. Andy saw what was happening and looked around frantically to give his child to someone else to take in. It was all that the others could do to keep the remaining children inside the church, they were screeching and trying to escape which was precisely the wrong thing to do. All of a sudden, from nowhere, Pat grabbed the other arm of the child that Andy was holding.

'Go. I'll come back and help you,' Pat shouted.

Andy had run out of the church entrance and grabbed one of Keith's arms, which were both currently around Father Philip's neck. There was a rotten egg smell about him. Andy had a form of machete in the back of his trousers, which he was trying to retrieve. Keith smiled gleefully ear to ear at Andy. He rotated his neck, turning his gaze from Andy to Father Philip. He bared his teeth. Father Philip uselessly kicked out at him around the side of the child. Andy thrashed about hitting Keith on the arms to no avail.

Andy pulled and pulled at the machete with one arm, but it wouldn't come, as it was caught somehow on the belt loops of his jeans. Keith was not bothered about Andy at all. He was just an insignificant bug. Father Philip, however, was losing consciousness and the child was still crushed between The Vampire and The Priest.

Pat ran back to the church, dragging the wriggling child behind her, whose Mother continually shouted *Keiran, Keiran, Keiran* in a lost and distant voice. Lauren was just running down the church steps and saw Pat on the way back. She could see the boy's face tearstained, his eyes fixed on the ghoulish vision of his Mother that still repeated her lament.

'I'll take him, Pat,' she said. Lauren swung both arms around the boy and lifted him up to her chest. This shocked him, and he stopped struggling for a moment. She ran as fast as she could to the church. Depositing him at the back. Our Doris was there, still looking for her sword. She took his hand firmly.

'Watch him, Our Doris. His mother is calling him outside, and he'll be off with her if we don't stop him,' she said.

'He won't escape,' Our Doris said, and Lauren knew she would keep her word. She went out to gather more kids. The sooner they were all in, the quicker they could retreat back into the church, and this nightmare would be over.

Tony stood halfway down the churchyard, his feet firmly planted. He put his hand in the air and fired his gun. All the children hollered shrilly putting their hands over their ears, and the vampires froze and looked towards him. This gave a brief couple of seconds for the people to gather the last few children and bring them onto the consecrated ground at least.

Danny and Nigel tried the new tactic, at this point, of not attacking Stephen but grabbing the child, which worked. That was good enough for the moment, and they moved back into safety.

Sue, Terry, Sally and Wee Renee managed to get the two children from their parents, using their two knives, Terry's scalpel and the lit can of hairspray. Sally had to be so careful not to burn the children as they rescued them. The father had a four-inch gash on the side of his neck courtesy of Terry, which he clutched. The black tarry substance oozed through his fingers and dripped onto the pristine snow. His wife's clothes were on fire. Keiran's mother had pushed her down into the snow. More to stop the fire spreading to her than to extinguish the vampire. The fire was now out, but the apron now just hung by its neck strap, what little was left of it. The vampire's arms were both blackened. She walked off into the night, examining them. Now, she couldn't remember why her arms were black. The three women ran as fast as they could onto the consecrated ground.

Tony walked forward towards Keith who at least now had dropped one hand, due to Andy full-on punching it for the last few minutes. The vampire had also loosened his grip with the other hand around Father Philip's neck who could now breathe again.

Tony grabbed the child who just managed to wiggle out from between the two men and pushed him onto the grounds. As the three women were running past Sue grabbed his arm and started to take him in.

Peter Woodall who was not afraid of guns ran to attack Tony. He grabbed the arm which was holding the gun, pulling Tony's neck towards his teeth. Andy at this point found where the machete was caught on his jeans and with his other hand swung it around to work. It hit home three inches into Peters' arm. There was a dull thunk, and he knew he had gone through the bone. Peter squealed and backed away into the night. Tony turned his gun towards Keith, who rotated his head again and laughed cheerlessly into the frosty night.

'That won't hurt me, fool!' He snarled.

'It certainly shut your wife up for a while didn't it? You stinky piece of shit!'

Keith let go of Father Philip and retreated into the darkness. The Priest tried to run but got as far as two steps away from the church boundaries, when Norman grabbed him around the neck.

'Oh, no. No, you don't. I want you. You are coming with me!' Norman said. Father Philip was dragged back, his heels cutting through the snow beneath him as he was whisked away with the rest of the vampires.

'He's got me! He's taking me!' Father Philip shouted. He tried to clutch at anything at the sides of him, that he could pull himself away with. His fingernails grated on the wall, picking up moss and ice under the fingernails. He grabbed the edge of a pine tree. His grip not quite connecting with the bush, but getting thickly coated with the sticky, fragrant sap. All the time, Norman made a shrill clicking sound, which seemed to herd his flock away. The protectors in the churchyard could do nothing for him. He was another to rescue along with Gary and Carl.

They watched the vampires' journey towards the centre of Friarmere and to their various nests. Father Philip now was on the open road, ten feet of free air either side of him, nothing to grasp so that he could rescue himself. He stopped grabbing, and Norman made his retreat with Father Philip. Now the vampires could check a few items off their tick list and had not left with nothing. They knew where the children were. Where the group from Melden were hiding. Also, that Wee Renee and Pat had returned. The hostages would be pretty useless soon. They had taken something undoubtedly precious for themselves. The Parish Priest. All in all, it had been a successful mission. No vampires lost this time. They retreated seemingly happy with this, at least for tonight.

The rest of the adults scanned the graveyard for running children but could see none. They rushed into the church. Nigel and Tony stood at the doors, checking that none of their own were outside. Now the graveyard was silent and frozen again. A mist swirled in the emptiness around the graves. Freezing fog on its way for the night. No creature moved in the graveyard, the street or under the soft laurel bushes. It looked like they were alone again and they shut the large doors. Shutting out the freezing night and the terror. Using a pew, they pushed it in front of the door, so that no children could be opening its again quite so easily.

They counted the children, and all were present. This proved to be more difficult than usual as there was chaos inside the church. Most of the children, already terrorised, ran crying around the church or hiding under pews. They had never felt so much relief in all their lives that they had saved each treasured child. The little girl and boy whose parents were outside at the beginning were crying. They were in shock. Their dirty tearstained faces buried in their hands. Kathy and Sally held one sibling each, as they cried. They knew that Father Philip had been taken and began to check for everyone else.

Everyone seemed present and correct. It took a few minutes for Wee Renee to notice. Where was the fly in the ointment? Where was the person that usually annoyed everyone?

'Where is Tina?' Wee Renee asked.

Mark and Maurice stood under the trees in the garden of the house next to the church. The house was not empty, but the inhabitants were as cold as the deepest snow. The two vampires stood far into the shadows and had watched everything that had occurred this evening. Maurice still hadn't come up with his rescue plan. Not only for Gary and the man from Melden but all his former friends in the band. There was a way, somehow, he just couldn't think of it right now. It would come.

He was delighted to see quite a few members of the band come out of the church tonight, and they had fought so well. This was the first time he had seen any of them fight, and he was very impressed. No wonder they had survived the ambush at the Civic Hall. It gave him even more hope for their rescue. If he could just make the chances, they could manage the rest themselves.

Unfortunately, he had not seen Freddie, but he could see that there were a lot of adults in the church through the door open doors, trying to trap children inside. Freddie could be in there, although he could not smell him. He hoped Freddie was safe somewhere else. Out of harm's way.

Maurice wondered what Norman really wanted with The Priest. Undoubtedly it would be sinister. Or was this man another valuable hostage? His job was getting more difficult as the hours went by. Now there were three men to rescue. Mark didn't speak. Maurice didn't know what he was thinking. He was a bloodsucker, yes. But he was here with him, not fighting with them. Mark was always a joker. Maurice couldn't count all the tricks he had played on the rest of the band. Maybe this streak of mischief, of devilment had been magnified in death, and he just craved fun. Whatever, Maurice thought his heart was in the right place, even if he was conflicted. With Maurice's help and guidance at least, he was going to be an asset in the rescue of their friends.

Maurice heard a noise from afar. Very, very high up.
He remembered what it was. A jumbo jet.
Somewhere, life still went on.

6 - Barricade

There was lots of chatter between everyone in the church. When had they last seen Tina? Where was she? What was she doing? Was she fighting or just collecting children? They spoke to the children. A few of them said Tina had grabbed them and told them to run inside. Some of the men looked through the windows. The church ladies checked, and triple checked every corner of the church. At this point, they found Our Doris's sword that Tina had hidden underneath the desk in the vestry. They felt very guilty that they had not protected her or seen what had happened to her.

Wee Renee and Nigel talked and were sure that as they watched the vampires go home, the only person with them was Father Philip. They had scanned every vampire leaving, as they thought one of them must have a child. But they had no-one. Therefore, Tina must have been killed somewhere, beyond the church boundaries, as that was where she had last been seen.

Several of the group dragged more pews across the door and then put one under every window with a stack of hymn books on each one so that even Wee Renee and Our Doris could see out. They decided that they should have a sentry at each side that faced the street at all times.

Some of the adults had a meeting. Nigel had the idea that it was the Priest they were after right from the beginning. If they took a couple of children to eat, that was a bonus. Terry agreed and said that as soon as they had the Priest good and proper, they were off. Sue was unsure about this but didn't voice it. She remembered Norman's words in the school. He wanted other people who had still been in Melden at the time. Now they were back in Friarmere. The group had just been lucky that it was only Father Philip that had been taken.

Sally and Kathy still held the two children who had opened the door that night. Rocking them until they slept. They tossed and turned. It was going to be a long night for them and the children. Lauren had brought a bottle of whisky and a bottle of dark rum from the pub. She thought it would be good if the adults had a nip for the shock. Although, she would be strictly monitoring it, as they really did need to keep their wits about them this night. At the back of Lauren's mind too, was the fact that they were in a House of God. She wasn't strictly sure about the protocol for alcohol in here. Lauren confided in Beverly, who thought she was being overly cautious.

'Look, if you are that worried, go and speak to those that are left from the church. I am sure they won't mind considering the circumstances, but if they do, I tell you, I am insisting that anyone who wants some, has some. It doesn't hurt to smooth things over first though if you can, I suppose,' Beverly said. They both approached the church ladies, who were pleased that Lauren and Beverly had come to them to ask permission or advice. They were a lot more relaxed than Tina and said they were going to break out the communal wine as well. Then people had got three choices if they needed something to steady their nerves through the night.

They also brought up the fact that they would have to say something if anyone got drunk and sleepy, as it wouldn't do for everyone to be useless that night. The vampires could still attack at any time, and they all needed to keep their eyes peeled.

Norman dragged Father Philip quickly through the streets of Friarmere. Away from the church, into the centre of the village. Past the shops, one by one. His heels still cutting two grooves into the compacted snow and ice. No other person saw him or didn't let on and help him if they had. Who would want to take on a horde of angry vampires dragging the village priest by his neck?

They travelled out of the village now, up the hill. Father Philip was unaware if Norman was taking him to the school or The Grange. He was hoping for the School as at least it was nearer to all the other houses in the village and less sinister. Father Philip had been there many times and knew his way around but had never visited The Grange or wished to. When Norman veered off the main road to the left, he knew his wish had been granted. Soon the school was before them – dark and cold. It still had to be better than the gothic Grange high above him.

Norman sat Father Philip in the Headmasters Office. The Master would have preferred to take him up to The Grange really. He was far more comfortable up there, but he needed leverage, and the leverage was here. Also, Norman wanted to keep an eye on his two hostages. He knew that the others would come to rescue them at some point. Yes, he had a few vampires here. Some were at The Grange. Some were out on the hunt. A few had got injured tonight.

Mrs White was still trying to keep the unruly vampire children at bay. She seemed to have been able to control them when they were trapped up here. But they really could not be trusted. Earlier tonight she had taken a party of them out, but several of them had run away and had not returned. He had to give her two of his minions to help now with the children. They did not to think about danger or waiting for the right time to do something but would try and get food or just to nip another human, or even each other. They were single-minded about it. Today some were missing, and he had to assume they were either trapped or killed by the people that were resisting his takeover. They had not come to his call, which he had made outside the church and they would have heard it no matter where they were in the village.

Norman locked Father Philip in the office and went off find Michael. Norman instructed him to make three cups of sweet tea and bring one into the Headmaster's Office for Father Philip. The others were to go to the two hostages that he held, with a plate of biscuits. After Michael had brought the tea into the office, Norman told Father Philip that he had grand plans for the village and that Father Philip could be very instrumental in these.

'You obviously know, I'm not going to help you do anything destructive or evil,' Father Philip replied, drinking his tea. Norman still talked, of how he loved the village, how he felt at home. His voice had a lovely tone to it and rhythm. Father Philip thought it was very nice in this office. It reminded him of his own vestry. It had the familiar scents of wood, pens and furniture polish. He finished his cup of tea. Norman spoke to him kindly. He seemed to be an engaging, intelligent host.

Gary and Carl heard footsteps approaching their room. High-heeled footsteps. A woman. Carl looked at Gary – was this the moment? Was this Kate on the way to him? Another set of footprints jointed the first. A man's. Carl swallowed, with dread. The key turned in the door, and Keith stood the other side. He took everything in, his policeman's stare checking that they hadn't been up to anything. They hadn't. Then he swung the door aside, and Christine entered with a tray.

'Tea and biccies, sweeties,' she said in a light, cheerful voice. 'Compliments of The Master!' She put the tray down beside them. Keith watched them like a hawk for any indication that would make a move towards Christine. 'For my two favourite humans, delivered with love by Chrissy!' Keith rolled his eyes. 'I'll be back very soon for the tray and cups. I don't want you doing anything naughty with them, do I?' She giggled, cheekily tapping Gary on the nose with her fingertip.

'Fair enough,' Gary said. Christine walked out of the carpeted room, Keith shutting and locking the door behind her. Now her heels clacked back down the corridor on the hard, tiled floor.

'I hate to say it, but I think you are *in* there,' Carl said.

Father Philip had the sudden feeling that he was being hypnotised and lulled into a false sense of security. He shook his head.

'Are you thirsty?' Norman asked, and got out a bottle of wine. He poured a glass before the Father and put it before him. Father Philip had heard the tales from Liz and Our Doris. He knew that this wine would make him infected with the vampire virus. Knowing it, meant he could smell The Master's blood, wrapped up in the heavy scent of the fermented red grapes. The smell was musty, slightly sour with a hint of copper.

'No, the tea was plenty, thank you. I don't want a glass of wine at the moment,' Father Philip replied. The Master sensed that his hypnotism had not worked and Father Philip was wise to his blood infused wine.

The Master raised one eyebrow and put his finger to his lips as if to say shush. He waited until Father Philip spoke. He could wait a long time. The length of Father Philips life if necessary. Which he could make as short or long as he wished. However, he only had to wait about one minute.

'I know what that will do to me!'

'Ah right. Let us lay all the cards on the table. If you don't drink this, I will bring the other vampires in and between us we will hold you down and force it down your throat.' Norman regarded the man before him, letting it sink in. 'I would rather you do it willingly. It means so much more to me.' Norman said this with feeling as if the Priest would do it out of love.

'There is no way, that I am going to take that willingly,' Father Philip said finally.

'We shall see.' Norman said and touched his nose at the side. He knew something that Father Philip didn't. He stood up. 'Come with me.'

Norman took him through the hall, down a corridor and stood him before a classroom door. A piece of black cloth had been pinned over the glass window. He pulled the fabric aside and showed him through the classroom window. Father Philip took a look through. By the light of a candle, he could see two men. One man was in his late twenties, good looking but looking like he hadn't slept for weeks. He held a cup of tea in his hands sipping it. The other one was older, bearded, with a baseball cap. He was dunking digestives in his cup of tea. As Father Philip watched, half of Gary's softened biscuit dropped back into the tea. The man frowned and fiddled unsuccessfully in the drink quickly, then took another digestive biscuit and made the same mistake again.

'If you don't drink the wine, I will kill these two men,' Norman said matter-of-factly.

'Then you won't have them as hostages.'

'That is true. But I will still have you. You can be my new hostage and live in the dark room. I will still force the wine down your throat. And you will have achieved nothing. Their fate is currently in your hands.'

Father Philip looked downwards and nodded. He had no choice. The fact was, he would end up at the same point, whichever road he took. Better to save the men. Father Philip would, of course, put these men before himself. He was in a position where he could not see the bigger picture. Father Philip returned to the Headmasters Office, reluctantly but resignedly. Without a word, he picked up the glass, watching Norman. He took a sip expecting a trace of blood, but the taste was not as bad as the smell, and it was indeed a lovely red wine to drink. He sat down and tried to reconcile his actions now. At least by doing this, he had saved the two men, and by coming outside, he had saved the children. The Priest felt that he had done some good, whatever would happen now.

'Was that someone looking through the glass on the door?' Carl asked.

'Bugger only knows. I've been enjoying my tea and biscuits while I can,' Gary said.

'I'm sure it was.'

'Who was it?' Gary asked, finishing the remainder of his tea and scooping the dissolved biscuits out of the bottom with his finger.

'I think, you'll never believe this, but it is so dark in here and out there in the corridor. I think I saw a face, a man's, that I didn't recognise. And,' he laughed, 'a vicar's collar!'

'No. Never,' Gary said. 'In here? I doubt it very much.'

'It was for a split second before it went fully black again. He didn't look like a vampire either. I guess I could be seeing things.'

'Too right you are. Hey! You don't think they have put something in the tea?'

'I have only had a couple of sips of mine. You've drunk all yours. You would be worse than me.'

'Oh yeah. Must be shock then. Nice tea actually isn't it?'

'Yeah.' They began to hear Christine's high heeled mules coming down the corridor from a distance.

'Drink your brew quick. Neck it. She'll take it off you.' Gary said. Carl downed it in one. They could also hear the sound of Keith returning too, or as Gary has christened him, *the laughing policeman.*

The two vampires re-entered, with an addition, Christine's creation, Wayne.

'Was that lovely, sweeties?' Christine asked.

'It was bloody gorgeous actually. You make a grand brew, I'll give you that.' Gary said smiling at her. Christine fluttered her eyelashes at him.

'I have to admit, it wasn't Chrissy that made it. But I did supervise!' She said girlishly.

'Oh, and I was going to ask for another cup,' he said as if is hopes were dashed.

'No, no. I couldn't authorise that. I am sorry,' Christine said.

'I could,' Keith said.

'Ah, so you make the cracking cuppa?' Gary asked.

'I did not make that tea. But I can happily order the person who did, to keep making them. In fact, it would be a pleasure.' The very thought of making Michael provide a nightly tea service to his lover's husband was too delicious a prospect.

'Well, er…. keep them coming as much as you can then,' Gary said, very surprised at Keith's hospitality.

'Take the tray,' Keith said to Christine.

'Wayne sweetie, the tray. Picky uppy,' she said. Wayne shuffled towards the tray. Gary knew him. It was Wayne, the postman. Healthy, happy, bright Wayne. Something must have happened in his turning. The others you could hold a conversation with. They were lucid, at least for the most part. Just evil versions of their previous personas. But Wayne was different. He seemed like a shuffling mindless zombie. Eyes half closed, toes dragging on the floor, his only purpose was doing the bidding of Christine. Gary had seen him like this at the Civic Hall. He had yet to hear him speak at all.

'Wayne mate. You ok? It's Gary. Remember, I fixed your roof just over a month ago.' Wayne didn't reply. The other vampires didn't explain, why he didn't respond. They locked the door again and went to find Michael.

The party inside the church passed an anxious, sleepless night, but at it was at least uneventful. After barricading the doors, throughout the night, they had decided to block off the windows with drawing paper below a certain level to ensure that the children were not tempted. If you were below five feet, you could not see out of the church anywhere. They decided that this would rule Our Doris out of the window watching equation, but it was worth it to know that the kids weren't upset again.

Lauren still hadn't slept at four am that night. She was quite uncomfortable and was thinking that she had traded comfort for company. She probably wouldn't have lasted much longer without them smelling her and breaking in to eat her anyway. Lauren watched the others look left and right outside as they stood on top of the pews. Maybe she could snatch a few uninterrupted hours before the kids woke up, as she had finished her turn a while back. Lauren watched Terry pick his nose, thinking everyone else was asleep and smiled to herself.

Occasionally she heard one of the children awake. In particular, it seemed to be the initial two siblings that Kathy and Sally were watching. A dozing Liz and Sue were currently watching the rest of the children. They had just replaced two ladies from the church, who had now moved to window watch.

Lauren could hear Kathy explaining that children, could not be blamed for any of this as they are used to obeying their parents' wishes. Lauren heard an objection from a child, but could not understand the whispers. The boy who was older than the girl felt guilty about the fact that Father Philip and Tina were now missing. Kathy and Sally tried to explain to them that it was Norman that had taken their parents and made them into something else. They were sorry, but their parents could no longer be trusted – ever. This was a terrible thing to have to explain to a child, but it just had to be done.

Some of the other children listened. Under no illusion as to what had befallen their village. After all, they had been living in darkness with many vampires in their old school for a while. However, the reality of seeing their parents as these monsters was just too much for some of them.

One girl refused to speak any longer and was eating very little. This worried Liz especially as there was no Doctor available for counselling or psychiatric help. She did not want this child to go any further down a path they might not return from.

'While my blood works its magic, I want to discuss something with you,' Norman said to Father Philip in the Headmaster's Office. 'So, drink up.'

'Go ahead,' Father Philip replied.

'Obviously, I do not expect you to *save* me, to help me atone for my many sins. But I have secrets hidden in my breast that's only I know. I am what they call, in a relationship now, and I have to move on with certain things that are holding me back.'

'Who are you in a relationship with?'

'Not as it is anything to do with you, but a lady in Moorston,'

'A human lady or a vampire lady?'

'A beautiful vampire lady, named Penelope. That isn't the point! I need to talk to someone as past matters eat away at me.'

'You can say anything to me, I have heard it all,' said Father Philip looking down sadly at his wine.

'I doubt it. You see I have a brother and a sister,' he said. 'My sister is over in Melden.'

'I have heard of her. Her name is Anne, isn't it?' Father Philip asked.

'Yes. That is her,' Norman poured himself a glass of his own wine. The Priest watched its ruby descent into the glass. He was starting to feel a little dizzy. Norman took a large drink from the glass. He looked at a picture on the wall. It was a painting of the school. The blossom was on the trees, the sun was shining. This had certainly been painted in happier times. Father Philip gave Norman as much time as he needed. 'Anne has a strange obsession with me. It still affects me now,' Norman continued. 'When we were children she loved me in a way that an older sister should not love a younger brother. Do you know what I am saying, Father? I am on about matters that are taboo.' The Master said thoughtfully.

'Yes, I understand,' Father Philip said, 'and I am sorry for that. No child should have to suffer that. Go further if you need to, but I know what you are talking about. Incest.'

'Yes, although I do not like to name it. We were both alive then. It was before we got turned. I did not tell my brother or parents about it.' Norman turned to Father Philip. 'But it affects me so, and you are the first Priest I have come across. Well, that is not true. You are the first I have come across since I have decided I could talk about it. I just need to get it off my chest. I hate her, but she is my sister. I do not know what to feel. I have to put up with her, I cannot kill her. Do you understand, Father? She is my sister. She is my flesh blood. My brother Len, well…. he does not agree with what she does over there either. Anne, for her part, hates him back but at least loves me. I need you to help me through this Father. I do not understand why it still means so much, even now, but it does.'

'There are several options open to you,' Father Philip began. 'You could forgive your sister. That would be the hardest. Secondly, in another time, for another person, the proper channels might work. By this, I mean prosecution in court, counselling, medical help for her and you. I don't see that as an option open to you. Thirdly you could distance yourself from her. Do not visit her. Try to heal.'

'She is my sister. My blood.' Norman said sadly.

'And she is an abuser. Do you have another choice? The only other option is to carry on as if nothing has happened. Has that worked for you? No. That is what you have done for years, and you are stuck. All options are down to you, Norman. You take control now.'

'Yes, you are right. This way does not work. You know Father, my sister is insane, in so many ways. What if help had been given to her years ago? Neither of us would be where we are now. I will think deeply about this situation.'

Father Philip had been listening to Norman unburden himself. He was intrigued. The Master was indeed a fascinating man, on so many levels. Norman stopped talking, and The Priest regarded his glass again. While he had been listening, he had drained the glass, and now there wasn't a drop left. Norman turned away from the window to look at him.

'Now we get to the meat of the matter. Right now, what I want to know from you...' He walked over to Father Philip. His manner had changed. He was back to the vampire he had been earlier. Slowly he leant over the sitting man, placing his hands on each of the chair arms. He was six inches away from his face. Father Philip was feeling quite inebriated now. The room was swimming, Norman seemed large and godlike and glowing in the office lamp.

'What I want to know from you, is where is the unconsecrated part of the churchyard.' Father Philip's eyes filled up with tears. He knew he would have to tell Norman this. He had just made sure that the rest of the people in his church would be food or vampires too. He hadn't even thought about it. It hardly ever came up. Father Philip couldn't imagine where The Master had found out about it. But there was an area of the Church that was unconsecrated for people to be buried without faith, or of other religions. Father Philip nodded and begun to tell him. Norman listened.

Christine stood outside the door of the headmaster's office with Wayne. She had been eavesdropping the whole conversation silently. She looked at Wayne, and he retained her gaze. They drifted off and knew much more than was helpful to them.

After a very quiet and reflective breakfast, the party in the church started to plan the new day. They were sure that the vampires would be back tonight, with a new plan. Luckily, they couldn't get in, but Wee Renee was worried that they might find a way to deconsecrate the ground, now they had Father Philip. It seemed to be the very reason to take him, the more she thought about it. Whatever happened, they should prepare. Several of them wanted to go to the shops. Tony thought that if they could make some kind of flaming torch, and put several around the church grounds tonight, it would help immensely. Sue thought that today, they should break into the chemist to get more antibiotics, cold remedies, antiseptic and bandages, just in case. The others wholeheartedly agreed with this. Also, there was the issue with the removal of Ian's body from the butchers.

Our Doris set to making a list, assisted by her niece, Beverly. She walked from person to person, asking for any ideas, or items they wanted. The grocery list, apart from the food, had bleach, dog poo bags, hairspray, and lighters. Sally had set a trend off in the church, and now it was the *must-have* item. A couple of the church ladies thought that this was a little dangerous. One of them asked for a bottle of lavender oil from the chemist, for stress.

They soon were ready to go. A more substantial group than yesterday. Our Doris and Haggis were on board. So were Beverly and Terry. They took all the sledges out to return their shopping and unfortunately, the grim half-eaten body of Ian. Nigel was thinking hard about the torches that Tony had suggested. He said he needed fabric, lighter fluid or petrol, and large sticks. Liz said she had seen plenty of fallen branches with the snow, and asked if they were suitable. They now had a plan. This afternoons craft event would be the men, stripping branches of their smaller offshoots and leaves, the women cutting up cotton fabric. They just had to find some. Nigel said if they found a pipe, he would try to get some petrol out of a car, other than that, they would use lighter fluid from the shop's tobacconist area.

After looking through the pub windows, to check everything was secure, their first stop was the grocery shop. They picked up everything on their lists. A large box of cotton Christmas tea towels sat in the corner, which they took for the torches. Fifteen large gold cans of hairspray noisily rolled around in their bags on the sledge.

They decided to break into the chemist next. This proved a lot easier than they thought, as between Terry and Nigel they managed to negotiate all locks and security devices. Luckily there were no vampires in there to dispatch. The ladies put all the items in bags. Terry rummaged excitedly around in the pharmacy area, picking up this and that. Wee Renee was almost nostalgic about the poisoning of the wolves.

'Do you know, Our Doris, I actually miss it. It was fun for a while, trying to guess if it would kill them or put them to sleep. I miss your house too,' Wee Renee said.

'You're not wrong there. I miss my own nest. In some ways, Anne's gang was easier. I might be wrong.' Our Doris replied.

'I think you remember it with rose coloured spectacles, Our Doris. Those wolves and her wolf vampires were vile,' Terry said.

'You're right Terry. Give me Norman any day over them critters,' Pat said sniffing.

Wee Renee wandered off to look for something. Pat rummaged around in the ladies' area. She picked up tampons and sanitary towels and threw them in a bag.

'Oh dear,' Liz said.

'They're not for me. Never in this wide world. But with so many lasses, it's bound to happen sooner or later isn't it?' Pat asked. 'Besides that. They could be handy for other emergencies.'

'Good thinking!' Wee Renee said and opened a fresh carrier bag. She filled it with the contents of the condom shelf.

'I like your optimism Wee Renee,' Nigel said sniggering, 'especially in these times. But I don't think you are going to need all them until the snow thaws. I mean, I don't know if you've got a boyfriend already, but you would have to go at it like rabbits to use all them.'

'You will never believe what we could do with these in the tinsel triangle!' Wee Renee replied.

'Well, you never cease to amaze me, Rene,' Pat said nudging her.

'Do you know what you can do with these? Carry water, use them as a rubber glove, keep food fresh or suckle a baby animal.' Andy and Liz looked at one another – what baby animals was Wee Renee thinking of? The mind boggled. She continued happily with her next juicy tip. 'Guess what, boys. Latex is flammable; they can be used as a firelighter! And now imagine where you've had these before.' Wee Renee was in hysterics. All the women were laughing. The men were stony-faced. 'I tell you what Nigel, in my younger days, I would have used all these in the usual way. I tell ye!'

'That just warms my heart, Wee Renee,' Nigel replied, starting to laugh with the women.

'Let's get this Ian then,' Terry said. Just to change the subject.

They went next door to the butchers. It was a short but sad time in there. Danny and Andy took Terry in the back to have a look at Aidy. Terry now could see what was inside the vampires. They all helped load Ian onto the sledge which they had pulled inside. At one point the bin bags and carrier bags drifted off with a gust of wind from the door and both Ian's legs and one arm was exposed in the daylight.

'Oh god. Poor, poor fellow,' Our Doris said. 'No wonder you had to come back for him. How absolutely terrible.'

They lashed the body down on the metal sledge with Tony's bungee cords and dragged him outside. Pat had been rummaging around behind the counter. She put something in a paper bag and quietly put it in her pocket. Pat was the last out and shut the butcher's door.

Heavily laden and with lots on their mind, they made their way back, through the iced slush and virgin snow. All the way through the village, they did not see a single person again. Sue knew people were surviving, however. At one point, out of the corner of her eye, she saw a curtain twitch, and a what looked a normal woman stepped back away from the window.

'I know her,' Pat said. 'She's named Beryl.'

'Should we call?' Sue asked.

'Maybe another day. She's obviously safe there. Probably safer than us. I'll call in at some point when we are straighter.' The conversation got back to the subject of Ian.

'We will put him on consecrated ground, under the bushes. Put the bins in front of him, so that the children don't find him,' Wee Renee said. 'Until the ground is thawed, that is all we can do.'

'What about this though?' Bob said. 'We want loads of massive sticks, and the kids could help to find those. But if they are playing a game looking everywhere, they might find Ian,'

'You're right there, son,' Tony said.

'How about this?' Sue said. 'We drag Ian round the back of the church, just keep him on the path, with a couple of us either side. Then we tell the kids that they must stay at the front of the church, to look for the sticks, as it could be dangerous around the back. Once we have got the sticks. They go in. We drag the sledge back round and put Ian under the bushes.'

'Brilliant, Mum,' Bob said.

'Yes, that will work,' Nigel added. 'The quicker we find the sticks, the whole process can start. We need a light on all this whole situation.'

When they got back, they did just that. Before knocking on the door, Pat looked up at Laura, who was on lookout, she mouthed the word *shhhh* and put her finger up to her mouth. Laura nodded and watched them drag up the large sledge, with the obvious body shape strapped on it, beneath black bin bags.

Ian was placed at the back of the church, with Nigel and Tony guarding either side. No children ran around to the back as they were too busy finding large fallen branches from around the tree line at the front.

After they had done this, the group had potentially twelve torches and there was still more that could be foraged for tomorrow. Some branches were too big for the children to carry. If they were still there tomorrow, there would be some mighty torches made.

While the children were tasked inside to cut the tea cloths into strips, the rest of the group hid Ian. They dragged the sledge to the edge of the bushes in the top corner of the churchyard. Rolled him off the sledge and deep under the bushes. He couldn't be seen already. One of the church ladies pointed out that there was a load of old plant pots around the back, and they should pile these in front as the bins might be needed.

Wee Renee said that she was going to say a few words for Ian if anyone was interested in staying. She thought a couple might stay, but was surprised to see that every single adult wanted to pay their respects, whether they had known Ian in life or not.

When they went inside, all the cloth was cut, and it was time for lunch. Today seemed to be the day for instant mashed potato, with ketchup, as nine out of ten children wanted that. Pat ate her tripe from the previous day, the other adults ate cold tins of beans or spaghetti hoops.

Pat's secret bag of stash from Ian's butcher's shop was revealed to be several cooked lamb bones for Haggis, which he threw up and down the church between chews. They skittered under pews and tables as he threw and chased them, wagging his tail. At least someone was happy.

More cake was consumed. Our Doris had picked up three Dundee Cakes, which were eaten just after lunch. Wee Renee said she wanted to have a meeting about a *Plan B* in the Lady Chapel and everyone should bring their hot drinks. She had picked up a mixed box of fruit and herbal teas. She now drank an orange one. The tag from the teabag wrapped around the handle of the mug. She had also picked up ten bottles of lavender oil from the Chemist's Shop. She thought everyone needed a *wee bit of healing* and went around dabbling spots on people's temples and wrists. The whole church smelled of lavender, which was relaxing and mind clearing.

When they were all seated in the Lady Chapel, Wee Renee began.

'Right, cards on the table, I am worried about tonight. I think something's afoot. I feel it in my water. I wish we had a Plan B and we need to think of one. I don't want to stay here another night. Where can we go tomorrow with so many people? Anyone? Let's brainstorm. There has to be somewhere.'

A few people that had been in Melden thought of various places, but the church ladies advised them that each one had been smashed up with their doors wide open.

'As well as location, I think we need to think about getting more weapons,' Pat said. This comment was strongly supported now that most of them had only one weapon each.

'I wouldn't mind a sword, like Our Doris's,' Bob said wistfully.

'Aye, lad. We'd all like one of those, but they don't have an armoury in Friarmere,' Wee Renee said. She was about to say something else, stopped, thought for a few seconds, her eyes excited. 'I'm a silly wee hen,' she said. 'What about the hardware store?'

The others felt an instant jolt of elation. They knew this was it. This was their Plan B.

'I think it would be perfect, considering it all. It is quite big. There must be lots of stuff we can use or adapt,' Wee Renee said. She continued to think out loud and now spoke in a crestfallen voice. 'But it's doors have those large glass windows, and it is a public building, a shop. Plus, the other big windows too. Maybe we could at least get ourselves tooled up there?'

Danny was thinking about the hardware store too.

'There is a big back room there that Gary says he had been in. They do workshops there, about DIY. I have a feeling that there are no windows in that room. That might be ideal for our purposes. There are shutters on the front now. Maybe we could enter from a different direction so that the vampires don't know we are there,' Danny added helpfully.

Pat looked at her watch. It was two o'clock. Now they had thought of a Plan B – it was too late to go. If they could just stop the kids from going out tonight, they should be fine for one more night. If they had turned Father Philip and Tina, they couldn't get to them anyway. But if they had made them like Michael, there would be trouble and some tough decisions.

They decided to use the time before dark usefully. All the men went and stripped the branches for the torches. Then they wound a few strips of tea cloth around. Wee Renee's special torch came next, a condom opened out and laid the length of the cloths. Then more were wound around this with the ring of the condom peeping out. This would be their firelighter. The finishing touch was a good squirt of lighter fuel. They wouldn't last all night, but it would be interesting to see how long they did. They could replace them when they went out and decided to light four, in position, just before it went dark. During this time, Kathy, Sally, Lauren, Liz and Beverly got the kids on a project. They knew the dark was on its way and it was all they could do to keep the kids from going hysterical. This was their primary objective. However, Terry wandered over at one point, with Andy and Nigel.

'What are you doing, kids. That looks fun?'

'Making an advent calendar,' Liz replied. Andy looked at the other two, and they laughed and shook their heads.

'Liz, advent calendars started on the first and what are they building up to? Christmas isn't looking too merry at the moment!' Andy commented in astonishment.

'Oh, go over there by the window, if you can't be constructive, Andy. These kids will look forward to opening these doors. Killjoy!'

'I can assure you, Andy, Father Christmas will come to them all. I will make sure of it!' Wee Renee said finally.

They didn't argue, but hoped as much as the kids, that she was right.

7 - Unconsecrated

After their evening meal, the men went outside to position and light the torches. The ground was so frozen that it was impossible to position them no matter how hard they tried to force them. In the end, they managed to wiggle them into flower holders on various graves, which seemed to work.

Wee Renee was correct about the condom, it did indeed make a brilliant firelighter. The fires lit up the front of the church, pavement, and roads quite well. They were surprisingly bright. Little golden sparkles reflected back from the frozen faceted snow.

After the decision to move the following day, there was a lot of planning to do. Hopefully, the group wouldn't be interrupted so that they could make the move as seamless and as safe as possible. They had decided that in between watches, people would write lists or things to be aware of, on paper. A notebook was left for this purpose on a large table near the door. This usually held hymnbooks on Sunday's and Orders of Service. A small party of rescuers was there chatting about tomorrows arrangements.

Pat was on duty, standing on a pew. Her eyes darted this way and that in the failing light. She amused herself by eating a large jar of beetroot with a fork, occasionally forgetting and putting her fingers in the purple vinegar.

She was stressed out. Being one hundred percent vigilant was tense and tiring and she really just wanted to relax. She would be letting the group down, however. This time of day was the optimum time for an attack. She wanted this watch. Then she knew at least, that she had done everything. Tonight, they wouldn't be getting in without Pat spotting them. Nevertheless, it was exhausting – looking outside at a constant white landscape, concentrating, didn't half give you eyestrain.

If she admitted it, she preferred Our Doris's house to this. This place made her grumpy. It was uncomfortable. It was boring. She generally had had enough. There was an awful lot of banging and screeching coming from the kids' area. She couldn't concentrate.

'Listen, if you kids don't pipe down, I will shove that game of *Hungry Hippo's* up your bums,' she shouted.

'Aye let's have a few carols,' Wee Renee said, trying to diffuse the situation. She waited until the game had been put away and then led them in a bought of carolling, which they loved but the *planning committee* needed her more and had to keep asking her to come over.

'Will you carry it on for me, Pat? Someone will do your watch,' Wee Renee asked.

'No chance. I don't want to, and you know full well I can't sing!' Pat replied. Our Doris said she would do it, but when she started singing, she realised she only knew Elvis songs, which none of the kids knew. Besides that, when she sang in her husky voice, for some reason Haggis started to bark. They rang out deafeningly throughout the church from corner to corner. An echo that hurt everyone's ears.

In the end, Lauren, who had by that time had a few nips of her own hospitality took up the mantle. She was quite the little performer, doing actions for each carol, which the children loved. Andy nudged Danny.

'What do you think?'

'Liz will go mad if she hears you talk about Lauren, but yeah she's fit,' Danny replied.

'I wasn't on about for me, you prune. I was talking about you.'

'Oh yeah. Ok.' Danny looked at Lauren for a while and licked his lips. He went into a long stare and Andy thought he wasn't going to reply. Then he blinked suddenly and continued. 'No Andy, she is a bit too young for me,' Danny continued to look at Lauren who was now bending over. He coughed. 'How old do you think she is, about 20?'

'Yeah.'

'Nah, she wouldn't look at me. She'd think it would be like dating a pensioner,' Danny said resignedly with a sigh.

Norman made plans throughout the first part of the evening for his next attack on The Church. His Lieutenants, Christine, Keith, Kate and Michael, were brainstorming, and later they would each tell their group of vampires what the plan was. Nine o'clock was to be the time, so several of them went out for a short while, to see what fun they could find.

There was also the matter of patching up a couple of Norman's vampires. Michael had been set the task of seeing to the wounded again. The worst, he considered, being Peter Woodall, who had what Michael called, a semi-amputation. Michael thought that the rest of this arm had to come off, but Peter was strongly against it. The triage room, as Michael had christened it, was now set up in the school staffroom. There were sofa's, tables and strong lighting in there. Without, medical supplies, he was forced to use everyday items on the repair of the vampires, not as proper medical supplies would have worked anyway. The staffroom worked well for Michael. Not only could he treat his patients here, but it seemed to be his job to continually make cups of tea for Gary and Kate's husband. Plus, the staffroom had the added bonus of a microwave. All in all, it served every purpose he asked of it, and Michael had made it his own.

After Peter's protest about the suggested procedure, Michael had told him that he would speak to The Master to decide the fate of the semi-amputated arm. Peter agreed, and Michael went off to talk to Norman. He knocked crisply on the door.

'Enter,' Norman said.

'How do?' Michael said as he entered, shutting the door behind him. Norman raised one eyebrow. Michael was getting too familiar.

'Could I borrow you for a moment, to look at Peter's arm. It's only held on by a rag of skin, but he won't let me pinch it off and finish the job.'

'I would rather a vampire keep his arm if you could. What about we let it dangle for a couple of days and see if it will right itself?' Norman replied.

'I really think you need to see it. It's never going to right itself in a thousand years. Plus, the bit that's been cut off is going green and smelly. Talk about the funk of forty thousand years. Jacko knew nothing. He should smell Peter's arm.' Michael said, shaking his head. Norman looked at him quizzically. He had no idea what Michael was on about.

'Which of them is Jacko? Is it one of my vampires?' Norman asked. Michael laughed loudly for a long time. Norman waited for him to cease in silence. He flared his nostrils in anger. Norman didn't like to be the butt of a joke.

'No. *Michael Jackson is Jacko*. Another famous Michael,' he smiled, as if he was in good company, 'That is a line out of the song *Thriller*. You're missing out if you haven't heard that. That is right up your alley as well.' He said.

'Quite,' Norman replied. 'Anyway, I'm not moving, so fix it together for a while. I'm not ready for Peter to lose his arm. You're dismissed.'

'Hmmm...very nice, I'm sure,' Michael muttered quietly, as he went back into the corridor. If Michael was truthful, he was pleased with this outcome. Cutting off the vampire's arm would be something to avoid as Peter would probably get really nasty about it. Although amputation was inevitable, when it happened, Michael could blame The Master. Also, he could do something he loved to do. Michael could say *I told you so*. He would relish that.

Michael explained the situation to Peter who was happy with the outcome. Now he had another problem. What could be used to stop it from flopping about and tearing off? He had a look at the small piece of skin which attached the two parts. There was a chunk of flesh attached, which had dried. The ribbon of skin was going papery and thin. Never in this wide world would this arm stay on. He looked through the drawers in the staffroom, nothing caught his imagination. Michael had an idea.

'Wait here,' he said, walking over to a key rack, and picking up the caretaker's keys. Off he wandered, whistling. Kate, who was in the hall talking to Christine, looked up.

'How's my lovely lady?' He asked. Still hoping that she hadn't heard about who they had got hidden in one of the classrooms. He didn't think she had as she actually carried on the conversation with him. Good.

'Fine. Looking forward to later,' Kate replied.

'Yes, about later, I was hoping we could go on a date after. It's been a while since we have enjoyed each other's company, hasn't it?' He asked desperately. Christine looked from one to the other as they spoke. She was quite amused about it all.

'I don't know how I'll feel. Shall we see how it goes?' Kate replied.

'Right you are, lovely lady,' He said and kissed her on the cheek. Christine giggled.

'Do you want one?' He asked Christine.

'No! Certainly not! What would Wayne sweetie think if he walked past?' Christine replied.

'Probably not much,' Michael replied and turned on his heel, making his way to the Caretakers Room. Christine scowled and looked back to Kate.

'It's not Wayne sweetie's fault if he bumped his little head badly on my basement steps, just before we turned him. I mean, I did push him ….. only in eagerness. I didn't know he would get hurt and it would ruin his natural vitality.'

'Back of the head caved in. It will do it every time,' Kate said coldly.

'Luckily it didn't spoil his looks, Kate!'

'No – just brain damage. As long as he can still satisfy you, who cares?' Kate said.

'You're right. Wayne sweetie can still do the business all right. I make sure he does. Several times a day! He's still having a lovely time, even if he doesn't know it,' Christine said thoughtfully.

Michael entered the caretaker's room and very quickly found what he wanted neatly stacked on a shelf. As he locked the door, he got an idea. Michael decided to go on a little detour. He peeked around the corner of the corridor that contained the hostage room. The room with its light bulbs taken out. There was no one there. He would just take a sneaky peak. A little heads up about the competition. Rolling his feet, so he made no sound he walked to the classroom door and lifted the black fabric. There was Gary, sure enough, with another man. Much younger than himself or Gary. Michael pushed his glasses further up his nose with his middle finger to get a better look. Gary saw the glint of the glass in the candlelight.

'Ayup Michael,' Gary shouted in greeting, loudly. Michael dropped the black fabric and quickly made his way back to the staffroom. Hoping that no one had heard Gary. He looked left, right and behind him in the corridor. Michael would be in trouble if anyone found out he had been there. What was doubly annoying was that he knew Kate's husband was more attractive and muscular than him.

By the time he entered the staffroom, he had even more patients waiting. He sighed loudly and didn't hide it. Stephen was also lurking about in the corner.

'What are you here for? You didn't get injured.' He asked.

'Bored. I thought you might need an assistant.'

'You are offering to be my nurse?' Michael asked. Stephen stood with his mouth open. Assistant sounded better than nurse, but he wouldn't squabble about the title. He didn't know what to say to this. Finally, his brain kicked in.

'Yes.'

'The jobs yours. Sit down next to Peter.' He said. Stephen plopped himself down to one side of Peter and looked back at Michael for further instruction.

'The other bloody side of him, Stephen! The side with the arm swinging!' Michael said crossly. Stephen crawled over Peter. His large form catching the limb and pulling the arm, it tore another half inch.'

'Watch it, clumsy,' Peter said.

'Am I on candid camera?' Michael asked. They all regarded him silently. 'Hold the arm up. Jam it up against the other bit. The stump. So, it looks in the normal place.'

Stephen grabbed it and pushed it upwards, it made a mushy sound. He then pulled it back down and wiggled it back up in a different place a few times. Let he let it drop again.

'Peter, do you want the hand facing forward or to your side?' Stephen asked.

'Er, let's say er…to the side of me. Yes,' Peter replied. Stephen pulled it back down again and slushed it into place, smiling at Michael.

'Ready.'

'Are you sure you have finished?' Michael asked. Stephen nodded. 'Well hold it still.' He unrolled a four-inch strip of the gaffer tape he held, then cut it. This he placed on the opposite side to the flap of remaining skin. Now the arm was attached in two places. He continued to peel four-inch strips off the roll until he had gone around the whole arm. 'How does that feel?' He asked Peter. Peter stood up and made a little twirl, the arm didn't move one inch.

'Great thanks, but I think some is stuck in my underarm hair.'

'That is the least of your problems, Peter. I'm moving on to the next now.' Michael said.

Peter moved to the edge of the room to watch the other repairs. Stephen was smelling his fingers and wrinkling his nose. Michael watched him. If Stephen thought it smelt rank to him, then it really was rotten and beyond saving.

'Who's next. Take a seat,' Michael said. The mother of the two children moved forward. Both arms were burned and her hair. She held them stiffly forward as if they might shatter into a million pieces if she put them down. 'Is it just that?' Michael asked.

'What?'

'Barbequed arms. Extra crispy?'

'Yes.'

'Then my able nurse can best help you there. Speak to him and find out what he's doing with his facial burns.' Stephen was wiping his hands on his jeans still and was concentrating on that instead of being Michael's nurse. The woman got up, and her husband sat down.

'I've been slashed in the neck,' He said. It sounded like the slash had gone through and punctured the windpipe or voice box. The voice was gravelly, thick and wet. There was a whistly wheeze about his words too.

'I can see that. Stephen, get up and speak to his wife, while I deal with this neck.' Stephen got up, and Michael sat down. The man still held his fingers over the gash. He had for hours. It wasn't healing. 'Alright, you can take your hand off now,' Michael said confidently. The man took his hand off, and an artery full of dark blood shot out at Michael's glasses. 'Put it back on, put it back on,' he shouted. The man quickly replaced the hand, and the jet stopped.

'Hells teeth! That nearly went into my mouth. We are going to have to be quick here. Stephen, grab that coffee table and pull it towards me.' Stephen did as he asked. Michael cut off five large lengths of tape. Each one, he stuck the end to the edge to the coffee table. Then he picked the final one up and turned to the man. 'When I say go, take your hand off. Try not to squirt on me too much.' The man rolled his eyes towards Michael.

'I'll try,' he replied thickly.

'Go!' Michael shouted. The man took his hand off, and the jet began again. Michael forced the tape over the gash and grabbed another and another, taping them around the wound and further round the neck to secure. By the fifth, the blood had just about stopped, and Michael let a breath out. 'I'll stick a couple more on. Just to give you reassurance.' Michael did this and then as an afterthought said, 'see if you can find some polo neck sweaters somewhere. Give it a bit of support.'

The man seemed happy with his new tight black collar and the thought of his swish new polo neck sweater look. He went to exit the room, with his wife.

'Hey, you two. As much as you might want to, don't go out fighting tonight. I might be on a date later so there will be no Doctor in the house. Understand?' Wordlessly they both shut the door behind them. 'That goes for you too,' he said to Peter, pointing his scissors at him as he observed him crossly of the top of his spectacles. 'Last patient. The lovely Diane. Take a seat.'

'Look what the bastards did to me,' Diane said as she sat down. He looked at the nose perfectly split down the centre. A nostril either side.

'If I can get it back together, it will be fine with a bit of makeup.'

'You're not going to use tape on me are you?'

'No, no. Of course not.' He was going to, but she obviously wasn't up for that. He looked around the room for something else to use. 'Actually, I might have to.'

'No. I'm not having all that round my head, sticking to my hair. No. Find something else.'

'Bloody hell, it's not a Private Medical Practice. I've got nowt else, Diane.'

'Please Michael,' Diane asked and fluttered her eyelashes at him.

'You ladies!' He replied but loved the attention. He looked around the cupboards, the shelves and then ended up in the stationary cabinet. 'Aha!' He shouted after a minute or two. Michael walked back to Diane a smile on his face. 'All because the lady loves.......' He shook his hands open, something rattled, and she looked down. 'Bulldog clips. I can offer m'lady gold, silver or a lovely pink.' He said. Diane seemed happier with this prospect.

'Pink,' she smiled.

'Pink it shall be. I think we might need two or three. Ok.' Michael put the others back on the coffee table and sat down beside Diane. 'Close your little eyes. This might pinch,' She did as he asked and he held her nose together at the top. He took the first bulldog clip, it was only a little wider than the bridge of her nose, but he still tried to force it on. It was in position for a brief second then it pinged back off her nose, somersaulting in the air and clattering to a halt in the corner.

'Ohh, I am a butterfingers,' he said. Michael put the next one a little further down, which held and then another one at the base. 'Ok you can open your eyes now,' he said.

She did, to see that he was taking the vision in. She fluttered her eyelashes again. 'It looks pretty cute, actually Di. I think once it knits together, it will be grand.'

'Thanks, Michael,' she said and stood up. The Master entered the room.

'How are you getting on?' Norman asked.

'Just finished. I am really getting the hang of it. In fact, I think I have a talent for it. Four satisfied customers tonight.' Michael replied. Norman handed Michael a carrier bag, which was full of old newspapers.

'It is nearly time,' Norman said. 'Never mind lambs to the slaughter, we are going to bring the slaughter to the lamb.'

In the church, the evening had arrived, along with so much worry. They lit the candles inside the church. Sally and Kathy constantly read stories to the group of children to distract them. Lauren was frantically acting out the stories herself, to make them laugh. Hungry Hippo's had been put in the bottom of the wardrobe with the Holy Robes. The children would never find it there. The adults said there was a total ban on going outside tonight, no matter how much they wanted to. They would only be safe as long as they stayed inside the building. Terry suggested that Norman might burn down the building somehow, by shooting some kind of flames onto the roof of the Church. 'That's a possibility. He could launch flaming stones at us too. Smashing through the stained-glass windows,' Pat said, putting a Wagon Wheel chocolate biscuit into her mouth, whole.

'There are endless ways he could get something in or get us out. But we can't plan for it all, can we?' Beverly said.

'There is the fact that Michael Thompson could come onto the grounds whenever he likes and do whatever he wants,' Liz said through tight lips.

'Liz, he is one insignificant man to overcome, love. Just imagine him on the lav. We'll do it!' Our Doris told her.

This warmed their hearts. They looked at the massive doors to the church. They were safe and dense, but they were made of wood. Not good. Another worry was that these were the only entrance and exit to the church.

Looking through the main window of the church, Andy stood on watch. He had been on duty for about two hours, and his legs were going stiff. Not a person was about, living or dead. Our Doris was the next person who had volunteered for the watch to relieve Andy. All the others had other duties or were looking after the children. Andy said she could for a few minutes, just until he got the use of his legs back. He didn't know whether to sit down or walk around. Unfortunately, she was so short, that Andy had to stand her on a stack of hymn books just to see out of the window. Haggis started growling and pacing up and down the church. Then he ran and stood underneath where Our Doris was on watch.

'Something is going on,' Wee Renee said and became alert. The others looked through the windows. It was still the same. Not a soul was in sight. The mist swirled undisturbed still, illuminated by the torches.

'There's nowt in sight. All clear,' Laura said, who was also on watch. Haggis still growled.

'What is wrong with Haggis, then?' Bob asked. 'He doesn't growl for nothing.'

'No, he doesn't,' Beverly said, who had also known Haggis all his life.

'Maybe he thinks you are in danger Our Doris,' Lauren said. 'That you're going to fall.'

'Aye come down. After all, you are still taking antibiotics. That goes for you too Terry and Liz. Don't overstretch yourself,' Wee Renee said, but she still felt that something was about to happen.

'Stay vigilant, though everyone. It may not be why he is barking.' The adults walked anxiously around the church. The children hugged each other. Just a quiet growl, deep inside Haggis' chest. Occasionally he made a puffing noise and stamped his front legs. For a few seconds, they thought they were in the clear, as Haggis stopped doing what he had been doing and stood rigid. He was listening. Then there was one enormous loud bark that came deep from the bowels of his stomach, and he got up from where Our Doris stood and ran over to the back of the church. The opposite direction to the road, and main entrance. The area at the back, against the bushes. Where no one at all stood watch. He stood up on his back legs, his front legs on a pew and was listening again. A snarl came from his lips, and he sniffed upwards twice. Something was coming.

'They are here,' Wee Renee said simply.

'I tell you there's no one about and I've been watching the roads. They could not creep along underneath the bushes. No one is here,' Our Doris stated truthfully. Andy went up to her.

'Come down, Our Doris. Let me have a look, chick?' Andy said. She did as he asked and he jumped up in her place.

'It's as quiet as the grave outside, quite literally,' he said, 'she's right.'

'Look, four of us are on watch,' Laura said. 'Me, Our Doris, Nigel, and Danny. There's no one been around the front.'

'What about the back?' Wee Renee said slowly, closing her eyes to the thought.

'There's no entrance at the back, is there? I thought it was just houses at the back,' Terry said. Haggis's growls grew louder.

'Wait a minute,' Tony said. He drew up a chair removing some of the papers from the window. These were the advent calendars that the children had made earlier. Outside, standing just behind the bushes at the back of the church, where there were not many graves stood Father Philip. At the side of him were Keith and Stuart. They could see Tony through the window, all the colour draining out of his face, his mouth open. Keith and Stuart smiled and waved. Keith had Father Philip by the shoulder, policeman style. He could not look at the church, his gaze was cast downwards. He certainly was unhappy about all of it, but nevertheless had still done this deed. Keith turned to Stuart.

'Are you ready?' He asked.

'I have never been more ready in my life,' Stuart replied. They both took a step forward onto the church grounds, pushing Father Philip in front of them. Nothing happened. They took another step. Still nothing. As the two of them moved out of the gap with Father Philip, many white faces became visible behind them. Through the hole in the bushes, came the others.

As the vampires teamed into the churchyard, Norman put his hand up.

'Wait, my children.' He shouted. They all immediately halted. 'Where does it go? All of it?' The Master asked Father Philip. The Priest did not answer but kept his gaze downwards. 'Look at me, now,' The Master said. Father Philip's face shot up like he had just received an electric shock. He could not move his eyes from The Masters' face. He pointed with his hand.

'That way, ten feet around the church, in all directions. Past there is consecrated,' Father Philip said. The rest of the vampires started to walk around to the church door excitedly. Christine danced and twirled as she made her way to the front. This seemed to be a joyous occasion.

Tony got down from the chair and looked back at his friends. He didn't even know if he could tell them, what he had just seen. His breath seemed trapped in his throat, with his voice.

'What?' Pat asked. Tony's mouth opened and closed then suddenly the spell was broken.

'Prepare yourselves. They are here with the Father.'

The Master still held Father Philip in his gaze. The Vicar stood like a statue and could have been mistaken in the dark for one of the ornate grave carvings.

'Wait here. I still may need you.' Norman said and followed the others. Father Philip's feet were rooted, but he very slowly turned his head towards the church. Wee Renee jumped up on the chair that Tony had vacated and stared down at him. Others jumped up beside her, taking the papers off the window to see him.

'You wee rat!' she shouted. Father Philip nodded once and then closed his eyes. He didn't want to look in their eyes anymore. He couldn't bear to do it. The group were startled back to reality with the noises at the church door and looked away from The Priest. Everyone apart from Wee Renee who continued to shoot daggers at Father Philip with her eyes. Keith and Stuart started to bang on the church door. Panic rippled through the inhabitants of the church. The children were screaming. Kathy and Sally were trying to contain them. The two church women had left their posts and calmly walked up to the Lady Chapel. They knelt and began to pray.

Father Philip stood alone now, in shame. All the vampires had run past him and gone to battle. As the Master had moved away a little, his will over The Priest had lessened. His resolve to move now was far is stronger. He looked to the left and right of him, as he couldn't look up into the eyes of Wee Renee. Her judgment was harsh, real and fair. And he deserved everything her eyes said.

To the left, he saw some shoes popping out from behind a gravestone. He needed to get to that person to see who it was. The grave faced the church, with only about ten inches behind it, and the overgrown bushes. He managed to move towards it, with leaden feet, to the gravestone and saw that Tina lay behind it. She had apparently been injured last night and maybe crawled here for shelter and died in the cold.

Father Philip clutched at his heart. It ached for what he had done tonight and how he had failed to protect anyone, especially Tina. No more, he thought, no more. Father Philip lay down on top of Tina's cold body so that The Master could do no more harm to her. He spread out his dark priest's robes, concealing himself and her in the night, under the laurel bushes.

8 - Smashed

Outside of the large wooden door of the church, the rowdy vampires yelled, and the weird clicking sound could be heard. Someone kept screeching. Pat knew it was Christine.

'How is this happening? We are on consecrated ground. How could they come through the back, like that?' Wee Renee asked, turning to the churchwomen. 'Has he unconsecrated it, somehow?'

'No, that is the unconsecrated area, where we bury people of any faith. They can choose to be buried here, whatever place of worship they attend. Their Minister or Priest comes and consecrates a patch just large enough for them, in their faith.' The lady said, looking back at Wee Renee blankly.

'And you didn't think to tell us,' Pat chimed in, while pulling her leggings up higher.

'I thought everyone knew!' The woman replied, indignant.

'Well, we obviously bloody didn't',' Our Doris said, wagging her finger at the woman.

'If I had known this, that we were never safe, we could have gone earlier - taken our chances in a building that had never been consecrated, because that is basically what this is,' Wee Renee shouted angrily.

'Oh no, you're wrong about that,' The other woman said but didn't elaborate. The others waited, but she said no more to reassure them.

'Tell us what you mean then,' Lauren said. The woman shrugged.

'Look, I've had just about enough of these games. You're playing with everyone's lives here, and you don't give a monkey's,' Pat snarled, cracking her knuckles and moving towards them. 'Well I do give a monkeys, so either you tell us exactly what you mean, or I'll take this length of rubber hose I have, and beat you down. Don't think I can't. Both of you.'

One of the women swallowed, her eyes brimmed with tears.

'Ten feet around the church is unconsecrated. I don't know why. And that patch, where they entered. Everything else *is*. The building, the graveyard and the main path up from the gates.'

'So, are you saying, we could give them a wee push off the circle round the church into the grounds, and they would be up the creek, without a paddle?' Wee Renee asked.

'Yes!'

Come out, come out, wherever you are a group of them sang. Laughing joyfully, Norman reached the front. He instructed Michael to do as he had asked. Michael was holding a carrier bag full of newspapers rolled up very tightly into long thin tubes. He bent down and began to shove them all the way along the bottom of the wooden front doors. Inside the church, the people could hear the vampires shouting and an occasional rustling of paper.

'It's a note!' Exclaimed one of the ladies from the church as she saw the first little piece of paper that peeped under the door. When they saw the others start to appear and Wee Renee saw that it was newspaper and not notepaper, she guessed what they were doing.

'No, they are going to set fire to the door,' she whispered. The second she said it, they heard the crackling sound of fire as Michael put his lighter on the newspaper. He went across the row of tubes from left to right systematically lighting each tube. He didn't move on until the each one was well and truly alight. Some of the paper was damp and the night was cold, but newspaper burns so easily, even under those conditions. As he had rolled them up into tubes, they syphoned the smoke down, under the door and into the church.

'We knew it would be fire, didn't we, Terry?' Pat said to him. He nodded sadly. The group looked at each other, searching for inspiration. They had not planned for this. Assuming that just another fight was on the cards, they had weapons ready, but no masks. Currently, their fate inside the church was either being burnt alive or dying from smoke inhalation.

The humans in the church had to decide very quickly. Should they try and fight now and maybe save the doors from burning. Or stay safe, and perhaps smash the windows for air. This would also mean a way in again for the creatures. Where they could pump more smoke or fire into the sanctuary. There was only one thing for it. They removed the pew from the front of the doors, took up their weapons and made themselves ready.

Smoke was coming in quite thickly now, and the horde of vampires were cheering outside. Baying for blood.

The children started coughing, Kathy and Sally told them to pull their sweaters up over their noses.

'We need to let fresh air in quick,' Bob said.

'Right, we are going out. Do as much as you can to push them on the grounds, they are performing keyhole surgery. Let's open the wound,' Wee Renee said.

The two ladies that were from the church congregation said they would look after the children as they had no weapons. They didn't really want to fight unless it was absolutely necessary. Every person who had come from Friarmere Band and Melden held their weapons ready.

'Get ready,' Our Doris said.

'Open it.' Wee Renee stated. Danny opened one door, and Tony opened the other. The double doors swung open, and there were the vampires. They still could not enter the church, and if the children were kept in the church, they would be safe. Tony pointed his gun up, intending to kill Michael. He wasn't there, and the other vampires were not afraid of it. After all, it did not kill them.

The air was cold and tense, as it wrapped itself around the group of humans. The slivers of burning newspaper drifted lazily up, caught by the wind. They rose into the night for a moment then dropped onto the snow, where they were extinguished. The virgin white, ruined.

'Charge!' Wee Renee shouted, and the people of the church surged outside. They outnumbered the vampires, by nearly two to one. But the vampires had strength and the night, where they had perfect vision. The humans did not. And it was suddenly extremely dark outside the church, as the doors were opened.

This was because Michael had wandered on to the consecrated ground and snuffed out every one of the torches they had made, by picking them up and throwing them into the snow. The vampires had even more of an advantage. He now stood proudly at the back with Norman.

After being in a very well-lit church to an unlit churchyard, the group suffered an immense shock to their eyes. It felt like they were wading through ink. They blinked quickly to adjust, but it wasn't happening. On this cloudy night, it really was so black outside. Dangerous even without obstacles, vampires with deadly teeth and twenty other people all swinging weapons about.

Beverly, Kathy, Terry, and Laura went for the vampire duo of Christine and Wayne. Wayne was still very much like a zombie and in Christine's thrall. He lumbered around using his arms like clubs. Swinging them in all directions, just trying to hopefully connect with a human. However, he was slow, and for some reason, he seemed to trip constantly. Christine darted this way and that. She had long red nails that she tried to scratch everyone with. In a deft move, Beverly got behind Christine and yanked her head back by her hair, shouting to the other two women to slit her throat. To avoid this fate, Christine wrenched her head back away from Beverly. Her head jerked upwards against her attacker's cast iron grip. Unfortunately, most of her hair and scalp remained in the heroine's hand. Beverly's hand and arm, immediately became wet, the long blonde hair, clinging instantly to the blood, as it lost its head.

Beverly yelled in disgust and threw Christine's scalp onto the consecrated ground. It smoked and turned to ash, without catching fire. There would be no repair from Michael, for Christine. Christine whooped maniacally in her anguish. As she glanced back, she managed to just glimpse the last few strands of her hair disintegrate.

'You're mostly bald now. I think you should know,' Laura said. Christine's hands frantically went up to her head to touch it and then seemed to change their minds and both hover, shaking and rigid, two inches from her head. The crimson nails and the gory red mess of skull, perfectly matched. But Laura was pretty sure that it wasn't what Christine had planned to twin them with when she had painted them.

She moved quickly behind Wayne. Still making the awful whooping noise. Wayne continued to swipe around with his club arms, grunting.

'Protect me, sweetie,' she said in a quivering voice. Terry had a large staff from the church, which he was trying to hit Wayne with. Wayne was not quick, but he did keep managing to knock the end away from himself and Christine who he stood in front of. He was very slow, but he was immensely strong.

Terry still swung and stabbed the enormous thick staff, protecting the three other women, who continued to try and strike at Christine. Kathy had some of the stakes, from Mary's house, in her pocket. She was trying to get Christine first from the front then the back. Christine was more dangerous than Wayne. The original group from Friarmere had told Kathy, Beverly, and Terry, that she was one of Norman's special vampires. One of his Lieutenants. If they could just get her, maybe that would make a dent in his arsenal.

Danny, Andy, and Tony were trying to tackle Sandra and Tracy. Sandra and Tracy had both been lovers of their bandmate, Simon. They had united in death to kill him, and here they were again, a formidable tag team. The two female vampires moved as one, with a connection that was unfathomable. Like a pair of velociraptors, they crouched and dodged, moving super-fast, trying to trick the three men.

Tony held Sandra at bay, with one of the flaming cans of hairspray, which also gave the human's a great deal of light. A stake from Mary's house was in his pocket along with a knife. Andy and Danny tried to grab Tracy, missing a few times, as she leapt about, trying to get to Sandra. It was Danny however that managed to catch a hold of her by the wrist.

'Andy quick,' Danny shouted. Andy went for the other which she whipped about frantically, trying to provide propulsion away from Danny. Andy launched his whole body at the arm, and they had her. Danny kicked her legs backwards from beneath her, and the two men dragged her unbelievably fast, screaming towards the wall of the church. She arched her back, her feet finding the floor again and she started to pull against them. Sandra scrabbled in the air for her evil twin, but Tony kept the flame in front of her, dodging with her.

Andy kicked Tracy's legs repeatedly like he was trying to score the biggest goal at Wembley Stadium. Finally, her legs went again, she was dragged and felt her head resting on something, it was beginning to burn at the back of her head. Danny had put her head against an ornamental shelf of the church wall. A consecrated shelf. They saw her eyes roll into her head, this was taking too long, and she still struggled. Andy took his chance. He released the arm, and as fast as lightning, he grabbed her head, lifted it, then bashed her head on the church wall. Her eyes opened, teeth bared, black blood filled her upturned nostrils. He bashed it again, and again. This coconut was proving hard to crack. Then it did finally. The struggling stopped, and Tracy fell to the floor. That fight had used a lot of their strength.

Immediately they turned to help Tony, running to grab Sandra's arms. This proved easier than Tracy as she also had the added threat of Tony to contend with. Danny ran with unexpected speed and underestimated where he was, going for her hand but ended up grabbing her upper arm, which was more dangerous as he was closer. Andy snatched and caught one of her wrists.

'Got her?' Tony asked.

'Yes!' Replied Andy. Tony stopped spraying the hairspray and dropped it to the floor, he knew another few seconds, and it would have been empty. It clattered and rolled down the path of the church towards the front entrance noisily. He ran around the back of Sandra and grabbed her around the waist. She was going to take the three of them. Sandra was even stronger than Tracy.

They pulled her back onto the front of the churchyard, amongst the graves, where the consecrated ground was. Immediately she started screaming, and they felt her struggles decreasing. Her strength was draining away. Now their hands felt more powerful than her efforts. She curved back, her head was near Tony's neck, but she had her eyes closed, screaming in agony. How quickly she could have escaped if only she had seen his pulsing vein, two inches from her teeth. Tony let go of her waist with one hand, she was like a clock winding down. The power running out of her, like a battery.

He took the knife out of his pocket and calmly slit her throat as it curved upwards, exposed to him. He cut it unevenly but very deeply. His knife smeared with her dark fluids. Her black blood dripped thickly but hastily down to the ground, instantly transforming into a hint of fire and then a puff of smoke. Gone forever. She lay dying just two seconds in their arms. Then they dropped her on the ground where she toppled over to her front as she fell, her head was tilted back, the edge of the cut landing on the corner of a grave. Tony stamped on the back of her neck which split into two easily. The head left the body and rolled forward. The body remained in its place and started to smoke. It shook as the underneath caught fire burning from the bottom up. Rolling down the hill, her head eventually settled alongside the empty can of hairspray at the bottom. Still, on church grounds, it finally roared into flames.

Four humans went after the formidable pair of Stuart and Keith. Sue, Bob, Our Doris, and Nigel. Sue had a lit hairspray. Our Doris naturally was wielding the sword.

Nigel was a strong, fit man, and Bob was glad to be fighting alongside him. Bob had given Nigel the rundown on the vampires. Nigel wanted to take the worst ones out first. Bob had told him that these were Keith, Christine, Stephen, and Peter. Now one of them was here. Bob had described Keith, which sounded pretty bad. Keith in the flesh, however, had surpassed even Bob's vivid adjectives.

Bob had his long pokey knife sharpener from Ian's butcher shop and stakes in his pockets. Nigel had two of his very long, broad knives from the kebab shop, one in each hand. Keith seemed like he was not prepared for this new foe, with his fearsome weapons and backed away hissing. Keith had meant to pick his battles tonight. With who and when *he* wanted. He wasn't expecting two to target him.

They tried to move forward, so Keith would have to back onto the consecrated ground, but he didn't fall for that move and launched himself forward at them, away from the graveyard. At one point he managed to grab Bob's coat by the arm, but luckily it was just a couple of fingers of fabric. Bob took this opportunity to shove the metal sharpener into him, upwards. It entered just below Keith's ear. It did not go very far as Keith had already started a backward trajectory, after seeing what Bob was planning. If he had stayed still or moved forward, it would probably have killed him.

Keith's head swivelled round to look at the others. He decided this was not working for him tonight, turned and ran out through the unconsecrated part of the land at the back. The bushes rustling behind him.

'Coward!' Bob yelled.

'Next time we'll get you good and proper,' Nigel shouted.

Stuart and Our Doris were sparring. He had been a sensible man, a policeman, and was now a deadly, intelligent vampire. Our Doris had her trusty sword, which she swung with all her strength and moved forward. Just as he was going to dodge to one side, Sue lit the hairspray again. She had stakes in her back pocket which she planned to use tonight.

Stuart stumbled backwards and fell onto the consecrated ground grabbing hold of one of the gravestones to steady himself. His hand smoked and sizzled. He pushed upwards and started to scream. Sue forced him back again. Our Doris couldn't get a good swing on her sword because other graves were in the way.

Stuart was trying to make his way to the back of the church to join Keith. Our Doris moved to the other side and had to slash in the opposite direction. She wouldn't be as accurate in this position. The sword connected with the vampire but only managed to slash across his stomach. Cutting through several layers of clothing, but only a thin line of skin was caught. Keith's head appeared out of the bushes, firstly clicking then shouting.

'Run Stuart, we'll get them another night. Run you fool!' Keith shouted. They looked round to see where Keith had yelled from and Stuart used this chance to run around Our Doris, off the consecrated ground and into the bushes to join Keith.

Pat, Wee Renee, and Liz, three ladies who were hell-bent for revenge had decided to target Norman. Liz was out for killing him tonight, she thought it would all be over if that happened. Pat and was trying to attack his arms with her lump hammer as they lashed. Wee Renee was working as hard as she could to get him in the neck with her machete. She wanted to take off his head. Liz held a large cross and a stake. It was his heart she wanted. He was slowly retreating towards the back of the church even though he was certainly putting up a good fight. Three of the best fighters were after him and not landing any blows whatsoever. He glanced over and saw that Sandra and Tracy where dead and wasted. This made him furious, and instead of defending himself, he went on the attack. He knocked the cross out of Liz's had with his sleeve, and managed to grab her by the throat. Her hand prodded the stake forward but his arms were so much longer than hers, and she could only hit thin air.

'Oh, my lost sheep. Your shepherd is here now. How I have waited for a chance at you. Vegetable eater,' The Master said. Wee Renee and Pat were behind Liz, so could not get a clear shot at Norman. Luckily for Liz, some of the others who had been fighting Stuart and Keith ran to help.

Norman saw the number of people with weapons that were about to attack him and made an unholy scream. It pierced the night, vibrating eardrums painfully. The other people held their hands over their ears. Wayne was distracted for a moment, and it was at this point that Kathy closed her eyes to the pain and managed to shove a stake straight through his heart.

'No sweetie!' Christine shrieked, reaching for him. It was too late, he was gone. Wayne had been released from his weeks of torment. Now he looked peaceful. Christine stood up clutching her fists, walking away from her dead mate. Norman's scream had startled the children inside who began to run outside. They seemed as if they were drugged, unaware of what they were doing, eyes staring into the night. The two churchwomen that were watching them jumped down the steps in front of them, with their arms open, gathering them forward.

Christine made to retreat towards the bushes, but revenge was on her mind. She grabbed both women at the bottom of the steps and rammed one of the woman's heads onto a spike that had been there a hundred years, to tether various animals outside. It pierced through her temple and deep into her brain. Her death was instant, and she remained impaled on the spike.

Christine grabbed the other woman around the neck, putting her between herself and her attackers. Norman disappeared through the bushes.

'I'm Christine! And I aren't scared of you. You are my prey, my food. You are nothing!' She shouted. Her head, bloody and mostly hairless, tilted back slowly then, horrifically fast, came down, biting down on the woman's neck. She snatched out her scream and her throat with her teeth. Then, covered in blood, as it sprayed everywhere, the snow absorbing the woman's life, she spat out the chunk she had in her mouth.

'Thank you!' Christine screamed at the woman in gratitude. Then disappeared into the bushes, snow falling from the leaves onto the body of the dead woman.

The bushes had closed behind them as if they had never been there. The Churchyard was empty again. The exchange had left three more vampires neutralised. Two of the humans were now dead too.

The group took deep breaths. Trying to take in what had just happened.

'Light the bloody torches again!' Our Doris shouted, and they jumped out of their shocked state, to attention. Some of the men ran in, fetching the spare torches. They lit the torches they had, while a few stood on guard at the bushes.

Beverly, Kathy, and Sally took inventory of the children, who were all present. Wee Renee went inside and removed one of the large crosses from the church. She walked around to the back of the church, Pat, Sue, Our Doris, and Lauren followed. She stood before the snowless gap in the bushes.

Bending over, she shoved the cross into the ground right by the entrance.

'I bless this ground with love and light. The whole graveyard is under your protection. Cleanse it of the dark monsters and keep us safe tonight,' Wee Renee said. This strangely moved Lauren and Our Doris passed her a tissue as she could see tears dripping from her chin. Haggis watched the ladies consecrate the ground from the path behind them. He no longer felt like barking. The bad things had gone. So he sat down and began to clean his underparts.

The five ladies, freezing cold, waited for a moment. Maybe expecting a further occurrence. But then they and Haggis walked around to the entrance. Terry and Nigel shut the doors behind them. Bob took in the state of the people and the manic looks of the children. Tonight was going to be a long night.

'Do you think they will come again tonight?' Bob asked anyone who would listen.

'No, not tonight, son,' Tony said. 'I think they have taken a beating.'

'Not tonight, but they will tomorrow. In the morning, I think we will be leaving here,' Wee Renee said. No one argued with that. Two sieges in the church were enough for anyone.

9 - Nuts

There was an awful lot of crying from the children most of the night. Half of them had seen the death of the lady impaled on the spike and had told the others. Sally and Laura were doing their best to keep it together. Terry wasn't good either. All in all, he was a sensitive man and what had happened tonight would rattle even the strongest brain.

Wee Renee thought that the two ladies from the church should be wrapped in a Holy Alb and put with Ian. About six am, four of the men went outside to deal with them in the dark.

As Nigel and Tony approached the lady at the front, they could see the blood, frozen in icicles from the spike to the snow. Her eyes were closed and peaceful. She was locked in her dying position. Her blood and hair had frozen to the spike.

They could not free her, and in the end, Nigel got one of the flaming torches and *defrosted* her a little. The consequences were the smell of burning hair and the dripping of blood, but she became free after about fifteen minutes of warming and tugging. It still took quite a lot of strength to move her.

The lady at the back was less of a problem, but her throat was hard to locate in the dark. That would have been a very nasty find for anyone. Her eyes were frozen – open forever to the horrors. She had been terrorised by Christine for a few moments before her death. Anyone who hadn't witness her murder would be able to see how terrible her last few moments were. Her expression was ghastly. Stuck in its horror, un-relaxed. The mouth was open, still projecting its last dreadful scream. It was now half full of blood, which had become a frozen plug. With the eyelids frozen open too, there would be no putting her face back to a peaceful position. Not until she thawed anyway. Finally, she was united with her missing piece, wrapped in the Alb and put with her friend, under the bushes with Ian and covered with the plant pots. The men rejoined the group. It was still dark.

In the morning, even before light, they decided they would have to leave. Now the un-consecrated ground had been revealed, even though they hoped that they had consecrated it again, there could be other areas they didn't know about. Besides that, Michael Thompson could always come in and smoke them out, night or day.

'Maybe they will use Pat's idea of flaming rocks. Fire got us out last night, didn't it?' Lauren said, she was a huge fan of Pat. No one could dispute, however, that the church was no longer safe. It had never been really. It did not have enough exits. One door to the church, and one gate to the churchyard. The vampires would find another way in tonight. It really wasn't comfortable either, although that was not a priority. Wee Renee decided that Plan B was now activated. Apart from that, there was still the issue of Gary and Carl to rescue, from the same beasts that they were trying to avoid.

Sue spoke to Wee Renee and Pat. It was clear to all of them that the children needed to run outside and play a little. They felt caged in and before going on their trek and being trapped again in another building for the evening, they should have a runaround. Plus it meant Sue could pack everything up, without them getting in the way.

'Aye, we should check the grounds first. There are probably a few things to deal with,' Wee Renee said. Of course, there would be no living vampires about in the daytime, but they never knew if Michael might be there lying in wait. Some of them went outside and tried to roll the three vampires away to the grounds near the front of the church. No one knew what to do with them to prevent the children having to see the filthy corpses. It was no use trying to put them under any bushes as children ran about so much. They were a horrific and bloody sight. It was decided that they certainly would not be put with Ian and the two church ladies. That would feel wrong. Unholy monsters, killers, and bloodsuckers did not deserve to rest on consecrated ground.

'Come on, put your thinking caps on. I'm sick of holding this,' Our Doris said, with Sandra's head underneath her arm. Pat had the *lightbulb moment* of putting them in the wheelie bin, as they were rubbish anyway.

'If the binmen ever get around to doing this area again, I am sure they will find a lot of filthy shit in the bins. We won't be the only ones dumping crap in there,' Pat said shrugging. Nigel thought they might be. He didn't believe hiding three dead vampires, one headless, in a bin was going to be as common as Pat thought. A couple of the men picked up the dead creatures and dumped them unceremoniously into the bin. There was a thick smear of black blood trailing from where they had been killed, right up to the bin. Their viscous fluids had been preserved partially in their runny states. There was some burning of the flesh that had been against the consecrated ground. But where the body was thicker, the stomach, chest and the top of the head, it remained the same. The base of them was hard, more like baked or brick-like rather than the ashy powder of Adrian in the butchers. The top of them was still wet. It was also showed that their blood hadn't frozen. Interesting.

The men walked around for a few moments kicking the other snow over the top to cover the grisly black evidence. Kathy, Sally, Beverly, and Laura said they would stand in front of the bins and supervise.

'Make sure they don't throw any snowballs!' Sue advised them, who had wild visions of a child getting a black snowball in the mouth and becoming infected.

Wee Renee thought that she would have a quick check around the back to ensure all was safe for them there. Last night they had shoved crosses in the ground, which were still in position. Several of them had been looking out of the back window every so often. They didn't want to get caught out again. The crosses were still embedded in the deep snow, all around it undisturbed.

She was singing *Jingle Bells* as she walked briskly around the corner. Someone had been alerted by the sound of her voice as she heard a groan. And she immediately looked to the left of her to see a figure lying on the snow, half concealed by a gravestone. She walked over to investigate the sound. *Was this an injured one of their party? Was this Michael Thomson waiting to trap her?*

Father Philip stood up, he had been lying on a deceased Tina all night.

'Pat!' Wee Renee shouted at the top of her voice. Pat's feet could be heard clumping very quickly around to the back of the church, to the aid of Wee Renee. Tony and Danny stood on chairs in the church, as they had heard her shout. The two men peeked through the window and were amazed to see it was Father Philip.

Pat stood at the side of Wee Renee. Father Philip waited until she was there before he had addressed the two of them. His face and hands were raw with cold. It was only the fact that Tina lay beneath him, protecting him from the worst of the frozen ground in her warm clothing, that he was still alive.

'I'm sorry, I had no choice,' Father Philip said. 'I carry his blood in me,'

'We know what it's like, you know. There are three infected in there. You could have had the antibiotics and resisted him!'

'I've not been a snitch deliberately. I had no choice but to tell him – you simply don't understand. When you are there, carrying his blood, that is all you can see. Before you know it, you've told him everything.'

'I simply don't believe that, you snake in the grass. Call yourself a man of the cloth?' Wee Renee said.

'Please forgive me. I would like to make amends. Let me come back inside the church with you. You cannot make me feel any more terrible than I already feel,' he said sadly.

'Oh, can't I?' Wee Renee exclaimed. She walked up and slapped his face.

'Is that it?' Pat asked.

'He is humiliated enough,' Wee Renee replied.

'Not for me, he isn't!' Pat ran up to him and gave him a swift kick. He crumpled to the ground and Pat and Wee Renee walked off. Tony turned to Danny with his mouth open.

'Did I just see Pat give the Vicar a kick square in the nuts?' Danny said.

'Yes, you did!' Tony replied, his eyes huge with shock and merriment. They both laughed.

The children had a small play outside. It was much less riotous than usual. They needed normality, and this just wasn't it. While they played, most of the adults loaded provisions. Clothes, food, blankets, and as many small crosses from the church as they could get, stacked on the sledge and in everyone's backpack, even the children's.

Soon the church was empty of everything that they could possibly use. They set off on their journey at about eleven o'clock in the morning. They were aware that they were leaving a lot of footprints and this could easily be traced back to where they would be staying.

'Those bloodsuckers will follow us here, there is no question,' Laura said, looking behind them at the torrent of tracks they were leaving.

'What I am hoping is that there will be enough weapons there so that we can defend ourselves. We're sitting ducks in the church.' Wee Renee said.

'Hobson's Choice,' Pat said simply and shrugged.

The day was dull and grey. Their mood was the same. They said little. Walking again from hell on earth to a new, uncertain nightmare tonight. How many more days would they have to do this? How many more nights? Where was the fresh hope? Was there anyone else alive at all here? They needed help and rest and shelter. Most of all they needed some piece of mind.

When they got into the centre of Friarmere, again not a soul was about. From what they could see, only the horde of vampires had passed through last night. The freezing wind whistled up the main street. When they spoke, their voices went a long way. Their words seemed to seek out company and returned to them even lonelier. Each shop looked cold, empty and eerie. They now lived in a ghost town in the day. A hotbed of evil at night.

The hardware store had shutters at the front. These had small holes so that you could see through them and inside the glass of the shop. There was no way in at the front.

A few of the people took the children to the grocery shop and told them to stuff every one of their pockets with as much food and drink as they could. Our Doris, Terry, Tony, and Sue went with them.

First, they checked out the back of the shop to make sure that were no vampires lurking in the dark. While the kids, looked excitedly for treats and goodies, the adults ferried out carrier bags of useful food, drink, and other items, and put them on the pavement. Sally, Kathy, Beverly, Lauren, and Bob, took these bags and began to stack them in the alley behind the hardware store while the remaining group negotiated a way in.

The back entrance to the hardware store, firstly had a gate to the alley, inside there, was a small yard. The door to the building was metal and reinforced. It looked like a strangely shaped key gained entry. None of them knew how to pick locks, so for the moment, they were stumped.

'Look up yonder,' Wee Renee pointed. Above them on what looked like the second floor was a small window that was slightly open, with steam coming out. 'There, that's where we will get in,' she told them. They looked up at the window. How high and small it was.

'There is no way anyone can get through there,' Danny said.

'I bet I could,' Wee Renee said.

'I could as well,' Our Doris informed them, 'but I'm not as supple as Wee Renee.'

'Look how far it is up!' Liz exclaimed.

'You've heard of ladders,' Wee Renee said, 'now let's go find some, and I'll go for it.' Andy found some ladders from the back of a house two doors down and put them up to the window. The top rung sat a couple of feet below the small window.

'Right. I need at least two fellas' holding them at the bottom and someone to be my eyes, who can stand back,' she said. By this time everyone was back from the grocery shop. Tony and Andy held the ladders, Nigel stood way back in the alley, with Our Doris and Haggis, so they could they had a good view and could help if required.

Liz and Lauren stood in the street. If Michael Thompson was sniffing around for any reason, they wanted to know. Norman may catch up with them in time, but it was no use sending him their address, via Thompson. Wee Renee threw off her backpack and scrambled up with surprising agility. She slowed down for the last few steps, and they could see that her legs were wobbling

'I'm not fond of heights, you know,' she shouted down.

'You're doing great, love,' Our Doris shouted. From where she stood, the window looked too small. Wee Renee was tiny, but there were limits, even for her. All of them didn't know if she could get through or not, it would be a close call. They hoped she could, as there was no other way in and no Plan C.

She reached the window and fiddled under the small gap, with the hot air coming out. The latch opened wider, and she pulled the window open to its fullest. She was unsure herself as to whether she could get through. Wee Renee carefully shoved her head in and looked down. The window was above a stairwell. A small landing was below as the stairs turned, changing direction. It was still quite a drop down there. For sure, if she dropped down, she would break her legs. This had to be done very carefully. She drew her head back and thought for a moment, left the window on its largest setting, then came back down the ladders slowly.

'I'm going to throw some things through there. I need lots underneath to give me a soft landing. The group gathered backpacks, clothes, and blankets. Instead of Wee Renee going back up, Danny and Tony took turns going up and throwing stuff through the window. They could not get their head and shoulders through to see where they were throwing, but a great deal of paraphernalia went through.

Andy managed to get two quilts that they had previously and shove them through the little gap. A couple of the kids had sleeping bags, and nearly all the backpacks were dropped in, as long as they didn't contain anything breakable or sharp.

Finally, everything they could possibly use was in there, and Wee Renee said she was going to go for it.

Up the ladder, she went again. She got her head and shoulders through and looked again. There was a small mountain underneath her for landing, and only a few items had fallen astray. Pat watched for quite a while as she tried to pull herself through holding onto the windowsill inside. She got half her body through, her hips and legs were dangling and thrashing outside. 'Go on Rene!' Pat shouted.

She hooked her legs around the window outside and seemed to be trying to rearrange herself for the fall. Wee Renee had found a set of metal pipes to the left of the window inside. She grabbed hold of these to try and pull herself through. Easing her legs through inch by inch, the plan was to drop them down first, before her body. Most of Wee Renee was on the left now, through the window, holding on to the pipes. Her legs would come through to the right of her.

It was a good job she was so light and amazingly strong, or this couldn't have worked. As she looked down, she realised if she didn't' get through, everyone would be without their possessions. She hadn't thought of that.

Finally, the last of her popped through, the momentum of her legs coming free, she used by letting go and plopping down below. Everything was very soft and comfortable beneath her as she fell. She bounced back on the pile, banging her head on the wall.

She stood up, rubbing her head and looked around. Back up at the tiny window she had emerged from, she could just about see the winter sky. The others were shouting out, asking if she had hurt herself.

Wee Renee walked down the small set of stairs and turned to the metal exit door. It had a bar on it and a peg, which was currently unused. This would disable the door if placed in a particular hole. She pushed the bar, which opened the door. All the people and children cheered, and she smiled, grateful.

The humans all rushed in out of the cold. Haggis ran into the shop ahead of the others, and all sledges and food were brought in. Nigel shut the door behind him. They had got here safe. Plan B had worked. They shoved the sledges against the door and put the little peg in its hole.

'Do you know you are a little marvel, Wee Renee,' Nigel said.

'Superwoman, I would call her,' Our Doris added.

'Aye, get away with you all, it was nothing,' Wee Renee said to everyone, clearly embarrassed.

'Nothing my arse. I wouldn't swap you for a gold pig,' Pat said, putting her arm around her.

Through a door from the back hallway, was a large room, with two enormous wooden tables. These tables had vices attached either side. There were metal shelves on two sides of the room full of various bits and bobs. Half tins of paint, tape, boxes of nails and screws, sealant, bolts, and washers. This was the workshop that Gary had done some training in. Apart from the two tables and the shelves, it was empty. The room smelled of paint and pinewood. Past the tables on the opposite side to the hallway door was the main shop.

Sally and Kathy told the children to sit down and rest. They were not to be allowed in the main shop. It was far too dangerous. All the food was shared out, as it was now way past lunchtime. The children sat cross-legged against the wall of the workshop.

The adults walked into the hardware store to investigate. The light lay in stripes across the shop as it squeezed its way through the small slits in the shutters. Lauren discovered just by accident that the front door was actually open, and it was only the shutter that was keeping them from the outside world. That was a little bit worrying. The hardware store was also not very warm. They could see their breath as they talked. It didn't help as it had so many metal implements for sale, conducting the heat away. But that was the good part about it too. That was what they were here for.

10 - Hardware

The adults started to look around the hardware shop, taking inventory. Letting their minds run wild with ideas for new and exciting weapons. Most of them felt that all their Christmas's had come at once. This was just what they had needed. There were some interesting combinations of tools that they could use. There was a discussion as to whether the children should have tools too. Bob was firmly on the side that they should have a little bit of something, even if it just gave them confidence, and this was the persuader. Everyone agreed as long as there was a strong safety talk about not using the weapons on each other for play fighting. Kathy and Laura felt that the children were under no illusion what the real threat was. This situation had changed them, and they had not seen them play fighting once.

Over the last few days, they had witnessed at least two battles, if not more on previous occasions. Weapons meant life and death now. Watching someone get beheaded or chopped up, took weapons right off their *things to play with list* and onto the *I am going to die – this will help me*, list.

These children were much older than they looked now. So a little protection for themselves, a small hint of comfort and security would be fine. Small items were picked out, that the children could carry themselves. Bob had significant input in this and between him, Beverly, Sally, Kathy and Lauren, they chose quite a few little axes and knives. All of these had plastic shields which could be removed but could be carried easily and safely by children.

Some of the men thought that lighting was crucial especially after last night. This was something that had been discussed even before the last battle, at the planning committee meetings by the church doors. They started to look at battery-powered lamps that were on a strap. Ones that could be worn on the head or even around the neck. Terry took lots of little lights and torches through to the workshop as these would be ideal for the children to hold, and the ladies began to distribute these too along with the mini weapons. Pat said she was considering donating her toffee hammer to the children. If she found something far more deadly, then a special child could have that. Surprisingly there was a lot of interest.

There was a feeling of uselessness and burden amongst the children. They couldn't fight and knew the adults had a lot to think about apart from feeding and protecting them. Bob, Terry and the five ladies that had looked after them the most, gave them a little talk. They told them they could be useful to the cause. When they were walking outside, they could hold the lamps and torches, so that the adults had their hands free for weapons. They also gave them a small item of protection themselves.

The children were very grateful to have them. They felt like they were being trusted to be part of the group. Some were still very withdrawn, they could not get the sight of their parents faces out of their head, and they had to have an adult with them nearly all the time to console and counsel them. Terry seemed to be doing an excellent job of this. His training as a dentist and having to reason with children who were having teeth procedures seemed to be paying off. He seemed to have turned a couple of them completely around, but the two children that had opened the church doors to their vampire parents two nights ago were still in a worrying state.

Pat and Our Doris were extremely excited to find several cast-iron fireside companion sets, complete with pokers, which they said would be invaluable.

The pokers were a good weight for swinging and stabbing, but not too heavy to be cumbersome. They were about two feet in length, so could be used in the same way as a small sword. Pat found a longer one on its own at the back of the shop. This was nearly three feet in length and had a hook on the end. Nigel informed her that it was a poker for barbeques and she decided the hook might lock into a skull or fold of bone and not come out – so she would stick with the companion sets with Our Doris. Wee Renee said she would take this if no-one else wanted it. The hook on the end of her cheese knife had proved very useful, and she had an idea of how she could use this item.

Anything long would be useful. Putting a distance between the vampire's teeth and their necks was always a good idea. There were quite a few broom handles. Some of these were metal, the others wood. Danny and Tony had found large knives and began to tape them to the top of them, to make spears or lances. Soon they had created twelve and decided to stop at that. Danny found some nail gun ammo, which would cheer up Gary when they rescued him. He would put that on the sledge for taking later.

During the search for the light's, Andy had made a discovery. Some of the lamps had daylight bulbs. This caused a ripple of excitement throughout the group. Until they tried them, they wouldn't know if these would kill their enemies or just protect the group from harm. At the worst, even if they made no difference, they were at least another light source. It was worth a shot, so they picked up these 5too.

Bob had been wandering around looking for lots of small weapons for the children. He had decided to look through the plumbing section for long pieces of pipe. These could be used for battering a vampire or poking hard into the soft flesh, without the nasty sharp end to accidentally cut anyone else with. As his mind was thinking about brass, he began to pick up anything that was shiny and yellow. One item was very interesting. It was a thick copper ribbon that was about three inches deep. Bob didn't know what it was for. He took some heavy scissors and cut off at length. Bob had a plan for it. He laughed to himself.

His mind drifted back to his lengths of pipe. He thought that the vampire's flesh was soft enough to pierce without a sharp entry if you put enough force behind it. This would probably just cause a nasty round bruise on normal skin, but he was willing to try out his theory the next time he encountered one. He thought he would tape something soft to the end so that he could put more force behind it. He looked around and caught sight of a large roll of loft insulation. Some of that would do. Bob set to work to fashion his invention.

Tony wandered over at some point and asked what he was doing with the 'lagging'. Tony listened, then took a hammer and flattened the end of the copper pipe, so it now had a point. He also bent the other end so that Bob wouldn't be pushing on cut metal. After that came the lagging. It ended up an excellent weapon, and Tony and Bob had requests for a couple more of them. Bob said he wanted the glory for every vampire they killed, as it was his idea.

Wee Renee found some plant sprays, which she said they would be able to utilise in various ways, but did not elaborate. She said that when they left, they would be taking them.

Pat was now testing out different hammers, just in case she mislaid her club hammer inside a vampire. She had decided that she would try and find one that was a little lighter so she could carry lots of other lethal weapons. Pat currently was testing out a tent mallet. The lightness was right, but as she squatted on the floor, banging it down, she felt there was way too much bounce. This position on the floor, also meant that flatulence was becoming an issue to hold in. Then it became impossible.

'Bloody tripe,' she muttered. Andy looked at Danny, she thought they couldn't hear her.

'Most noises that come from her are entirely involuntary,' Andy said knowingly.

Tony had moved on to some circular saw blades. He smiled as he stroked the sharp circles. Tony knew exactly what he was going to do with these.

'What are you going to do with them?' Sue asked, picking one up. They smelled oily, and she wrinkled her nose. 'These can only be used for close combat, and we have got tons of weapons like that, plus the stakes.' She held one between her two hands. Making a slicing motion in front of her.

'You are not getting it, Sue, are you?' Tony replied. He took the large circular saw blade off her and lay it flat in his hand. Then went to throw it like a frisbee. Her eyebrows shot up.

'What the hell!' Sue exclaimed.

'What's that?' Pat asked, her arms full of pokers, rope and plant spray bottles. She was currently working hard on sucking two Uncle Joe's Mint Balls.

'Circular saw frisbee,' Tony mimed the action again for Pat. 'I just invented it.'

'Lethal and very nice. Just check they don't act like boomerang's when I am about!' Pat said. The sweets clicked against her dentures as she struggled to talk. She clumped into the back room. Sue folded her arms, gave him a long look, then walked off too.

Sue thought this was just as dangerous, if not more so than his gun. Why did he have to always pick something like that? Sometimes she felt like she had two children.

Sue entered the back room to see all the people in there, frozen silent in fear. The children's eyes were wide, and they clung to any adult for comfort. There were noises outside the back door. Feet and voices.

11 - Vigilante

Wee Renee rushed to the back door listening. She looked up at the little window she had climbed through an hour ago. It was still clearly light. No matter how high she jumped, she wouldn't be able to see through it. Whatever, it was light, and unless Norman had made a few more in the likeness of Michael Thompson, they *had* to be human.

'Hello!' She shouted through the door.

'Hello?' A man's voice said questioningly. 'Who is that?'

'It's me, Wee Renee. Who are you?'

'I'm Joe, and I own this bloody shop,' he said.

'Oh, I am sorry. Just a minute,' Wee Renee said. Immediately moving the barricade and peg from the door, it swung open to reveal Joe, with three other men behind him. He was a big man, over six feet and hefty. Joe had long dark hair in a ponytail and a black leather biker's jacket on. He held a large, lethal axe in his hands. The other men with him were also tooled up. Every one of them was tall and well built. They were a formidable foursome.

'I'm so sorry, we have broken into your shop,' Wee Renee said. 'We didn't know if the owners were dead or alive, but it was just what we needed.'

'I understand. These are grim times,' Joe said and walked in, followed by the other three men. The youngest one shut the door behind them, putting the peg back in. There were lots of shaking hands and exchanges of names that both parties would find hard to remember. The other three men were Rick, Darren, and Craig.

Darren was blonde, stout, in his thirties and seemed to know a few of the people from Friarmere Band. He had played Tuba in a rival band and had met them a few times at different contests. Rick was good-looking, with dark brown hair. He was the tallest of all the men and looked about nineteen or twenty years old.

Craig was about fifty and was the slimmest and smallest. Like Gary, he had a look of quiet understanding and seemed to know his way around DIY.

Joe looked around at the eclectic mix of people. The Friarmere group couldn't tell whether he was angry or happy at his squatters. It was also quite a shock to see so many children sitting in the back room of his shop. Safety regulations were running riot through his head. But also, he was amazed and thrilled to find so many live humans, surviving the horde.

'So, what's your story?' Joe asked. He didn't know who was the leader, or if they even had one.

Wee Renee cleared her throat, and in her Scottish musical accent, briefly told him the tale about the infection within the band, the people dropping out of circulation one by one and then the fight in The Civic Hall, which he had heard about. Then she told the four men the parts that they didn't know.

'We escaped over the tops in the snow, and for over a week we were in Melden. These are some of the people from there,' she said and introduced each of them. 'You will find out sooner or later I suppose, but you might as well know now, that a few of us are infected.'

'What?' Darren said, a little angrily.

'Wait. Hear her out,' Joe said calmly.

'Infected, not turned,' Wee Renee emphasised.

'We have found a way to fight it, so all is well. And we are getting stronger,' Our Doris said.

'Thank you for being so honest with me,' Joe said to Our Doris.

'So the next part, you don't know,' Wee Renee continued. 'Over in Melden they are in a similar situation to us, but they have another threat. It is Norman's sister Anne. She is just as lethal as him, but crazy too. She turn's people not just to vampires, but a kind of a wolf-vampire.'

'Do you mean werewolves?' Rick asked.

'It's easy to say that, isn't it and it would cover it nicely. But I don't think so, because these are in the same form twenty-four hours a day, every day of the year,' Terry said. 'There are so many differences, even within the clan. Some are quite bent, with dog-like faces. Some are just a bit hairy. I don't know why she has such a varied mixture. But yes, myself and Our Doris are infected with that strain, as we unknowingly drank her blood. We are fighting it and taking antibiotics. She can sniff us out though, that is clear. Her pack of real wolves can smell us too.'

'I am infected with the regular strain,' Liz added with her finger in the air, smiling. 'Just so you know. The Friarmere Strain. He had his hands around my neck last night. He called me *vegetable eater*.' She shook her head and looked at the floor.

'So, you have got two deadly predators and their minions after you?' Joe asked. 'Haha... what a lot of hiding prey I have run into!'

'Yes, you have, but we're thriving,' Pat said loudly and burped before continuing. 'Norman has got two of us by the balls up at the school too. So, we are getting them back, sharpish!'

Rick laughed at Pat's frankness. He already liked this group.

'Ah, so that's where they've been,' Joe said. 'We have been smoking nests out. That must be the main one!'

'Apart from The Grange, you mean,' Sue said.

'The Grange at the top?' Craig asked.

'Yes!' Sue replied. The four men looked at each other. Joe shook his head, and Rick squeezed his eyes shut. They didn't know.

'We never went as far as that,' Joe said.

'That's where his house is. A home he actually bought. Conveniently for him, ten minutes away is the school. This is where he was holding all these children, and now he has two of our friends,' Wee Renee said.

'The plan was that we were going to rescue them with some of your stuff if you don't mind,' Danny said.

'That's fine, by me,' Joe said. 'You fancy some company?' The whole group was ecstatic. These men were a definite asset.

'So, what have you been up to in Friarmere?' asked Laura.

'We have been watching houses. Rick watches them with his binoculars. We go in and check in the daytime. We check for any human activity going on in there first. Sometimes we find one of *them* inside. It's rare to find just one, we've learned there will usually be another hidden somewhere. In a cupboard we haven't checked, in the attic, the glory hole, who knows, but we often hear more than one scream when we torch the house,' Joe said.

'We have also found a couple roaming outside at dusk before the main lot come. We tied them down put something flammable underneath and burned them,' Craig said.

'Have you been burning vampires alive then?' Bob asked, his mouth open.

'Yeah, we have been doing that quite a bit mate,' Rick replied. 'It was supposed to be a deterrent to them. We have been firing out any nests we find and also setting the odd fire, so they think we have just found another one for burning.'

'I had this idea,' Joe said, 'It must have been a rubbish one, though. I thought that living people would see what we are about, and know they aren't on their own. Next time they saw a fire, they would know where we were. But no one has come out and said can we join you? Or even will you protect us? So I don't know how many are left. That is why I am so glad to see you lot.'

'You've seen no-one?' Nigel asked.

'No,' Joe answered.

'But I was in the pub,' Lauren advised them. 'It doesn't mean we are the only ones left. I mean, we have only just found you too!'

'I can't believe we missed you!' Craig said. 'If the pub was open, I would have seen the light on and been in for a swift one.'

'Oh no, I've mainly been opening up until around three, then I'd disappear. There was no way the vamps were coming into me at night and getting a swift one!'

'That explains it,' Rick said smiling. 'We haven't been getting up until then. We usually have a plan to watch certain houses at night, before we torch them. We've mainly become nocturnal.'

'Nice!' Our Doris said, nodding. 'I had a hamster like that.'

'What we have here,' Danny said, 'are four vigilantes then.' He laughed joyfully.

'I suppose that is what some people would call us. I feel uneasy about that actual word, but we have seen the two vampire policeman and know we are cut off. These actions are out of desperation. Who is going to help us and take our village back if we don't?' Joe asked honestly.

'My thoughts exactly,' said Wee Renee. 'Well now we are here, and we have dispatched quite a few of the critters in both villages. You won't go wrong with us.'

'I can tell,' Joe replied.

'What do you think we should do now?' Andy asked him. It was now nearly dark, and there was only a weak light squeezing through the shutter windows.

'We need to get out of this village at some point and try and find help. We don't know how many of the vampires we are working against. There seems to be a lot more of them than normal folks now. If only we could have a checklist and tick them off when we are done.' Joe said.

'There are some at The Grange, at the school and who else knows where, if you have been finding various nests willy-nilly. We really are dealing with the unknown in so many ways,' Terry said, thinking aloud.

'If some of these kids' parents are turned, perhaps the parent is lying in their house waiting for the child to break free and run to them. It's horrible,' Beverly said.

'We can't burn every house down in the village systematically. That would take too long. So we need to get out, but not to Melden.'

'You do know you've probably been spotted and are lucky to have got this far?' Pat asked.

'No, what do you mean?' Craig asked her.

'You four are just as targeted as us, I bet. There is one infected with Norman's blood that has not resisted, but Norman has not turned him. He was on the committee for our band, his brother played baritone and is one of the buggers now. A real nasty one too. His name is Stephen. This bloke I am talking about is named Michael, and he can go out in the day and undo any good work that you have done. He could trail you anywhere, if all of you are inside at the same place, you will be done for. Especially when you have been going in, just before night-time because he could run and get Norman Morgan. When you are saying to me, the fires will draw the living, they could also draw the dead.' Pat sniffed in punctuation and looked at them all out of one eye.

'What does he look like, so we'll know him,' Rick asked. Pat thought for a moment, her eyes surveying the ceiling for inspiration.

'A nonce,' she said.

12 - Training Band

Father Philip had retired to the Vicarage. After limping home, he had entered and thrown himself down on the kitchen chair. His original plan was to take a lot of painkillers. After having second thoughts, he had decided to suffer. That was what he should do. Suffer, and rot in hell. Pat and Wee Renee were right. Why did he deserve to have pain relief of any kind?

He did, however, decide to have a glass of whisky. Very painfully he walked over to his bureau where he kept the whisky, taking a glass and the bottle. Father Philip returned to the table. He filled the glass and took a large drink. It burned. It was good.

Soon the bottle was empty, but he wasn't drunk. Just a little numb in the brain and the balls. When had it gone dark? Maybe he was drunk. A little face looked in at him, a child's face. The boy squatted on top of Father Philips blue recycling bin so that he could clearly see him. The vampire child cocked his head to the left jerkily. The food was inside, and he couldn't get to it. He scratched at the window. Father Philip wasn't scared. Just resigned to the fact that he was getting stalked. The boy licked his lips and drooled. Tasty human.

The vicar managed to get up out of his wooden kitchen chair and make it back to the bureau. It would have to be brandy now. He dragged his feet as he returned to his seat. A little girl had joined the boy. He waved and cracked open the seal on the brandy. There would be more tomorrow.
Father Philip would go – get out, he knew where to go. He needed to be away from the beasts, he didn't want to become one. The Master had made sure he was halfway there as it was. He needed to be away from humans. He didn't deserve to be around them. To have their company and comfort. To kill himself was a sin before God.

He had seen a lovely place on a Sunday walk. He would go there, well out of the way. He had camping equipment, supplies, heating. In the morning he would go.

Father Philip knew he wouldn't make it to bed, or even to his sofa. He got onto the cold kitchen tiles, curled up and cried until he went asleep.

The two children watched until just before dawn.

Michael's medical room was full tonight. Peter Woodall was back again. He wanted Michael to cut the hairs on his armpit as the tape that was helping to keep his arm on was stuck to them. Peter had tried to put up with it, but he had not been able to rest all day. He had lain in the dark, but it kept him awake. In his words, *it stung like a bastard*.

'I'm not really here for this. Trimming hairs. Couldn't you have done it yourself.'

'I tried, but I couldn't see to do it and get my hand under.'

'That'll be your moobs,' Michael replied.

'What?'

'Admit it, Woody, you were a big bloke when you were given The Master's gift. You had moobs. Man boobs.' Peter looked at Michael and sighed.

'Just get on with it,' Peter said. Stephen helped Michael take Peter's V-neck sweater and flannel shirt off. Michael sat down beside him and picked up his scissors.

'Right Nelson,' Michael said, beginning to raise Peter's arm.

'Nelson? I'm Peter.'

'I was trying to use humour. It's like casting pearls before swine, with you lot. I'm going in *Peter*,' Michael said. He lifted the arm and went to trim the armpit hairs. The tape had definitely stuck to them, Peter was right.

'Oohhh!' Michael exclaimed.

'What?' Peter asked, worried.

'Er, nothing, nothing. I am still a little worried about keeping this arm, Woody. That's all.' That wasn't what Michael was talking about, although the arm was now entirely black and withering. It felt very light too. *It was probably just a shell full of that green powder they had inside them,* he thought. *A husk.* There was no chance of this joining up and pumping their black blood through it now. There would be no veins left.

The fact was that the tape had pulled at the armpit hairs, the skin was unnaturally soft there, and the armpit skin has pulled away and free at least two inches from Peter's body. It had a white tear down one side, and Michael could see inside Peter. 'I'll just do my best, here Peter, but I think they maybe damaged your armpit as well. You might find it's still stinging tomorrow. It definitely isn't my fault though.'

'I'll get them for that,' Peter said sourly as Michael snipped away at the armpit hair.

After Michael had avoided the blame for Peter's armpit, he told them to decide amongst themselves about who was next. He wasn't in the mood tonight.

Keith automatically sat down. He had a small hole, a short distance away from his ear.

'I can put some gaffer tape on for you. That is all, Michael informed him. 'Your type of skin doesn't stitch. Not as I have thread anyway,'

'It's small enough for a plaster, isn't it?' Keith asked angrily.

'Yes, I suppose it is, but you could have done that yourself. Why come to me?'

'It's your job. Not mine,' Keith said finally and remained in the seat. Michael rummaged around in the medical kit and came out with a medium sized square dressing. He placed it on Keith's neck, pressing a little bit harder than he had to. He gave Keith a sarcastic smile.

'I fixed what Little Lord Fauntleroy gave you. Next!' Michael shouted. Keith curled his lip at Michael and removed himself from the room.

Stuart sat down next, as Christine said she wanted plenty of Michael's time. He could see her problem and had no idea about what he was going to do. Stuart lifted his polo shirt up, sadly. There was an eight-inch gash across his stomach. In two areas it was quite deep, and a little black bubble of intestine peeked out of each one.

'Mmm…. nasty. How did you get this?'

'Sword wound.'

'The sweet little old lady, did this? What a little gem.' Michael said laughing.

'Are you enjoying my discomfort?'

'Oh no. I didn't mean that. I just meant…well, fancy that!'

'I see. Can you fix me?'

'A bit.' Michael said and started to cut off lengths of tape from his large roll. 'You're not a hairy man, luckily, are you Stuart?'

'No.'

'Very, very good,' Michael commented before taping Stuart's stomach up with three good lengths of tape. 'You'll be all right with that. I've tucked everything in, nice and sweet. You're good to go and signed off to fight!' Michael said proudly.

Stuart got up off the sofa, with no comment or thanks and then only Christine remained.

'I'm all yours,' Michael said.

'Ooh sweetie, don't flirt with me yet. I'm still in mourning a little for Wayne. That wound hurts more than the one I need you to attend to.'

'Right… er ….ok. Take a seat then,' Michael said.

Christine sat, then fussed around arranging her skirt and folding her ankles girlishly. She fluttered her eyelashes at him. Michael was amused at this new Christine. What had happened to the competitive vampire of the last few weeks? Both of them not speaking and trying to score points.

'I knew you'd like me once you needed me and didn't have Wayne sweetie as a henchman,' Michael muttered quietly, as he began to examine her bloody scalp

'I always liked you, sweetie. I don't know what you are talking about,' She replied. *Amazing,* he thought. *As if I buy that one!* Michael took a good look at her head. Three-quarters of it was bald now. The hair and scalp ripped off and burnt on the consecrated ground. What remained was a large skull covered with patches of dried black blood. The remaining peroxide blonde hair had apparently blown up in the winter wind and stuck fast to the scalp in a few areas. Its pale yellow stained and stuck forever.

'I'm sorry to say, your hair won't grow back, Christine. All the hair follicles have gone,' he advised.

'Oh sweetie, are you sure?'

'No chance. So let's think about how we can make your head look nice. Maybe we can find a wig somewhere.'

'Yes! A lovely wig. Maybe a Farrah Fawcett one. I can see myself like that,' she said excitedly.

'That might be a tall order. We will have to look for a wig when we go into houses after humans. I don't think we have found one yet, have we? We will say that when the first wig is found, you have first dibs on it. What about that?'

'Yes, lovely.'

'But what shall we do until then?' Michael asked her, while considering the situation himself and rubbing his chin. 'Bobble hat?'

'Oh no, sweetie!' She exclaimed, astounded that he would suggest such a thing. 'I don't do bobble hats.'

'You can get some nice ones now, Christine. Don't dismiss it straight away.'

'It's just not Chrissie. A bobble could never be chic or stylish, could it sweetie? Go on admit it.'

'Well, I think it is a hat or nothing. You are going to have to have something on it. Bits are going to get stuck to it.'

'Hmm..' Christine said, rolling her eyes, this way and that, for a few seconds. She was considering all kinds of hats available. 'I'll settle for a sequinned one!'

'That might be as rare as the Farrah Fawcett wig! Think of another kind. What about a white Stetson? No, no. That is probably just as rare. I think around here, you will either get a bobble hat or a flat cap, and that's it.'

'No, sweetie. I know someone who wears sequinned hats. One of the living from the old Friarmere Band. She has one on now, and I have seen her in another one in the past. I think she will have some in her house.'

'Who?'

'The one with the boy that The Master wants to collect, Adam's friend.'

'Oh, you mean Sue. Yes, she does like to wear a shiny beret. If we both go, we might find one that you like from her house. Would that be good enough?'

'Yes.'

'First things first. We need to wrap your head in something. Michael rummaged again in the drawers, near the microwave and returned with a roll of cling film. He took any remaining hair that she had dangling downwards and lifted it up, pressing it on an exposed patch of the skull. 'There, it's neat now.' He wrapped the cling film around her head, several times. She now looked like she wore a very strange coloured swimming cap. 'Come on then. Let's finish the job. We might just have time before tonight's inaugural parade!'

Christine and Michael set off for Sue's house. Michael was sure it was empty and also unsecured. The Master had broken the lock on the back door a couple of weeks ago, to search it. Michael had stepped in and invited all the vampires in, he remembered. When they arrived, it was dark and empty. Even the cats were out for the night. Michael and Christine and started to nose about. They looked through the drawers in the kitchen, the under-stairs cupboard, the living room sideboard. No luck.

Undeterred, they made their way upstairs. Neither knew where to find Sue's sequinned beret collection. In the end, Michael found a bag, containing hats, scarfs, and gloves at the bottom of Sue's wardrobe. Christine waited patiently as he rummaged through them, laying all the ladies hats onto Sue's bed so that Christine could make her choice. She fancied the gold one, which Michael fitted for her.

'It really suits you,' he said.

Gary and Carl were sitting quietly in the pitch black of the classroom. They were half asleep as they were pretty weak now. The Panettone had gone, all the children's trays had been checked, and there was no food available. Today the vampires didn't seem to want to feed them. They hadn't been given tea and biscuits from Christine either. Where was she? Once they knew who the high heeled mules belonged to, they realised that they had heard them many times.

'I am so hungry,' Carl said

'Same here. It's astounding how quickly you deteriorate, isn't it?' Gary replied. 'A minute ago I thought I heard a cornet play, jeez. It must be my brain, yearning for the good old days!'

'Yeah, you are imagining it,' Carl said. 'It's the hunger and all the freakishness of our situation.' Gary nodded, relaxed back, then immediately jumped up again.

'I am positive I have just heard a baritone warming up, far away. Didn't you hear it?' Gary asked. Carl listened to the absolute silence. Now Gary couldn't hear it either.

'No, there's nothing there.' On Carl's last word, they heard the unmistakable sound of a harsh trombone. Then a horn cut through the night. The two men caught their breaths and looked at each other. A bass drum beat a couple of times. 'It must be the gang coming to tell us that they are rescuing us!' Carl said excitedly.

'They are telling everyone else they are all coming too!' Gary said, a little worried.

'Maybe it is some kind of war cry from the gang. To get the vampires outside to them so they can nip in the back to us,' Carl replied.

'I don't know. It must be a part of a bigger plan. I can't figure it out at the moment. I am just glad this saga is nearly over.'

The whole band started off, bass drum beating time, and the rest of the brass instruments joined with him. Gary looked at Carl, his shoulders dropped – all the excitement and anticipation drained out of him.

'That is not our lot. It's out of tune. It's not together. I don't even recognise the playing, never mind the piece. What the hell's going on?' Gary asked flabbergasted. 'That sounds like a bloody training band! That is definitely not Friarmere band!' Gary's brows were furrowed. He was desperate to see who was playing. Looking through the windows was useless, and he sat back down. The view from this classroom looked out over to the side of the building. The sound seemed to be coming from the front and the main playground. Carl started to get a bad feeling about this.

'I can't see bugger all,' Gary said to Carl angrily. All he knew was that a brass band, an awful brass band were playing about fifty feet away from where they sat.

It was indeed a brass band, a re-formation of the old Friarmere band. Old and not improved, plus some new and enthusiastic players. For many weeks the instruments had been in storage. In cold wardrobes, in The Grange, and in musty cupboards. Apart from the need to tune them, there were other complications

Christine walked at the front holding the banner saying Friarmere Band, which they had taken from The Civic Hall after the others had left. Michael carried the banner the other side of Christine. Norman walked behind them with his baton conducting the band. No idea of whether he should be beating in bars or beats. Peter was trying to play the bass drum, which should have been no problem to the percussionist. He had it strapped over his shoulders, but his usual drumming arm was severely injured. So he played with the other arm, the drum swinging harshly to one side as he did. He was struggling with the one arm, the snow and the sudden inability to keep time. Norman wasn't helping either. Swinging the baton in circles did not give Peter anything to follow.

There were a couple of each instrument in the band, but the sound was terrible. The vampires, however, could not hear this and were just joyous again about making music in a group. They set off in procession from the school to walk around the village.

Norman had a plan. Not only did he have his own brass band, which was absolutely wonderful, but these chords might bring out a curious human. Coming out to see if this was a real brass band, telling them that they were not alone and giving them the all clear. What Norman hadn't realised was that if they had any ear for music, they would know that something was wrong. It certainly was a haunting sound.

What this band also signified was that Norman wasn't worried about anything anymore. He had *arrived*. The band announced this was their village. Their rules, no discussion. Loud and proud they would play, whenever he liked.

He cast his mind back to the previous night's discovery. This would show the people burning his children what he thought of them. They were nothing. Last night he had found out where they stayed, just by chance. After the battle, he had returned to the village, for feeding and comfort. He needed time alone. Freedom to be himself.

On his way back, what should he spy, but four men, with the smell of petrol about them? They carried many weapons. From their discussions, he was now sure it was the vampire murderers. He followed them silently, slithering along the roofs, which he loved to do. He watched them enter a house at the opposite end of the village to the school and The Grange. He hung upside down from a gutter, observing them laugh through the windows. They took pleasure in burning his children. He was so angry but only had fifteen minutes before dawn. Tomorrow he would take them. Probably turn them to replace some of his fallen vampires. Let them see if they could tackle the whole of his vampire army. He thought not.

Then after turning them, they would make another trip into the churchyard. Michael had his instructions tonight. If these four men loved fire, their luck was in. Because there was going to be one almighty one at St. Dominic's tonight. All in all, he was looking forward to this evening's activities.

The band wound their way through the streets of Friarmere, down from the school on the hill and into the main village. They did not follow music but tried to play Christmas Carols, the best that they could, which was terrible. They played a lot slower than they thought they did, and every carol, no matter how merry, became a slow dirge under their musicality.

Norman still conducted as he walked, occasionally turning backwards, smiling at them. His chest puffed with pride as he thought about it all. *A brass band of his own folk.* Oh, how Anne would be jealous of this. What an achievement!

13 - Parade

There was no traffic sound. No people going about their business of an evening. No shops open. Nothing else going on, whatsoever. From a great distance away, the group in the hardware shop began to hear the brass band, approaching from afar.

At first, they could not tell how harmonious the playing was. It was just the distinctive sounds of a brass band playing. The sound of the bass drum carried through the cold night air. Booming through the snowing village, the brass instruments distant but growing stronger.

'That drum is out of time,' Bob said almost immediately. As the band got closer, they could hear how tuneless the players were.

They were trying to have a crack at Carol of the Bells, which is usually quite a quick melody. But with no music to read, no musical direction, and people trying to play with vampire teeth, they woefully could not manage this carol. The cacophony increased, and they entered the High Street. Most of the occupants of the shop crowded behind the metal shutters, their eyes to the slits in the metal. As the noise got louder, second by second, they started to see what all the racket was about.

Christine and Michael held the embroidered banner that said *Friarmere Band*. Norman stood behind them proudly conducting the band. Peter was playing the bass drum but could be seen just banging his beater, every so often, with no intention of rhythm. There was also Colin on tuba, Keith on trombone, Stephen on baritone and a few of the other ex-members. A couple of new eager players had got involved but didn't look like they could even buzz the mouthpiece, let alone hit a high C.

'It looks like Diane is on Principal,' Andy said to the others, who could not find a spare slit to watch through.

'She couldn't manage Carol of the Bells even on second cornet when she was alive, never mind on Principal,' Pat said and sniffed. 'I bet she is well chuffed at getting that seat!'

'Aye, she will be,' Wee Renee said casually.

Sue wasn't looking through the shutters, so didn't realise that Christine was wearing her gold sequined beret.

'Oh, God. Look at Vincent's eye!' Danny commented. The people that could see out of the shutters turned their gaze to the Tuba player. He had a hole instead of one of his eyes. Inside the hole, framed by the white dead skin, it looked silvery. The skin had moved around the lip of the mouthpiece. Inside his head, the suction held it fast. There was just now a deep channel to his brain. A thin line of black issue glistened in the street-light.

'Oh no, look how deep that baby is in his head. That is disgusting!' Liz exclaimed as quietly as she could.

Joe was quite amused about Vincent's new orifice and was stifling laughter without much success.

'Eh, Joe. That's him we were talking about,' Andy said, pointing out Michael Thompson. 'He is the only living one in the group.' Joe scrutinised the man through the shutters, then turned around to Pat before he spoke.

'You were bang on when you described this guy. He looks exactly like a massive nonce!'

From Friarmere Park, Maurice watched. He had his fingers in his ears. Playing off key always set his teeth on edge and Maurice could abide it no more now he was one of the living dead than when he was a living human. Why couldn't they hear it, if he could? Maybe it was a work in progress. That was the only excuse. He wondered what the point was. Maurice thought very hard about it, furrowing his brow. They were very bold to do this in a village that they had raped and pillaged in. It was like they were announcing that it was theirs. They owned Friarmere and all that it held.

He had realised precisely what Norman was up to in fact. To understand The Master was to conquer him. Maybe this was the key. He was still flabbergasted. They were announcing where they were in Friarmere. They were holding instruments so couldn't fight as quickly as usual. Was this so necessary to do? Did he really have to rub it in everyone's faces? Norman's arrogance could cost him the game. Maybe this was his *Achilles Heel*. Tomorrow a group might hear them coming, and lie in wait. Ah, but what group? Maybe his friends who had made the journey from St. Dominic's to the Hardware Store. Yes, unfortunately, they weren't difficult to find, even for him. He wondered how tonight would play out.

14 - Bell

Carol of the Bells stopped, and Norman announced that the next carol to play would be *In the Bleak Midwinter*. Liz couldn't imagine how this would sound because, at the best of times, that was slow and plodding. If they played Carol of the Bells as a dirge, how would they play this? This would be interesting.

Just as they were about to start, and Peter Woodall beat his bass drum twice, they heard the sound of the handbell. They had last heard this two nights ago, outside the church. Maybe tonight, they would see who was ringing it, as only Tina had seen him the other night and she had no idea who he was.

Ringing his bell, the golden brass gleaming, proudly walking down the High Street towards the group of the vampires was Mark. He was carrying one of his milk crates in the other hand, and the bottles clinked along as he walked. As he reached them, he put the crate on the ground. They, in turn, put down their instruments and happily went to greet him.

'Who wants some?' He said. The vampire band crowded around his crate.

'Who's that?' Terry asked.

'One of our band. He's a vampire. But he didn't' give us away when he saw us leaving,' Laura said.

'Bit of a maverick. Does what he wants to. That's Mark all over. Decent bloke before he was turned, actually,' Tony advised them.

'He was on percussion with me, Laura and Woody. He taught me loads on the drum kit,' Bob said sadly.

'Who's Woody?' Sally asked.

'The one playing the bass drum now. Peter Woodall. Another decent bloke before all this. The one whose arm I nearly took off, the other night,' Andy said.

'The plump one,' Liz advised Sally.

The people in the hardware store could not see what was going on because they could only see the backs of the vampires.

'All varieties,' they heard Mark say.

'What the dickens as he got?' Sue asked, who still had no slit to look through. From her low slit on the shutter, Our Doris spied one of them drinking out of one of the bottles. The contents were dark. The light shone through the bottle as it was emptied, now the glass could be seen as a dark, thick claret colour.

'He's got blood in the bottles. He's peddling pints of blood to the rest of them!'

'Well, bloody hell,' Pat said. 'What do you think about that?'

'I think, *whose blood is it?*' Wee Renee said mysteriously.

'Hmm.... Mark was always up for a bit of a business idea,' Tony said thoughtfully. 'He probably saw this as an opportunity. At least he's not playing with them in the band.'

'Or fighting alongside them, against us,' Liz said.

'Maybe another potential good egg,' Wee Renee said.

'We haven't seen him doing this before. This is a new venture, I think. If he is just trying to peddle blood to them, then that is probably the least of our worries.' Rick said.

'Maybe or maybe not,' Terry said.

'What do you mean?' Kathy asked.

'It's the openness, the confidence about this scene, I don't like. They are playing music loudly in the village. Certainly not bothered about attracting attention to themselves. Now we see this enterprise from Mark. They now are living a normal life, to them anyway. A new culture has emerged. Life in Friarmere is now this. Nothing is stopping them. They are becoming civilised, with their sales or bartering of blood. They have no fear or shame about being a vampire. It's fascinating really.'

'Aye, you are right Terry. This does change the way we can maybe defeat them. That is a brilliant observation,' Wee Renee said.

Pat was clutching her stomach and had been all day. She said it was a bug, but Wee Renee and everyone else knew that it was the tripe that she had eaten from Ian Butchers shop. Quite a few of them had said, it had been standing out way too long. Apart from that, heaven only knew what germs were in there with so many strange things, walking past the tripe to get to Ian's corpse in the back. But Pat said as it didn't' smell rank, it must be okay. Wee Renee had said she couldn't tell what it was like with the sheer amount of malt vinegar that Pat had drowned it in. Pat said this was a preservative anyway, so all was well.

'Oh shit!' Pat said suddenly and did the most enormous fart, which went on forever. It was loud, rasping and raucous. The others turned to watch, their mouths open at the sheer volume of it. Visibly they could see Pat's stomach deflating. It was quite amazing. Our Doris turned her gaze back to the slit in the shutters. All the vampires' heads had turned towards to the hardware shop.

Maurice shook his head sadly and backed away into the shadows. Of all the things to happen. Just when you are trying to spy on a horde of vampires, someone gets extreme flatulence. *You couldn't write it*, he thought. He hoped his friends would make it again through this siege.

What he didn't know was from above the building, on the roof of the Old Bank stood Adam, who was watching Maurice. He had been out on the roof's watching it all. Adam liked to be up here. He could see a good portion of Friarmere, and no one could see him. For the last couple of nights, he had been here. Adam had seen Norman and his gang wander around, attacking the church. He had seen Mark selling blood. Maurice walking alone, trying to understand it all. The odd human running through the night from house to house with supplies. He had also observed the four vigilantes, and Norman following them from the rooftops the other side of the road.

Adam knew that his friend Bob and all the other survivors were in the hardware shop. He had already heard all the humans and their conversations in there before the band had arrived when they were still off their guard. Adam didn't think Maurice was playing Norman's game, and Adam no longer wanted to play it either. He was in a strange no man's land of being dead and not loving it. The vampires knew Adam wasn't playing ball and the humans knew he was a vampire. To him, everyone was a predator, which meant that he didn't have many choices. He watched Maurice, obscured by the bushes to the front, but visible from his viewpoint. His mind ticked over with various scenarios and ideas. It may be, that a door had just opened for Adam.

15 - Bite

The vampires walked towards The Hardware Shop. Norman sniffed the air, and a monstrous smile crept across his face. The others who had finished their macabre beverages had just picked their instruments up. They sniffed the air too and replaced their instruments back down on the snow.

'Michael!' Norman shouted and pointed to the shop. Michael walked over to the door, squatted down and began pulling on the shutter, which was locked at the bottom. It didn't budge. The people backed into the rear of the shop, but alas, Norman already knew that they were in there. The vampires crowded around the entrance.

Inside it suddenly became even gloomier as their dead bodies blocked the streetlights out. There was a collective deathly moaning. All their eyes were up against the shutter, peering through the glass, trying to see into the darkness.

The group of survivors were not ready to fight. After battling for the last two nights, they were mentally and physically tired from it all. But they would just have to do it if The Master got in here. Wee Renee thought about the fact that the door was unlocked, and that nearly the whole front wall was glass. If it wasn't for the shutters, they would have had no protection whatsoever.

Norman regarded the shutter for a moment. He turned around, his eyes flicking amongst the objects on the snowy road. Christine still held the banner at one side. The other side, Michael had dropped to the floor, so that he could try and open the shutter. Norman took the banner off Christine. This was, of course, a banner with two metal poles that sat in channel's sewn at each end of the fabric. He took one of the metal poles out of the side of the banner and moved back to the shutter.

The Master put one big red eye to a viewing slit and looked at the people inside. Norman could see each and every one of them in the darkness.

Crouching down, he got his fingers under the shutter and started to pull. It was well and truly locked. However, he could feel that there was only one place where the metal was caught in the lock. If he could break that, he would be in. The gap was too narrow for his fingers. He put the banner pole on the floor and stamped on the end. All the time he stared, unblinking into the dark shop. He now had a kind of crowbar. Acutely pointed at one end. Much like Bob's new invention. Bob realised this and swallowed hard.

Norman placed it near to the locking mechanism, next to the ground. He wiggled the bar until it could get between the gap of the shutter and the stone floor. He began to pump the banner pole up and down while shoving it further into the gap. The people inside could hear the grinding of metal on metal.

Norman continued to pump and push. Now he could get his fingers on the other side. The shutter groaned. It was starting to give way. Our Doris at the front could see slightly more and more light coming underneath the shutter door.

With an unimpressive click, he released the lock. His hands shot firmly underneath the shutter and shoved it up. There he was in the door, large and menacing. He moved forward to enter. This was a public building after all, and now nothing could stop him from coming in here.

'Everyone get ready,' Joe shouted.

'Yeah, go hard or go home,' Rick added. Norman and his vampires were quickly in the room. Tony, who stood near the front, right next to the objects he most desired to use, could not resist it. He threw a circular saw blade at the group of vampires. Luckily for Norman, he saw at the last minute and punched it away. It flew across the shop, embedding itself into the wall.

Our Doris moved forward with her sword in both hands, and a fireside poker shoved into the back pocket of her brown corduroy jeans. There was not much room to swing her sword, and again it was proving quite useless. In fact, the sword was a hindrance. She could not fight in close proximity. The run and sweep through the air that she needed was unavailable here, with rows of shelves, and lawnmowers and garden rakes. She did manage to whack Diane round the head with it a couple of times. Our Doris was pleased to see the bulldog clips still holding the two parts of Diane's nose together, ping off into the night. Diane still held her cornet, and that flew across the shop skittering up to one corner. She seemed very agitated about this and ran to try and retrieve it. Wee Renee and Our Doris ran after her beating her on the back, as she bent to retrieve it. One with the poker, one with a length of rubber hose.

Danny approached Keith who he noticed had a plaster across the hole in his neck. As usual, he was irate and determined to take some scalps with him. Danny considered him to be the most dangerous vampire there, apart from Norman. He planned to try and keep Keith at bay, thus protecting the others. He had made a spear earlier, and he was trying to poke Keith from far away. Again, the closeness of the shop, the shelves, and all the stock made it impossible to do anything. Danny's spear kept getting caught up in various objects, which were hooked up on the wall. The vampire's efforts were proving just as irksome as he kept knocking items off the shelves too. This was like keyhole surgery for the both of them. There were boxes of screws falling all over the ground, and people were rolling around on them as they opened. Danny kept poking at him like a bear and was managing to keep him contained.

Several of the women stood at the entrance to the back room. Their only job was protecting the children who were now behind them. Joe whispered something to Rick and Craig. They nodded and moved towards the woman who began to step back and disappeared. Rick and Craig now stood in the doorway, with Joe and Darren in front.

Bob attacked Colin with a length of copper pipe. Trying to hit and pierce him at the same time. This didn't work, and Colin twisted him around, immediately biting him on the neck. Just like that. In a split-second, Bob dropped to the floor. The whole exchange between the two of them had lasted five seconds. Tony and Sue left the group they were fighting and rushed to Colin, who had decided at that point to flee.

Tony had thought that Bob's idea with the pipe was great. But he had decided to use it differently. Tony had hammered the tip of the pipe and had a point. The other end remained untouched. Always a fan of the very long-distance weapons – guns and circular saw frisbee's – he now had a spear or even a javelin. He held it out before him as he ran. Items knocked over in the shop, a tin of paint fell with a dull thud. Its purple contents glugged out of a gap on the lid. The smell of paint filled the room immediately. Tony shoved the spear into the back of Colin who was on his way out of the door. He seemed to be screaming anyway and holding his mouth. Liz wondered what was wrong with him. Maybe Bob has tasted bad. More of them stopped fighting the others to help destroy Colin. He wasn't just Sue and Tony's kid. He belonged to all of them, and they were having revenge.

Colin was firmly impaled on Tony's spear, screaming the unnatural scream that was becoming a familiar noise to the group. Sue took the sword out of Our Doris's hand and swung it out. The screaming stopped almost immediately. Colin's head flew off, his body began to drop down straight and forwards. Tony was still holding him on his long spear, so let go. He lay on the floor, the pole sticking straight up from his back towards the roof of the shop. Bob was on the floor close by. Unconscious or dead they did not know for now. The attack from Colin had only lasted about two seconds.

'He is lifeless now!' Norman shouted, looking over at the two of them. Which he was on about, they did not know.

Liz tried to take on Stephen, who had dodged Sue's swinging sword and slid on the purple paint. He had fallen into the corner where Diane's cornet had been minutes before and was trying to get up, but the slimy paint was proving impossible to negotiate, and he kept slipping back.

Liz avoided the spreading pool beneath Stephen who was still an incredibly strong and powerful predator, even though he was badly burnt. She had a diamond-shaped plastering trowel. Sharp, and metal. With all her strength she shoved it into his shoulder, the tip emerging out the back of him. Liz wrenched it back out, which made a very satisfying sound. She pushed it in back in again, at an angle. This was so easy. Liz had made an excellent choice. Apart from the fact that she had to get up close, it was a brilliant weapon.

Pat was still farting as she was fighting. She was currently fighting a new member of the band, that she did not know, with a two-handed approach. Fireside poker in one hand and trusty club hammer in the other. She had already caught their fingers between the wall and her hammer. They were now just a crushed and bloody mess. The fingers dangling off the ends of the meaty mash that were once digits. The flatulence now was painful and very potent. Although the vampires could not smell anything, the other people could. It was now swamping the smell of the paint in the room.

Tony was trying to reach more circular saw blades to throw at Norman. As he negotiated his way back to the saw stock, he fired his gun at Norman who got hit in the shoulder. This made him step back once, but he shrugged and moved forward. Tony's bullet was just a little fly. How insignificant!

Laura ran towards Peter, her former fellow percussionist. He was facing away from her, trying to grab at Andy, with one arm. Andy was trying to get him through the eye with a long blade, but Peter was dodging as much as he could, and Andy had managed to cut off most of his ear, which dangled down and had put several clean two-inch gashes in his cheek.

Laura grabbed one of the large pairs of loppers from the gardening section. She could see that Peter's arm was swinging around a little. The tape was lifting up, as the dead limb went withered and powdery and could no longer adhere to the desiccated arm. Currently held on by only two pieces of tape, Laura thought she would help him out. She opened the loppers and still behind him, clipped the arm cleanly off. The pathetic part that had been attached dropped down and broke apart as it fell. Peter turned around to her, as she knew he would and she was ready for him. The garden loppers were already discarded, and a sharpened drumstick was in her hand. Laura stabbed it forward before he even realised who had taken off his arm and it hit home, straight into the heart. It certainly did the trick as Peter dropped down onto the floor and the widening smears of purple paint. *How poetic for Peter to be killed by a drumstick* she thought.

Wee Renee decided that now, was the right time to use her new weapon, the firepit poker. A new member of the vampire band, a middle-aged man, stood watching the staking of Peter in awe. Inexperienced, unsuspecting and unaware that Wee Renee was running up behind him. She held the firepit poker low, the hook pointing upwards. When in position, Wee Renee stopped suddenly and brought it up swiftly between his legs. There was a crack from down there, she had broken a bone somewhere and an ear-splitting scream from him. She tilted the hook inside him, then brought it downwards. Not only did she see at first sight his genital cluster, but what followed was a whole stream of lumps and loops that smashed down on the floor along with a torrent of thick black blood.

'Aye, ye bastard!' She screeched with glee.

Joe was coming from the back with an electric chainsaw. The noise was immense in the shop, the cold metal objects seemed to quiver with the vibrations. The humans scattered one by one in front of him.

'Take them into the cellar, Tony!' Joe said.

'What cellar?'

'In the backroom. You'll see. Get everyone down there.'

Tony started pushing everyone into the back room. When they got into the room, stairs were leading down an extensive cellar. There were lights on down there, which gleamed out into the darkness. The lights were still off in the shop, the idea being that they did not give themselves away earlier. All the children were already down there and looked up at them. Lauren was dropping the bags of food down, and Sally, Kathy, and Beverly were catching them.

Joe and the other three men moved forward. Joe weaved the chainsaw this way and that in front of the vampires. They seemed terrified at being cornered by this weapon, and the monsters spewed out of the shop in terror. Stephen still slipped in the paint, one shoulder useless. He escaped with only inches to spare. He could feel the wind of the chainsaw in his hair.

Sue and Tony grabbed Bob's body and pulled it through the shop and down the steps. Laura, Danny and Andy stood behind the vigilantes with their weapons, shouting at their attackers. Joe moved forward for one last time with his formidable weapon. Now all vampires were on the other side of the shutter door. Joe passed the chainsaw to Rick, before banging the shutter down.

'Hold it!' he said to the others and rushed back into the shop. He returned with a metal rod and shoved it straight through the bottom lip of the shutter into the locking mechanism. Rick held the chainsaw, which still resounded throughout the shop.

Liz checked through the shutters.

'They're moving off. Some are still looking back at the shop. Don't turn the chainsaw off yet,' Liz said gasping. For a minute there was silence in the whole of the main street, apart from the resounding mechanics of the electric chainsaw. The Master lifted up his head and clicked his tongue. In unison, all the vampires turned and began to follow him.

'They're all going back up the hill,' she said. Rick turned off the chainsaw.

'How are we securing these shutters?' Craig asked.

'All of you come with me,' Joe said. They went over to the back corner of the shop. 'We are going to put that on the lip of the shutter.' They looked down at the massive blue generator. 'We should just be able to shift it between the lot of us.'

Eight of them struggled with the generator across the floor, even on wheels, it was one heck of a job. They rested one side of it against the shutter, two caster wheels on the lip. Joe pressed the brakes down on all four wheels, and the shutter bulged from the other side.

'Try shifting that, you dirty bloodsuckers,' Joe muttered. Liz rechecked the street. It was an empty frigid arctic scene again. They walked back to the cellar, and one by one disappeared down the cellar steps. Joe was the last, shutting the cellar door behind him and putting the two enormous bolts across that were in there. They were safe.

16 - Cellar

Freddie and Brenda were having a cup of tea and a slice of Battenberg cake in Jennifer's house. Jennifer was still anxious about Beverly. She gazed out of her kitchen window into the dark night, the walls cutting off the view of the snowy moors. Jennifer was ninety percent sure that her daughter was gone. Eaten or turned into a vampire. Would she come back here for her if she was? If that happened, she would probably give in and let Beverly bite her. That was better than the alternative, which was this. Living for the rest of her life knowing she didn't say the right things to save her daughter - to stop her from going on this foolish rescue mission. She had lost one sister and a niece. Wasn't that enough?

Freddie had not been doing well for the last three days since the others had left. But today Brenda thought he was looking a little better. A small pinkish hue was back in his cheeks, and his eyes seemed brighter. He wasn't struggling as much to get in and out of his chair either. Plus, he was actually asking for food rather than Brenda and Jennifer having to force it on him.

'I've just been listening to the weather, Bren. A woman in London came out of Harrods and thought she saw a snowflake. She was so shocked she fell over and crushed her Royal Doulton figurine. Someone posted this on Facebook and its gone crazy, questions in Parliament and everything. All the Waitrose supermarkets are out of Artisan bread, and Humous and all the trains have been cancelled. The Prime Minister has ordered every gritter, even the famous 'Freddie Salted', to be sent to London to protect the Seat of Power. Jamie Oliver is starting a campaign for all Northerners to send our hand knitted cardigans to London to help them cope.'

'Really?' Brenda asked wide-eyed. Freddie couldn't last long and burst out laughing.

'No. But it's about as plausible as anything else, as to why the gritters haven't got through and rescued us,' Freddie replied, raising his eyebrows.

Throughout their married life they had always laughed at any hardships or misfortunes, and it helped them over the years. Black humour was their thing and neither took offence. Brenda was currently laughing with him as he ate his third piece of cake.

'Look at you! Your appetite seems to have returned. When I came into the bedroom just two days ago, I didn't know whether to pull the sheet up, instead of down,' Brenda laughed hysterically at her own joke.

'It's good to see that you can laugh about me dying like that. I suppose you will be off with a young buck, after me. You're sex mad, that's your problem.' Freddie was half smiling and looking at her across the room until she looked back. He winked at her. She screeched with laughter.

'Freddie, you know what I am like!'

'Like a pig at a 'tater in that respect,' Freddie said. Brenda's mouthful of tea spurted out over Jennifer's coffee table. She tried to compose herself, picking up a tissue and wiping herself and the coffee table down. 'Oohh, you dirty girl,' he said, just as she had taken a mouthful of Battenberg. That exploded out, and she began to cough, reaching for her cup of tea and relief. Freddie's spirits were certainly back up. When she had calmed down, she seemed wistful.

'How do you think they are getting on in Friarmere?' Brenda asked him.

'Well, they aren't back here yet, rescuing us. So, it mustn't be over. I hope they have got the kids they went for. But really, would you fancy your chances against Gary, Wee Renee, Pat and Our Doris? That's not even thinking about everyone else. Whatever's going on, I can guarantee they are giving that Norman a right bloody headache! Have you poisoned the meat?'

'I have Freddie, but they are not taking it,'

'Well keep doing it, they are howling all right,'

In the cellar, it was hushed, apart from the occasional rhythmic noise of Haggis panting. Sue was holding Bob in one corner rocking him, her tears falling on his face and Tony had his head in his hands. At the other side of Sue, Pat and Wee Renee had dropped to their knees. *How could they have failed to protect him*? This boy, who had been a shining light to them all. Our Doris was openly crying, stroking Haggis. She thought he would never say anything about her *Easter Egg* again and she was determined to have her vengeance good and proper on all the vampires. In the silence, they could hear nothing above them. Lying above them in the shop were the three dead vampires. Joe would remove them when it was safe in the morning. Terry had an idea, but the situation was delicate.

'Sue, I'm sorry. I wondered if you would like me to try something? I don't know if it will work,' Terry asked.

'Bless you, Terry. Please try anything,' She said, her face tear-stained and turned towards him.

'You see, I have some injectable antibiotics from the pharmacy. I could inject Bob near to the wound. If it was just a quick bite, which it seemed to me and if he has not suffered a great blood loss, maybe we could save him. After all, he has not ingested any blood from any kind of vampire,' Terry explained.

'Oh, Terry. That is a great idea. I will try anything to have Bob back,' she said gratefully.

'We really will try anything. Any ideas, please come forward. Please anyone,' Tony said desperately.

'I have an idea,' Wee Renee said. She took a cross out of her bag and put it on Bob's forehead. Nothing happened. No smoke, no burning, no reaction. 'He isn't one yet,' she said quietly.

Tony was pale and disbelieving about the events of the last fifteen minutes. He had lost his only child.

Terry was now ready with his syringe and antibiotics.

'Ok, can I get in and let's try this,' Terry said, squeezing past the people that flanked Bob from all sides. 'Now, I'm going to gently remove the scarf.' Sue looked away, Tony closed his eyes. They didn't want to see the mess that Colin had made of their boys' neck. Pat's eyes opened wide, she would face it, if Bob had taken it. Wee Renee watched, but her hand was over her mouth, to perhaps stifle the oncoming scream. Our Doris put her head on Haggis's back, burying her eyes in the Westie's fur.

'Oh my god!' Terry exclaimed. Sue feared the worst. She thought that her son's throat was ripped out, and Terry had discovered it. That there was no hope with a thousand syringes of antibiotics.

'Will you look at this please?' Terry said.

'Well I'll be damned,' Pat said.

'I don't want to look,' Sue sobbed. 'Don't make me look, Terry!'

'I promise you it isn't bad,' Terry said.

'Yes, look, Sue, look! It's marvellous.' Wee Renee said excitedly. They all lifted their heads to see what was so wonderous. Underneath Bob's scarf was an orange metal band around his neck.

'What the hell is that?' Sue asked. Soon the other adults walked over and started to look down at Bob. They all gasped when they saw what he had on under his scarf.

'It's brass. It's a brass neck!' Wee Renee exclaimed.

'What it is,' said Joe, bending further to confirm his suspicions, 'is a length of copper strip used for roofing. Clever lad. I never thought of that.'

'Get it off him then,' Our Doris said. 'We still need to see his neck.' She pulled off the copper strip and underneath his neck looked red and bruised.

'That's beginning to bruise,' Terry said. Our Doris held up the strip for everyone to see. There were teeth marks in the copper strip, but they had not punctured the metal.

'No holes at all. He's not been got!' Our Doris said happily.

Terry examined his neck, could feel a steady pulse and said he thought it was a little pinched and that is why Bob had probably passed out. Sue picked his head up and started to hold him again and rock him, crying now with relief. Her son was still alive and unbitten.

Bob took this opportunity, to come around. Bleary-eyed, he took in the sights around him. His mother's face alarmingly close. The crowd of people looking down at him, in the cellar. He had no recollection of how he got there.

'What happened?' Bob asked.

'Colin bit you and then started screaming. We killed him after though. We got him, Bob,' Pat said.

'What you put around your neck saved you, Bob,' Terry said smiling.

'Joe, how much of this stuff have you got?' Wee Renee asked. 'We could all do with one of these miracles.'

'Sodding reels of the bugger,' Joe said. 'The supplier only sells in massive bulk. I can't get rid of it!'

'Well, you will now!' Pat said. 'This is a game changer.'

Everyone started to calm down, and Bob sat up against the wall taking it all in. He still felt a little dizzy and discombobulated, so sat quietly, blinking at the scene before him, waiting to start feeling normal again. Sally and Kathy thought that the kids were a little shocked about all the fuss with Bob, even though this was now resolved. They started a game of I-Spy, which kept them good. Lauren and Beverly began to try and prepare food for all the children, and soon they were eating. They had made a meal of wraps, with mixed chilli beans, cheese spread and a few chopped tinned tomatoes on that they were trying to pass off as vegetable fajitas.

Pat was trying out a new recipe. She was mashing barbeque sauce into a tin of spam, with a screwdriver. Bob watched her work on it for a while, as he came to.

'What are you making, Pat?' Bob asked.

'Pulled pork,' she replied.

'Eat your heart out Nigella,' Tony said laughing. Pat tried her concoction, by sucking the screwdriver clean. She wrinkled her nose. It was a failure.

'Haggis!' she shouted, putting the can of flavoured spam down on the floor for him. He was glad to have it, and Our Doris thought now, he would be farting all night. If it wasn't Pat, it was him. Thinking it about this, both of these incidents of flatulence were down to Pat. She was glad she had brought that bottle of Youth Dew in her pocket.

Bob's throat was sore, so his meal was two tins of custard. Terry was spreading a tin of beef curry over a long-life naan, which everyone thought they would copy tomorrow night. They could tell by the way he was eating it, that it was delicious.

In the wake of the disaster with the pulled pork, Pat was now eating all the sausages out of a large tin of sausage and beans, with her fingers.

'Does anyone want the beans out of this tin? I'm not having them, because of the obvious,' she asked.

'Aye, I will love,' Wee Renee replied. Taking the can off Pat, she sat quietly in the corner, drinking the beans out of it.

After the stress of last night and tonight, and the walk over here, they soon began to see eyelids drooping. Wee Renee started to sing lots of carols to lull them to sleep. She sang for so long that her voice started to go. There was still the odd child awake, staring wide-eyed around at the adults waiting for the next problem to terrify them. Our Doris took over. Singing in a deep husky voice for such a small lady, she began to sing her favourite Elvis songs. Tonight, Haggis didn't bark as he was fast asleep. His feet twitched, and he puffed his lips every so often. Pat's pulled pork recipe had sent him straight into a wonderful sleep.

'This reminds me of the war, Rene,' Pat said.

'What do you know about the war? You're not that old!' Wee Renee said amusingly.

'My mother told me over and over again. You know I still have the Anderson Shelter in the back garden. She used to take me in there with a candle, me and our Jackie, especially in winter. We would sit in there for hours and she would tell me what it was like. Course, as I'm still in the same house, now she has gone, the memories are all still very vivid.'

'You've got some marvellous memories, Pat. You know. Those ones, and the romantic ones about Dennis you were telling us about,' Kathy said. Pat sighed and smiled, nodding knowingly at her.

'I've had a wonderful life, love. A wonderful life,' Pat said. It was a night they would never forget.

Gary and Carl could hear something. Little noises coming from outside the classroom doors. Whimpers, scratching, bumping.

'I think we have a visitor or visitors outside,' Gary whispered to Carl.

'Sounds like a dog to me,' Carl said.

'Could be a fox.'

'Yes. Or badger.'

'It's night-time so it might be a nocturnal creature.' Gary stopped for a moment then shouted out to the scavenger outside. 'We haven't got anything to give you, and we can't come out, boy. You'll have to try elsewhere. But be careful or else you will end up someone else's dinner!'

The noises stopped as he spoke, and he thought he had startled the animal away. Then the scratching got even more frantic and the whimpering.

'They'll go away soon,' Gary said.

It took fifteen minutes for the noises to stop. Not long after that, Gary and Carl dropped off to sleep. Dreams of woodland animals, cavorting round Friarmere in their heads, now it was silent, and the animals were gone.

But the creatures weren't gone. The two of them sat back and waited for another hour. Maybe the food would come out at some point. It was in there, they could smell it and hear people in there. They could wait for a few more hours yet, as they never got cold. It was boring out here and the food was so scarce. After a long while, one of them sensed that dawn was coming. It was time to leave. There would be another time and another place for these two vampire children. Tomorrow they would feed.

17 - Rescind

Maurice started to slowly walk home after he had seen the vampires come out of the shop and go back up the hill. He had a lot on his mind. Maurice had noticed that Peter and Colin were missing, especially seeing as though there was a bass drum and tuba left on the snow outside. There also seemed to be a horn, but he didn't know who that belonged to.

In Maurice's opinion, his old group of friends were doing well. They were picking them off one by one. Yes, new ones were being made all the time. But Colin and Peter were both significant kills. Keith and Stephen were better, but those two were a good start. He needed to think about what had to be done next, but he was stumped. Taking some lesser ones down himself might work, but it would be tricky.

Maurice also wondered, how he could use this new confidence of The Master. Parading through the village with his vampire brass band must open new opportunities for attack. However, they were living on human flesh, and he was still on frozen liver. The Master's vampires were bound to be stronger. If only he had some allies. Maybe the humans would listen to him if he approached them. No, on consideration he was sure they would think he was one of Norman's spies.

As he walked along the street, a figure followed him from above. Adam slipped a little, jumping from house to house and a bit of giveaway snow dropped down onto Maurice, who looked up. A young milky face looked down at him. A face he had never seen before, but a vampire face nonetheless. Adam dropped down next to Maurice.

'Hello, what's your name?' Adam asked.

'Maurice.'

'I'm Adam. I am a friend of Bob's. Do you know Bob?'

'Yes. Plays percussion with the band.'

'I want to say I used to be a friend, but I still am a friend. As far as he is concerned, he can't be friends with a vampire. But I still want to be and have the best intentions,' Adam said. 'You probably don't believe me, do you?'

Maurice didn't reply, and Adam was unsure if he had explained his situation correctly. 'Do you even know what I am saying?' Adam waited for a reply but didn't get one. Maurice was dumbfounded but nodded. Somebody must be watching over him and his situation. This boy was exactly what he needed. Adam continued after seeing Maurice nod. 'I want to help you. Am I right in thinking you are fighting against them? You are, aren't you? Well, I want to too.'

Maurice didn't know what question to answer first. This young vampire talked so fast. Maurice had the idea, he was lonely and had been building this conversation in his head. It had all tumbled out at once, as soon as he had had the opportunity.

They began to hear the chink of empty bottles. Mark was coming along the road towards them. Adam went to get back on the roof, but Maurice put his hand on the young vampire's arm.

'No wait. He's all right,' Maurice said simply. Mark reached them. The three vampires stood in the middle of the road. Adam squinted at Mark, taking everything in about him.

'What are you doing giving them that? I saw you earlier, and I've seen you before,' Adam said. 'That is human blood, you are harvesting for them.'

'It keeps them sweet,' Mark said. 'If I give them this, then I am some use to them. Norman leaves me alone. After this, I go home to read. I like to read.'

'We need your help with the old band. Adam here, who is a friend of Bob's is going to help too.'

'How are you going to do that?' Mark asked.

'First thing is, I know where they are keeping the other two. I could help you rescue them, and maybe we could find another way to get the whole gang out to safety,' Adam replied. 'It's a start, isn't it?'

'Why would you want to do that?' Mark asked. 'What's in it for you?'

'They might let me go with them, wherever they go. I've got no mum anymore. Didn't have a dad. I just want to be with Bob and his Mum and Dad. They are my family now. However much Norman thinks we are kin, we ain't. I will find some way of not biting him now I am not near The Master. I don't have to do his bidding. The further you get away from him the better it is.'

'You're right there,' Maurice said.

'Yes, that is how I feel too. The closer I am to The Grange, the more I am compelled by his will. That's why I prove I am more useful elsewhere. I don't mind being a bloodsucker, but I don't want to be a puppet.'

'It's obvious we are all of the same mind. Let's go to my house for a meeting, it's not far,' said Maurice. 'We might get spotted here, and that wouldn't do. Let's sort all this out in private. It needs proper planning. They are in more and more danger every day,' Maurice said, leading the way.

Unfortunately, Stephen and Vincent had not gone back with the group but had instead gone for sustenance in one of the local houses. The two injured vampires had made a new kind of friendship and understanding and were often together. They had returned to the scene of the earlier battle, for the two instruments remaining on the street and thought there was no harm grabbing a bit of refreshment on the way. Vincent spotted them first, with his one useful eye, as they turned the corner, catching Stephen and shoving him back around. They both peeked around the side of the building and watched the three vampires walking away into the distance.

'What are they up to?' Stephen asked Vincent.

'I don't know,' said Vincent, 'but I bet it's not for the good of The Master.'

'Shall we follow them?' Stephen asked wickedly.

'I can't be bothered, all three of them are useless. What could they be up to, really? The three of them couldn't fight their way out of a paper bag,' Vincent said. 'Let's just pretend we haven't seen them. They are more trouble than they are worth. Maybe they are the first three founder members of the vampire losers club. Who cares?'

Maurice invited the other two vampires into his house. They came in and sat down on the edge of the sofa. This was too weird. Mark and Adam waited silently for him to start talking.

Maurice stood at the window, he pulled back the curtain a little, then moved a small piece of newspaper that was taped to his windows. He surveyed the street. It didn't look like they had been followed. He turned back, took his cap, coat and scarf off and laid them on the back of his chair.

'We're in here, but we aren't safe. I suppose The Master could just walk in,' Maurice said. He got up and checked through his curtains again. Maurice was making the other two nervous.

'You could try and rescind his invitation if you're worried about that,' said Mark

'What's that?' Maurice asked.

'You say that he is no longer welcome in your home. No one can get into my house only me. But as The Master has never tried it, I don't know for sure. I was taken outside Christine's house delivering milk, so it has never come up.'

'How do you do it?' Maurice asked. 'I invited him in when he first bit me.'

'You just say, *I rescind your invitation, Norman Morgan* and he can't come in.' Mark said.

'Who told you that?'

'You'd never believe me if I told you,' Mark said smiling.

'Go on – try me,' Maurice insisted.

'Ernie told me,'

'Ernie Cooper told you! How does he know?'

'He's read it in a book, or something.'

'There's a book on it? Where?'

'Wee Renee's house. He's been in there with Lynn, looking for people. Luckily, they didn't find any because Lynn is a right little devil now. Taken to it like a duck to water. What's worse is, it was me that bit her in the first place! She has ended up more vicious than me. Who would have thought it?'

'How interesting.'

'Yes, she's at it every night.'

'I didn't mean her. I meant what Ernie found out.'

'Oh. He went in and saw some books and all this stuff stuck on her living room walls. Lynn wasn't bothered about it, but Ernie remembered it was important before he was turned. He went back. And he keeps going back.'

'Cheeky devil. Wee Renee wouldn't like him nosing in her particulars, in his condition.'

'No, and he keeps going on about her triangle, or something.'

Adam's eyes widened. Wee Renee's triangle. This conversation was getting a bit sexy. He swallowed.

'He's what? Maybe that's how the bloodlust has taken him. I must say, I am surprised at Ernie. Apart from that, what's he up to?'

'I don't know. But he told me how to rescind invitations. You know as much as I know.'

'I wish I had somewhere I could make safe, and rescind The Master,' Adam said sadly. The two other vampires didn't know what to say to this, so Maurice continued.

'Well, I'll do that then. I rescind your invitation, Norman Morgan. Right we're safe, apart from Michael Thompson, I suppose. I have the option to bite him, but I would have to give in then,' Maurice said sadly.

'What do you mean?' Mark asked. 'You would have to give in then?'

'Well, I've never bitten anyone yet. I've been surviving on liver out of the freezer. After all these weeks abstaining, it would be a damn shame.'

'You are kidding me,' Mark said laughing. 'Bloody hell, Maurice. You don't know what you are missing.'

'I haven't bit anyone either,' Adam said, 'what's so bad about that?'

'How's that happened?' Mark asked. 'You have been with him and all those tasty kids. How did you resist that?'

'It suited him and me,' Adam advised him. 'For a start, he wanted me to look after all the kids inside the school and temptation was a lot easier to resist if I hadn't tasted human blood. I wanted to do it because I knew that it would be more difficult to be friends with Bob if I succumbed to it. So I have been living on animals. It wasn't a problem for me to do it either.'

'We are going to have to approach the others you know. The living remains of the band,' Maurice said, 'and tell them we are on their side.'

'Wait a minute,' said Mark', I'm not declaring for any side.'

'What are you doing listening to our plans and sitting on Maurice's sofa then?' Adam asked, crossly.

'All the more fun I can have, the better,' Mark answered, 'and letting them win all the time means I can't watch the fun. It's all a game to me, I enjoy it. I especially like watching Michael Thompson being pissed off, to be quite frank.'

'Okay, so we will go to them with a plan,' Adam said. 'But as we haven't got a plan, we are going to have to think of one fast. How about we distract the other vampires, say we want to join them or something like that. Call a big meeting in one area of the school, with Norman and all the vampire bigwigs, so that the people could get the two hostages out while we were doing it. But we would all have to do it in the dark or else they would know it was a trap.'

'I can't see The Master or the humans falling for that,' Maurice said, shaking his head. 'They will think we just want them out in the open to eat them.'

'There has to be some kind of a compromise from the humans. Some middle ground and a little trust, for that to work,' Mark said.

'What about if we do it when it's still dark? *We* have to then, let's face it. But what if we say we will provide a distraction on this day at this particular time. Then they can come along, with their own plan, just knowing that they will be safe. They don't have to tell us the how, when and where. Or they can leave it if they don't trust us. We can't trap them if we don't know the plan,' Maurice offered.

'Yes, I can see that would work. We will then have to nobble the vampires as soon as they twig on that we are in cahoots though,' said Adam.

'That depends on how we do it. Maybe we don't jeopardise ourselves. Life is hard enough as it is. It's not an easy existence being a lone vampire, is it?' Mark commented.

'No, we will act as shocked as them. If we are with the Master's gang, they can't exactly blame us. It could be any vampire. It is better if we can all save ourselves. It leaves us free to help again if we have to,' Maurice mused.

'Okay, we will work that bit out. That is the only part we can plan for. We've got a few hours until daylight, and then we need to sort this, and quick. From what I can see, those two aren't looking good up at the school,' said Adam.

'How do you know?' Mark asked.

'What I do have, at least, is free access to them.'

'Maybe we could warn them, to be ready. That would be a help too,' Maurice added. Adam nodded.

'Good idea. The problem is, if they have already decided to rescue the two of them this morning we won't be able to help anyone. I know – I've got it!' Adam looked very pleased with himself and looked at the others. 'What about if we go up to the school now, and make our plan up there in one of the classroom's as quiet as we can. It must be a plan that we can activate when we see *them* make their move. So, we hide where we can see access to the two men. When we see them arrive, we activate the distraction plan. The living guys don't have to know about our plan, they just need to benefit from it. Then if it happens today, we are already in situ to help them. We aren't doing anything else today are we?'

'You're a clever lad,' Maurice said.

'Well I do have to do my blood supply round,' Mark said agitatedly.

'If it happens soon, that is the last thing they will be thinking about. The vampires will be trying to chase after our guys, not waiting around for you to turn up with your crate. Anyway, as soon as we have done the distraction, you can run off. Do what you have to do, they will be busy. By the time the dust is settled, you will be sorted. Are you all with me?' Adam asked.

The other two vampires nodded, and without further discussion, the three of them walked up to the school in the darkness. No other vampire saw them, even though they were roaming around feeding.

Mark and Maurice were a little nervous as they arrived. It was normal for Adam to be here, but they would be questioned. The trio went through the front entrance and into the first classroom that used to hold the reception class. Adam left them there. He didn't have to remind them to be absolutely still and silent.

Adam wandered around the school, to see what was going on. The two men were still alive but dozing, the only vampire on duty was Kate, who sat in the Headmasters Office, filing her nails.

'Everything okay?' Adam asked. Kate stopped filing and looked up at him. She rolled her eyes, then returned to her nail filing. Adam knew she would be there for a while. This was his best chance to complete part of the plan. He returned to the two living hostages in the classroom, gently knocking on the door, they awoke, rubbing their eyes and Adam entered.

'Have you brought tea? Gary asked.

'Shhh!! No. It's better than tea.'

'At the moment nothing could be,' Gary said.

'How about getting out of here?' Adam asked.

'What?' Gary said astonished. It was the last words he thought he would hear from Adams's mouth.

'I don't know how or when your rescue will come, but it will. Just know you have friends on the inside too. There are three of us. Me and two of the people from your band.'

'Who?'

'Maurice and Mark. No-one else can be trusted though. No-one. When we know the rescue is happening, we are going to provide a distraction. Just be ready and be comforted with that knowledge. We will do all we can.'

'Why are you doing this?' Carl asked.

'Various reasons for all of us,' Adam replied. 'But now is not the time for that. Don't tell anyone about this conversation. Only your living friends when you see them again.' With that, he smiled and exited. Kate had still not moved, so Adam returned to the reception class.

He advised them of what he had just done. They whispered in there for about twenty minutes, going over various scenarios before deciding on one.

Adam went back into the school and prepared for their plan. Just as he finished he saw Kate drifting around the school a little, she seemed to be bored, but would never condescend to have a conversation with him. He slipped back to the reception class quietly, knowing that she wouldn't care where the hell he was.

'It's done,' he said. Mark took the first watch, while it was still dark. Maurice said he would sit behind the blackout curtains and listen all through the day. He was used to sitting in his living room watching daytime television, behind the newspaper and the curtains of his own terrace house. There was no more to say.

There they sat, as vampires do, in stasis waiting for their trigger.

18 - Familiar

Below the Hardware Store in the cellar, the survivors started to stir. They had not heard any noise since all the vampires had left last night, so apart from being quite cold, they had enjoyed a restful sleep.

The children seemed to feel a little better, and one by one the adults woke. There was a moment where everyone noticed that Rick and Lauren had slept with their arms around each other. Sue and Liz had seen he had been talking to her a lot last night and it looked like something special was starting between them. A small glimmer of normality and hope. There was also a moment of shock when Wee Renee and Our Doris saw the condition of Pat in the morning.

She was lying on her back, snoring loudly, her mouth open. Around her nose and mouth, there was a thick yellow mucus. Wee Renee shook her shoulder gently, but she just continued to snore, muttered the word 'Dido' and remained asleep.

'We've got a problem,' Our Doris told the group as Pat lay snoring. 'Pat seems to have come down with a severe cold. There's snot all over her, and she seems to be in a deep feverish sleep.' A few of them scrawled over the others to take a look.

'Poor bastard,' Andy said. 'She is going to struggle now with all this.'

'Not to mention, we are all going to get it. This probably means a trip back to the chemist's shop,' Terry said miserably.

'I'm going to try waking her again, bless her,' Wee Renee said. She knelt over Pat and started to jiggle Pat's body with one of her hands. 'Pat, Pat, wake up love. It's Wee Renee,' Pat's eyes started to open almost immediately this time, and Sue's hand came over Wee Renee's shoulder, holding an individual pack of tissues.

'What's wrong, Rene? Are they back?' Pat said suddenly with a start. Her eyes were wide open, and she tried to raise herself up on her elbows.

'No, no. You rest easy for a moment. We can see your condition, and we just want to help you.'

'My condition? Am I pregnant? Am I dreaming?' Pat asked, clearly horrified and confused. The rest of the group were laughing now, which was making Pat angry. She was the only one not in on the joke. Then she realised what was wrong and sank back down closing her eyes. 'Oh god no. I've been turned into one of *them*, haven't I? Kill me, Rene. Don't risk yourself. Quick before I realise what I am and start wanting to drink blood. In fact, I'll kill myself. Oh no,' Pat said sadly. She actually believed she was now a vampire. This made the rest of them laugh even more, which they knew they shouldn't do, but they couldn't help it.

'Pat, no. You're not one of them. You just have a heavy case of the flu, love' Our Doris informed her. Pat lay for a moment considering how she felt.

'No, I don't. I feel right as rain,' Pat announced.

'Well, how do you explain the snoring and the sheer amount of mucous over your nose, and mouth? It's everywhere,' Terry said clinically.

Pat sat up and wiped the back of her hand across her upper lip. Sure enough, it came back yellow and slimy. They were right. She looked at her hand again forlornly. Then Pat burst out laughing. They were the ones not in on the joke now.

'What's so funny?' Wee Renee asked. Pat lifted her Russian fur hat, which was on the cellar floor beside her. Underneath was an empty jar of lemon curd.

'I scoffed it when everyone had dropped off. It was dark,' She still laughed as everyone else drifted off and prepared to leave the cellar. Pat still sat, trying to wipe the sticky lemon curd of her face with Sue's tissues. She would need wet wipes, she thought. The tissues were sticking to the curd and leaving a powdery residue on her face. The clean-up was further hampered by the fact that Pat had quite a hairy face for a woman. All the time she was muttering under her breath.

'They moan when I have tripe, now they moan when I have lemon curd. You can't bloody win with these lot.'

Joe popped his head out of the cellar hatch mole-like and instantly knew that they were alone, by the sound of the shop. He could see the generator still in situ, on the rim of the shutter door. Just as a *belt and braces* approach, Joe and his three vigilante friends checked out the shop from top to bottom. They announced it was clear. Everyone came out of the cellar, blinking in the daylight.

Breakfast was the first concern, so several of the women began to feed the children and then the adults as further arrangements were made. There was still plenty of food that they had taken from the shop yesterday.

Today's breakfast mainly consisted of cereal bars and cake. Joe had a kettle in the back of the shop, but only six mugs. They each quickly took turns with the mugs, either having tea or coffee. Wee Renee took Joe aside and apologised for the mess she had made of the vampire, with her firepit fork. He squeezed her shoulder amiably.

'Just to see you doing that was amazing. I couldn't care less about the mess. It's not a priority to me,' Joe said proudly. Wee Renee knew he wouldn't be cross with her, but old habits die hard.

The group were discussing what had been useful last night and there were various opinions on what were the best items to take. The fire pokers were going and anything that was long and sharp at the end. There were still a few spears remaining, and these were easy to make up, so a small task group started on this project.

The new *must-have* item was the brass neck. Joe made everyone a strip of copper, which Craig and Rick shaped with their hands, finally rounding off any sharp edges with a file. Now if one of the bloodsuckers lunged for them, they would get a shock.

Andy looked at the floor near to where Colin had attacked Bob and made a discovery. Colin's teeth lay broken on the floor. He picked them up and poked them. They were quite brittle and hollow. That was interesting to know. Wee Renee had a good look and decided to investigate more. She took Pat's lump hammer, made Andy hold Colin's decapitated head and knocked out a few more. She examined them closely. They were all hollow, more like a case of enamel rather than a whole tooth. Then she remembered they had a tooth expert in their midst and excitedly showed her find to Terry.

'I've got you your own fang,' she gleefully said pointing out the hollowness of it. He agreed with Wee Renee's findings and said he would look at them in more detail when he could. Terry put them safely in a zipped pocket of his jacket.

As they finished their drinks, they listed what they needed to do and prioritised. Today would be interesting.

Soon everyone was fed and watered. As always, it was imperative to use every bit of daylight to their advantage, so they prepared to leave. Everything was replaced back onto the sledges or into backpacks, and the whole lot of them collectively put on their coats, hats, and gloves.

Joe brought two extra reels of copper strip, in case they met other people who needed the protection and Wee Renee attached all the plant sprays onto the sledge. They wondered what she was going to do. Wee Renee kept her mystery and said they would find out in good time. The plant sprays were all tied together and hung from the back of the sledge like tin cans from a wedding car. They un-barricaded the back door, Joe locked it behind them, and they set off on their next mission.

The first stop was going to be Sue's house. She needed to get more clothes and outer garments, which would be useful to them all. Some of them didn't have hats, and she knew she had quite a few in her wardrobe, plus of course, she wanted to check on her cats. They started up the bank. Sue promised she would only take five minutes, so most of them would be waiting outside.

It was an uneventful journey. No sightings of anyone living or dead. When they stopped, and the icy footsteps, the noise of the sledges and the clattering of the train of plant sprays ceased, all there was left was ear-splitting silence.

On her way into the house through the back door, she immediately could tell that the house had been disturbed. She could only think that they had been in looking for her. Her cats were well and pleased to see herself, Tony and Bob. There was an enormous about of fuss again from them, and Sue left Bob, Tony and Liz to feed and look after them while she went on the hunt for her hats. Strangely, her hats, gloves, and scarves were scattered across the quilt on her king-size bed. What in heavens name had they wanted with them? She didn't think they got cold. Sue started to gather them up to take downstairs when she realised what was missing. Her lovely gold sequinned beret. She checked the floor and under the bed. No, it was definitely gone. That was more of a fashion statement than a warm hat. Who would want that? She wracked her brain as she stuffed everything back into the zip up bag and then she had the worst feeling.

Sue walked slowly down the stairs, the bag in front of her. She reached the others, and they could tell something was wrong.

'What's up?' Tony asked.

'I'll tell everyone outside. So I can say it once. See if anyone else comes up with what I am imagining,' Sue growled.

They walked down Sue's drive. The rest of the party were waiting patiently on the pavement. Basil, her ginger cat, trailed behind her, with his head cocked to one side.

'Okay,' Sue said. 'Here are some hats. There are more than enough for those who don't have any. But listen to this. I found the contents of this bag all over my bed. It's been rummaged through.'

'Maybe they were after your scent?' Wee Renee offered.

'Maybe. But I don't think so. I have a hat missing. Not a hat I have worn a lot so it won't have a lot of scent on it. It's a party beret in gold sequins. It's not warm. But they don't need warmth do they.'

'What are you saying?' Laura asked.

'Who needs a hat? Not for warmth, but to cover something up. Who likes glittery glitzy things in Friarmere?' Sue asked them.

'Christine!' Liz said. 'Her hair has been ripped off,'

'Yes. The cheeky thieving bloodsucker,' Sue said through tight lips.

'You don't know for sure,' Terry said.

'No. But if I'm right, I'm ripping it off that bitch's head and then burning it.'

'Aye, she was always a cheeky bitch. It would be her alright. I bet she has eyed that beret on you for a while,' Wee Renee said. Danny wandered up from the back of the group.

'Sue, I hate to tell you this, but I realise now she was wearing it last night. I never thought about it until now.' Sue flared her nostrils. She didn't want that back, but she'd make sure Christine didn't have it forever either!

'Right. Let's get on then,' Sue sighed. They walked a few steps towards Wee Renee's house, and Tony noticed that Basil was still with them.

'Go back Basil. You can't come with us,' he said.

Basil looked up at him, he understood but ignored Tony. He had decided he would not be letting his mistress go alone again. He knew his way around the top area of Friarmere well and was comfortable around here. Basil turned his head to Sue now.

'Look, Basil, I would love you to come, but at one point you won't know where you are and I will end up having to take you back,' Sue said. 'Go and get in out of the cold. We have a long journey. I'll be back as soon as I can.' Wee Renee walked over to Basil and picked him up. She looked into his eyes for a long time and stroked his head. Wee Renee passed him to Sue.

'It is his time to come. He is with us now. Basil is your familiar Sue, and he could prove very useful to us,' Wee Renee said mysteriously. Sue looked over at Haggis and bit her lip.

'Haggis doesn't have a problem with cats, he likes them,' Our Doris informed her. Sue put Basil back down on the snow, and as if he knew what the conversation was about he walked over to the little white dog and started to clean Haggis's head with his tongue.

'Good boy Basil. Clean the dirty hound up,' Our Doris said in amusement.

'Okay, he comes,' Sue said shrugging. The rest of the group set off to Wee Renee's house which was only a few houses away and across the road. Sue and Tony went back to get some cat food and a bowl for Basil.

Wee Renee said she wanted to check up on something, but she did not tell anyone what it was. In the last couple of days, more footprints in the snow had appeared on her drive. That was strange. She suddenly got worried that they had found what she had come for herself. The things that she could fight them with. They would change everything if she were right. She rushed inside and with a sigh of relief, started reading one of the larger books that she still had.

'Well blow me,' she muttered smiling. She read a little more then uttered. 'I can't believe it.' She looked at another part of the book and said, 'All right.' And that was that. She would not tell anyone what was going on, not even Pat. Wee Renee then went to the freezer, where she had several cloves of garlic, peeled and bagged. She had stored them up for dire necessity, which was now. Wee Renee boiled the kettle and mashed up the frozen garlic cloves in a jug, until they were defrosted and in a pulp. After that, she put the kettle on again and mashed away at them once more.

She took five of the plant sprays, and put some of the garlic mash in the bottom of each one. Then she asked the children to carefully fill them up with water out of the tap, put the spray tops back on and shake them, which they were happy to do. It made them feel part of the team, and they did the job well. Now the group had five garlic sprays, which they knew the vampires did not like. They were useful and safe. Some of the children could have them to repel the vampires but not endanger each other.

Next Wee Renee asked Nigel if he didn't mind syphoning petrol out of cars, with the length of rubber hose that she had beaten Diane with the previous night. She did not know how you did it, or how to get into car petrol caps. Bob was quite surprised that there was something Wee Renee did not know. Nigel, Joe and his three friends, said they would see her right. She gave them the other five plant sprays and said if they could find canisters to bring more back in, then please do. They were back within about an hour with everything full of petrol. Rick and Craig had also found various spare petrol cans in the backs of cars, which they had filled too.

Wee Renee had used the time efficiently while they were away and had cut up her tea towels into smaller chunks. However, the Gretna Green one was still intact, Ernie would have been glad to know. She had rummaged around in her glass bottle recycling, and several of her neighbour's bottle recycling until she had what she needed. While she did this, some of the children had been taken for a wash, and everyone had had a drink.

She asked Andy to fill up all the recycled bottles with petrol, and she jammed pieces of tea towel into each. They now had about twenty glass Molotov cocktails.

'You can't light these as well, you know. They will explode,' Joe said, with one of the petrol filled plant sprays in his hands.

'No, I know. But we can use them to spray petrol on the vampires and then chuck a match at the varmints,' Wee Renee replied. Joe thought it was a brilliant idea. Andy had one can of petrol left after making the Molotov cocktails. Wee Renee put this in her shed, for emergencies. Along with their weapons and their brass necks, they now had, twenty Molotov cocktails, five DIY flamethrowers, five garlic sprays and a ginger cat. They couldn't be more prepared. It was time to search for Gary and Carl.

19 - Ernie

Ernie lived at the bottom of the same street as Sue and Wee Renee. He had heard the group going past his house not long after it was daylight. Ernie recognised the voices and wished so much to be with them. Lynn lay upstairs in the darkened room. She would be cold, no respiration, no sound. Lynn would be like that until the evening. Ernie however, still liked the daylight, even though it didn't like him. He had helped Lynn to find humans, she was his wife after all. But he could not bring it upon himself to bite them himself.

He had been offered a pint of Mark's blood delivery. Lynn had an arrangement now with Mark, and he brought two pints a day, just like before. But still, he did not fancy it very much, even with the human aspect removed.

Ernie didn't know why he would rather live on animals, but he couldn't bring himself to take the next step. He shivered when he thought of it. Lynn thought this was hilarious and said he ought to *grow a pair*, which was not like Lynn at all.

She had always been the gentle one, the caring motherly, lovely Lynn that everyone knew and loved. But she had taken to this new life with gusto. He didn't think he would ever be the same as her and the others. Ernie wanted his old life back. He wanted to be sitting in his bandroom, working out his figures and booking up concerts. Going around the country, contesting. Ernie thought that would never happen again if he let himself become as she was. He ate animals before this, so he was doing nothing different. Ernie was sure that there was a cure for this, somewhere. In his opinion, it was worth holding out for. *It wasn't like he was getting any older, was it?* He could bide his time eating animals. It was fine. Ernie could make the choice in the future if the opportunity presented itself. Apart from anything else, just the very thought of biting or eating a human made him bilious.

When he had heard the others pass, he was delighted that they were still alive.

He didn't know how many there were outside, he couldn't look through his curtains. Ernie didn't know if all the humans he cared about had survived, but he recognised some of the voices. Wee Renee's, Pat and Andy's for definite. He also heard a couple of other voices that he didn't know too. Male and female, quite a few of them. It sounded like they had managed to gather a right lynch mob together. That suited him. Kill The Master and the others he felt pressured by. He could bide his time until the government came with a cure. He could always rely on the nanny state.

He wished he had not had to play a part in the battle at The Civic Hall, but alas he was a vampire and was compelled to do so by The Master. But The Master was not here now, and he felt like he could maybe do some good. While he had a responsibility to Lynn, he also had a duty to himself and to his village and the Band that he had loved so much.

The people outside had been more than friends, they were family too. He needed to help them if he could, but couldn't see a way that he would be able to. Also, with Lynn lying upstairs, that seemed ever more unlikely. If she got anywhere near the humans, she would think he had organised a takeaway delivery for her.

He didn't venture out much, so he wasn't likely to encounter his old friends by chance. When Lynn was out, he usually made a secret visit up to Wee Renee's house and thought of happier times. He didn't dare trek all the way to the bandroom and back. That was too far. She was never out longer than a couple of hours. The whole group of them had roamed around for a while when it was still a novelty. He had managed to pop into the band then a couple of times. Oh, how that was such a delightful treat. But Lynn thought it was silly. That life was long behind her, so she never wanted to walk over there again. So, he hadn't been. He was incredibly sad about that. But he found small pleasures locally, at least.

Ernie liked to sit on Wee Renee's sofa and remember that night when they had last been as one in there. The night they had been carolling and had gone back for a mince pie and some mulled wine. The old gang working together, talking about defeating the enemy, which was now him.

He leafed through some of her books. Ernie would on occasion find something fascinating, but he was lucky to remember it by the time he got home. He got very distracted these days and had short-term memory loss on a daily basis. However, Ernie remembered how it felt to be with the band before all this and wanted to *feel that* again. In the bosom of friends — warm, happy, belonging. That's what he wanted to feel again.

He regarded his hands in his lap and began to play cat's cradle with his fingers. That was all you had to do when you were a vampire. That, or play solitaire. Hmmm…. that was an idea. He picked up his playing cards and started to lay them out. This would pass the time. Soon he would be back to normal. Not long now, Ernie.

20 - Changes

The vampires were all asleep after the previous night's battle in the hardware store. Some were wounded again and even Michael, who did not have to sleep in the day, was resting now. It had been a long and tiring night. Three more of The Master's children were gone. The humans were putting a severe dent in The Master's army. A few more nights of this and he would be at a disadvantage. His current advantage was that they didn't know how many vampires he had. They didn't realise how close they were to really turning this around. He would have to make more in his image and fast.

Some of the ladies had agreed to stay outside the school and look after the children and had organised a snowball competition to keep them occupied. Not only were the children terrified to go back there, but they would just be a hindrance to the rescue of Gary and Carl. They would be safe as long as they stayed in the open, at the bottom of the school drive. The ladies explained to them that needed to be quiet for the moment, as they did not know if the vampires would wake at the sounds of children. So, they stood at the bottom, quite a distance from the school. As long as Michael didn't wake up, there should be no threat outside the school.

The band of rescuers walked up the drive. They did not know if Norman and his group were there or at The Grange above. Wee Renee and Pat stared up at the brooding manor house above them. Even in the day, it was incredibly creepy. It felt like it was empty, to Wee Renee.

'What do you think, Pat?' Wee Renee asked, gesturing towards The Grange, with her head.

'He's here, I think Rene,' she said and sniffed.

'Aye, so do I. Licking his wounds and watching over his captives, like a vulture.'

'Great,' Our Doris said, moving beside them. 'Gives us a chance to stake him.'

'Or you could just use your firepit poker on him, Wee Renee. You know, for a laugh,' Nigel winked.

'Yes, he wouldn't like that, the sexy pig,' Pat said, pulling her leggings up.

When they got to the front everyone tried to be as quiet as possible. They did not know where Gary and Carl were being kept in the school. Between garlic spraying and burning vampires, they were determined to go from room to room. Ripping down the curtains and just generally destroying this nest. Nigel had a few other tricks up his sleeve and said if they could open some of the doors and drag the vampires out into the daylight, then they would burn. This would only work if they were dozy and maybe, that would be an even easier kill for them.

Maurice, Adam, and Mark stood in the entrance hall, just in the darkness and safety. The rescuers were startled to see them. They felt deflated. Their rescue attempt had already been rumbled.

'We're still going for it, get ready. They are waiting for us,' Wee Renee advised the people behind her who couldn't already see the vampiric trio waiting in the gloom. Adam, they knew was bloodsucker as he had been looking after all the children. Mark, they had seen as a vampire previously and Maurice they knew certainly didn't like garlic and had been one of Norman's lot for the longest of all.

Maurice looked from side to side, checking they were alone and beckoned them in.

'Is he kidding?' Pat asked.

'He must be,' Tony said.

Danny opened the door, and in a loud whisper, Wee Renee addressed the group.

'Do you think we are stupid?'

'I am asking you to trust me for old times' sake. We would like to talk to you, but obviously, we can't come out there. We want to help you?' Maurice said, also in a loud whisper.

'Pull the other one, it's got bells on,' Nigel said.

'I don't know who you are mate,' Mark said, 'but he is telling the truth. We don't hang around with all the others, apart from Adam being made to look after the kids, in there.' Mark gestured backwards with his thumb to the school hall.

The humans knew that this was true. Maurice and Mark had not been at any of the battles of the last few days. They had also not been involved in the bloodbath at The Civic Hall. They had not seen them fighting. They had seen Mark peddling pints of blood, and they had seen Adam, watching the kids. But the children had told them that he had not bitten one of them.

Maurice had a spotless record. Maybe they were on the level.

'Put it this way, if we wanted to get you, we could have waited for you to come in and got behind you, couldn't we?' Maurice said helpfully.

'Okay,' Wee Renee said. 'I will come in, and a couple of the others. For the moment we will have a parlez, but that is as far as it will go for now.'

She stepped in, along with Pat, Our Doris, Danny, Sue, and Tony.

'I need to Bob to be part of this,' Adam said flatly.

'No way,' said Tony.

'I know exactly where the two men are being kept. You don't have to go through the main hall to get them, there is another safer way. I will tell you which classroom they are in, but I want to talk to my mate Bob. That's the deal.'

'Done,' Bob said and walked in. He had been listening behind the thick dark wooden frame of the entrance doors and had heard everything. Sue and Tony stood in front of him so that Bob could only slightly be seen. They all had the reassurance to know that they were wearing the *brass neck's* and that an injury to their neck would be more fatal to the vampire than to the person.

The door shut with the final ones inside, which were Nigel and Joe. The foyer was now quite full. The others stood outside trying to listen as hard as they could, but it was hard to hear all of it as everyone talked in hushed tones.

'Okay,' Wee Renee said, 'what can you do for us and why are you helping us.'

'For my part, I don't want to be what I am, and even though genetically I suppose I am part of their family, my real family and friends are you lot,' Maurice said. 'Surely you can believe that. I must ask as well, as I cannot see Freddie. Is he alright?'

'Freddie is fine and safe. Don't worry about Freddie. He is with Brenda,' Wee Renee advised him. She didn't say where he was with Brenda, and Maurice didn't ask. Just to know he was safe was enough.

'We can help you by distracting the vampires, and you can get the two people out, from the side,' Adam said.

'Why are you doing this? How do we know you aren't his lackey?' Bob asked.

'I'm doing this because I sort of want to come with you after,' Adam advised him.

'You want to come with us? We are getting out of this place Adam,' Bob said.

'Where are you going?'

'Why should we tell you? So you can all follow us?' Tony added.

'I don't care where you're going anyway,' Adam said. 'I want to come with you. You see, I don't like it here, and I have been going through all these changes but I am still Adam, and I don't have anything else to cling on to. I would love to just get back to everything I enjoyed – in fact, *anything* I enjoyed. It's the only thing that keeps me from staking myself. My one wish would be to play online with you again if ever we could.' Bob laughed at this statement.

'If you are on the level, then that is great, but I don't fancy my chances now, with your reflexes. Come on though Adam, there is no way you are coming with us. We couldn't sleep with you roaming about, just in case you got the munchies. You do realise you are a child of darkness, don't you?' Bob asked him frankly. Adam was shaking his head, but Bob continued. 'You think you are pure, but you have a demon inside you mate, no matter how much you don't want to admit it.' Adam looked crestfallen as Bob continued.

'Think about this as well, it would be more of an advantage to us if you were our allies here. Our eyes and ears in this village. Remember how we used to play games. You need to be our spy. Just like Call Of Duty. Stay here and tell us what the enemies are doing and then maybe I will survive long enough for you to be mates with me. That is how you can help us and if you do, and you prove yourself to not be evil, like Norman, then we can be friends again.'

'Have you consumed human blood, Adam?' Wee Renee asked.

'No, I've been living on animals. That's why I was trusted to look after the children.'

'Then there may be hope for you. I cannot say much more,' Wee Renee advised him. 'It is difficult, but there may be a future for you if you can manage to keep off the human drinkies. Have *you* drank human blood?' Wee Renee asked Maurice.

'I haven't,' he replied. 'I have been living on raw liver all this time, and it has been absolutely fine for me.'

'That is good. What about you, Mark?'

'I have to be honest and say that I have. But I do not want to run with Norman's gang. I just want to keep to myself, survive and live my life and at the moment I can do that. I like to watch the fun had by all though.'

'Fair enough,' Pat said. 'Lone wolf.'

'What have you got to fight them with,' Maurice asked.

'Garlic sprays, weapons, flamethrowers, chains,' Nigel said.

'Extreme self-protection, don't forget that,' Bob added. The three vampire's eyes widened.

'Wow,' Adam said. 'No wonder you have been kicking ass!'

'Okay, what about if we set a fire in the foyer?' Maurice asked. 'Then in the hall. There aren't any vampires in there. It is just used as a thoroughfare. They will all have to run in and try and extinguish the fire. This school has plenty of fire alarms that will go off and cause a lot of confusion.

'That's a good idea,' Tony said. 'Where are Carl and Gary?'

'Just the first classroom around the corner on the left. So the first door that you will come to on that side.' Adam told them pointing to the right. 'I have the key. The kids used to be kept in there sometimes. He took the lightbulbs out, so it is always dark. Norman thinks people taste nicer if they are scared. Especially kids.'

'You can't help but love that guy,' Tony said sarcastically.

'You can go around and open the door and get them out. The door is locked from the outside, that's the only way. They put a bit of glue on the inside of the lock from this side so it couldn't be picked open.' Adam took a key out of his pocket and put it in Bob's hands. For the briefest of moments, Bob felt the cold skin touching him, and he instantly looked up. Adam smiled at him.

'All right mate. I will be your eyes and ears here. Come back here after,' Adam said.

'Friarmere's still my home. I'll be back,' Bob advised him.

'Where are you three going to be, while we are doing all this tonight?' Danny asked.

'Going back into the front classroom. That's where we have been since last night. It will be quite safe. We will work on extinguishing the fire before there is a problem. Then we will sneak out later. We will just make sure that you get them out first.' Maurice assured them.

'There is a corridor around the side of the hall that leads to that room. The room is currently locked from this side by a catch on the top so that vampire children cannot get in. We will make sure that there is chaos out here and the vampires in here can't get them out from the inner door. That will really mess the plan up. We don't want your guys running out of the door straight into the fire. Get them out as soon as you hear the alarm,' Adam said. 'For everyone's sake.'

21 - Run

Maurice took one of the Molotov cocktails off Wee Renee. He brought it closer to his eyes.

'Well I never,' he said. Tony gave him his lighter.

'You know what to do, don't you?' Tony asked. Maurice nodded to them.

'Good luck everyone,' he said to the others, and they exited the foyer and quietly told the rest of the group what was happening.

As they walked around the corner to the classroom they did not dare to speak, just in case a pile of vampires lay in the classrooms they passed. They were tense and nervous.

Our Doris found herself hyperventilating a little. This was a do or die scenario. Any mess-ups would prove fatal. She realised that she was so worried because they were really gambling with Gary and Carl's lives, not their own. They were safe in the daylight.

It was quite clear which was the right classroom once they knew what the vampires had done to it. Apart from that, there seemed to be blood on the outside of the door and small handprints all around the handle. Wee Renee concluded straight away that not only had the vampire children tried to get through the corridor but also through this exterior door. She was glad she hadn't had the misfortune to see one of them, let alone deal harshly with one.

Sue breathed deeply and looked around at the others. Any moment they would have to become activated, and their muscles ached as coiled springs they waited. The key was in Tony's hand, and it was an inch from the door. They dared not open it until the distraction was happening.

Even though it was light, they knew that once the discovery of Gary and Carl's escape had been made, that they would be in great danger, despite it still being daylight. There was always Michael Thompson, forever a daylight threat. They heard the three undercover vampires shouting and at first thought that they were giving them away but then they heard a poof and a smashing of glass, so knew that they were keeping up their end of the plan. Good lads.

As soon as the vampires had started the fire, they flew back into the front classroom and shut the door. The three of them got under a tablecloth that the teacher had brought for the class Christmas Party. Who knew if they would suffer from smoke inhalation? It was all a learning process. If the fire escalated, they planned to pull down a curtain each, open the classroom door from the inside, which was unlocked and run out into the daylight. If the blackout curtain protected them currently, it must still be able to do the job, while they ran down to the shelter of Maurice's house.

That was the plan anyway, but they hoped they wouldn't have to go that far. Ten seconds after the broken glass sound, the school fire alarm was set off. As if by magic, the vampire trio could feel and hear the rising of the vampires' voices started to echo in amongst the school, including many vampire children's voices screaming.

'Now!' Wee Renee said. She knocked on the door, 'It's Wee Renee, stand back, we're here for you. Don't speak, it will give you away.'

Tony put the key in the lock and started to turn the key, which easily went part way and then either stopped or stuck. He pressed down the handle to open it. The door didn't budge. He turned the key harder, feeling that it wasn't all the way in. He knew that the final click wasn't there.

'Bloody shitting hell,' Tony said as he jiggled the key and tried to force it past its current resting place. He still was trying to be careful, because if he broke the end off the key, it was game over. Nigel now tried to turn the key, then Joe joined him pressing the handle at the same time. Joe was muttering about if he had been given notice, he could have brought a solvent. It seemed to be taking forever, but the whole process had only taken about thirty seconds. Nigel looked at his hand. It was really red. But it triggered a memory.

'My granddad's door was a bit like this when I was a lad. You turn the key, Joe. I want to try something.' Joe did as he was asked, and Nigel pressed the handle very quickly up and down. It was so fast it was nearly vibrating. On the last push down, he pressed really hard. Suddenly, it forcefully popped open.

Already a few curls of smoke came out of the room, Gary and Carl sat blinking looking into the daylight at them. Carl coughed shallowly. The rescuers could see they were already weak and pale, but most importantly, so thankful to see real living people.

In the hall, there was an enormous amount of chaos. Christine ran around with her hands in the air, yelling for the fire to be put out, but not doing a thing about it. There seemed to be a general feeling of not knowing what to do. The parent whose arms were burnt a couple of nights ago curled up into a ball in a dark corner of the hall. Stephen was extremely anxious as he had recently been burnt on the face and was worried about having his full body dowsed in flames.

Their panicked state was heightened due to the creatures only having a few hours sleep, and realising that not only was their abode in flames, but it was also daylight.

'Shall we chance going outside, Master?' Diane asked.

'That would be even worse for you than staying in here. We will work it out,' The Master answered crossly. The fire was starting to catch other areas of the hall, and Stephen wondered where his brother was.

Michael was in a locked classroom away from the vampire children. He lay on a pile of beanbags, in a deep sleep after a late supper of Red Wine and Gruyere Cheese.

He slept heavily, dreaming of the lovely Kate and how she would pleasure him. From far away he could hear her banging on his door. Desperate for his touch. Telling him to open it so she could climb on top of him. *Oh, lovely Kate, why can't you wait…. I'm a poet, and I didn't know it.* He smirked half asleep. The banging continued, more insistent. He opened his eyes. Was he still dreaming? No, it wasn't Kate, it was Stephen thumping and kicking at his door, and this was happening in real life. His heart was beating fast, shocked straight out of sleep. He looked up at the glass panel on the door to see his brother banging on it. There was something wrong. He could tell by the look on Stephen's face.

'The hall is on fire!' Stephen shouted through the glass. 'No one knows what to do.' Michael rubbed his eyes, he could now smell smoke.

'Bloody hell, you're a useless lot aren't you?' Michael said scrambling up off the beanbags. When he stood up, he found he was shaking. Michael unlocked the door and joined Stephen in the corridor. The smoke here was a lot thicker. 'Where is it?'

'The hall,' Stephen replied. Michael ran towards the hall, and right there on the wall was a fire extinguisher.

'You've just run past this to get me, you knob,' Michael shouted. He removed the fire extinguisher off the wall. 'There is another one of these in the staffroom, I've seen it. Go and get it,' He told Stephen. Stuart was twenty feet away from them and said he would get it, as he was nearer and rushed off to find the second fire extinguisher. *At least someone with an ounce of brains was getting it,* Michael thought.

He skimmed the instructions as the vampires ran around frantically, actually doing more harm than good.

'Someone get the hostages out!' Norman shouted. No-one had thought of that. They were quite a perishable item. The fire was right by the closest exit to the hostage's classroom. Typical, Norman thought, someone has got to go all the way around the school to rescue them. Humans are so much trouble.

One of the vampire children was running willy-nilly, screaming uncontrollably through the hall. Her dress caught the flames, and her screams escalated as her running velocity increased. The other vampires were unwilling to help her and so just watched her run around whilst she burnt. The vampires shrugged their shoulders at each other. Not knowing what to do.

Michael wondered why they were so confused. Surely, they would have known what to do when they were alive. But they seemed to be in a dire panic. Maybe it was because they had been woken up in the daytime. Michael started to spray the fire extinguisher around. First at the little vampire girl and then at the fire.

Stuart joined in after Michael quickly told him how to do it and he started helping Michael. At least one of them was useful. The fire was now under control Stuart went over and extinguished the girl vampire again, as she had started to burn once more, even though she had long since departed. *That will be the green powder igniting,* he thought.

It was finally over. Michael now knelt, hanging over fire extinguisher with the stress of it all. Norman and his children looked down at the charred wooden floor. Keith got right down on the floor, flat on his stomach and smelled it.

'This is petrol,' he said. 'And look here. Some broken glass. Someone has thrown in a Molotov Cocktail to burn us. As if I wouldn't know, with all my experience.'

They looked at Norman for instruction and guidance. He was so angry his lips pressed together making a white line. Christine still ran around screaming, but they ignored her. Mrs White was in a dreadful state over her lost vampire child and was trying to pick the child up to rock her, even though the child was roasting hot. Although she had done nothing to save the vampire girl when she could, choosing to stand still and stare at her instead.

The vampires waited in the smoky hall for Norman to speak, the air unnaturally electric. They were smoke stained. Their white skin highlighting the blackness perfectly. Michael had great sprays of dark ash under his nose. He was the only one really in danger. But he had been the one to save all of them.

'Come on!' Pat said, 'We haven't got much time. Move your bloody arses!'

Gary rushed out, and Carl began to crawl out. He was extremely weak. Gary started walking gently into the daylight down the side of the school to make his escape. Holding on to the wall for support. The daylight and snow glare was way too much for his eyes to take and he had to keep them shut. The brightness had delivered an instant headache, and he hadn't used his legs properly for several days. All this was hard, but he would do it.

'Come on!' Nigel said to Carl. As he raised himself up, one foot out of the doorway, he looked back into the room, and for the first time, his Kate stood in the open door to the corridor. In the smoky darkness, she had finally found him. This was whom Norman had sent to rescue them from the fire. She had meandered around the school until finally, she had arrived there. Uninterested from the beginning, she had never checked on them before. They were somebody else's job. Carl froze. This was the time.

'I have to stay here. I will find you. This is what I came here for. I'm ready to do this. It's fate. Thanks for the rescue and everything, but this is what I need to do.' Carl started moving back away from them.

'You have tormented him all his life,' Wee Renee shouted at Kate. 'Now let him go.' Kate just laughed dismissively.

'Never, old woman! He belongs to me, not you. Go and die somewhere,' Kate sneered.

'Aye, up yours as well,' Wee Renee replied. Then addressed Carl again. 'Show some restraint, Carl. Leave her and come with us. You're free,' Wee Renee pleaded.

'No, this was my reason for coming to Friarmere. You all know that' Carl replied. His jaw was set, and they knew his mind was made up. He was three feet inside the classroom now.

Joe entered the dark classroom behind him. He put a knife in his hand and a stake in his pocket. Carl drifted hypnotically towards Kate. Nigel quickly followed Joe in and gave Carl a plant spray full of garlic juice.

'It's garlic in there. Good luck mate,' Nigel said putting his hand on Carl's shoulder, which seemed to jolt him out of his trance for a moment. That was what saved him. She was drawing him in, and Nigel had broken the spell.

'I will be with you soon, don't worry,' Carl said as the men exited. He walked back to the exterior door and shut it behind them. What went on now was his business only. His and Kate's.

22 - Slug

Carl looked at Kate with teary eyes. She had never appeared more beautiful in all her life. The new vampire Kate was paler with redder lips and faint rosy cheeks. Her chestnut hair shone, and her figure as always was astounding. She glided towards him in her evening dress, and he felt his will dissolving. Now he saw her, the reality was a lot harder than he had imagined. She had become a dream. A stunning, gorgeous creature that effectively was his. His wife. His soulmate. How could he ruin this? He felt like he was watching the scene from above. His above self could tell how this was going to go down. It didn't look good for him. *What am I doing here?* Carl thought. Why didn't I leave with them? Or ask them to help me? Carl knew he was weaker than he usually was. She was certainly stronger. How was thing massacre going to start?

'Carl, my darling. I was going to come and see you. The Master says we can be together forever. Would you like that? To be in my embraces until the world dies?'

'Yes,' Carl replied, 'I want that.' In the back of his mind, Carl knew if The Master had said that, why hadn't she come before tonight? She had been sent to rescue them from the fire, it was as simple as that. She was a liar.

'Let's start that life now, my darling.' Right in front of his eyes, she lay down on the floor, offering her lovely self to him. The door and curtains were now shut so this room was dark, and she was safe. She lay close to the outside door. Kate reached up her arms towards him, and he immediately lay beside her. He touched her body, it was so cold. This was the beginning of his new resolve. This wasn't Kate. 'Let's make love, darling. It's been so long since I have felt your warmth inside me.' Kate said, smiling. Her small sharp teeth visible, close and dangerous.

He started to lift up the dress that she was wearing. Carl looked down to see she was wearing gold evening sandals. No stockings. Her legs were white and stunning. Her coffee coloured gown was silky and easy to slide up her legs. Now her knees were exposed perfectly and moving apart.

He brushed his hand on her cold soft flesh. She smelled of smoke and petrol from the hall and another earthier scent. Erotic but also like she had gone off. It was a struggle to keep his eyes away from hers as he knew she would try to hypnotise him and also to keep his eyes from where her teeth were in relation to his neck. Her legs were distracting him too, and he knew that would be dangerous as she was going to strike at any moment. Then he happened to luckily glance down at her legs, and something caught his eye. The realisation hit him. Why was he waiting to do this? He had waited long enough.

This was a monster, and he was playing her game. What he had seen was a red slug of blood slithering down her inner thigh. No, this wasn't Kate anymore. As he watched the slug's progress further down her alabaster legs, towards her sandals, out of the corner of his eye, he saw the briefest of movements. Kate's mouth was open, all her sharp teeth exposed, ready to bite. Carl coughed.

'I will get undressed,' he said, standing up immediately. He put his hands on the waistband of his jeans as if to take them down. She closed her eyes, thinking of how delightful the next few minutes would be. He tried to photograph that one moment and hold it in his head forever.

Carl took the stake out of his back pocket and threw himself fully on top of her. He raised the stake high, ready to plunge it into her heart. Kate screamed, her fingers scratching out at him. She caught his face with her nails. Her eyes were angry, and they were the eyes of a monster, yellow now. Her true self. The vampire succubus.

'You bastard!' She shrieked.

'No. You bitch!' He replied matter-of-factly and brought the stake down into her chest perfectly.

Kate's inhuman screeches simply stopped. Carl took a deep breath. He had done it. As he started to move off her body, he saw his next threat. The bottom of her evening dress began to move. Something was flooding out of her. From between her legs, a hundred slugs of blood seemed to be hell-bent on finding another host.

Norman worked it out after about twenty seconds.

'This was not to burn us. They could have done so much more. This was a distraction. Go to the men. Now!' Norman shouted. Keith and Stuart ran over the hot smoking floor and out of the door nearest to the classroom. Keith flung the door open to the dark hostage's room and saw Kate lying near the door, no longer one of their own.

Carl was standing above his dead wife. Stamping on the slugs, which moved on the floor, while trying to spray the others with garlic spray, as they continued to spew from between his dead wife's legs.

'Back off, Carl,' shouted Keith, who moved into the darkness of the classroom. Carl needed to escape as both male vampires could reach him in here. He pressed the handle of the door, which flew open behind him. The curtain was still across it, but the icy air drifted in, warning the two attackers of his escape route. Keith lifted the teacher's desk above him and threw it with great speed towards Carl. He tried to step back, but the desk pinned his leg and its weight would not allow it to move freely. A pain shot up to his groin.

He could also see a few of the slugs starting to make their way greedily up his jeans leg, and he couldn't do a thing about it. The garlic spray had been knocked out of his hand and had come to rest over the other side of the room. Carl ripped open the curtain as he tried to pull away from the desk, which created a great triangle of light between him and the two vampires. Norman, Stephen, and Christine arrived behind them.

The Master screamed in pain of loss. His beloved Kate, the first he had made here. His most trusted Lieutenant. His beautiful succubus was gone. He could never find another like her in a hundred years. Christine turned to see her Master crying tears of blood. The Master pointed at Carl. Carl knew it was a promise The Master would keep.

With all the strength he had remaining, Carl moved the desk away and fell backwards through the door, into the daylight. The light shone into the room. Across the ghastly sight of Kate, with the dead slugs around her, all the way up to a couple of feet away from the corridor door. It would be a few hours before they could chase Carl. They didn't know that it wouldn't take them long to find him. The desk had splintered as it landed. One leg had taken all its weight as it fell, and a shard of wood was wedged deep in Carl's thigh. The sharp tip pivoted on his nerve, as he tried to walk.

Carl passed out just the other side of the door with the pain. He was just a sitting duck. Luckily the sunlight killed off any slugs that had made it outside with him or those that had wished to follow him. With no consciousness of their own, they wriggled over the doorway into the cold daylight, just to smoke and wither.

The group of rescuers got to the end of the drive, where the others had waited. They quickly explained their deal with the three rogue vampires, who had indeed helped them and that Carl had chosen to stay, as his wife had turned up. Gary chanced opening his eyes to the glare and squinted around at everyone.

'Why did you let him?' Laura asked. 'He could have done it another time. Look at the state of Gary. He probably didn't know what he was doing. Don't you think he would be damaged enough? He had to be strong to fight her. He wasn't.'

'Laura, he would have always had this on his mind. You know that is why is here. He is an adult, and we couldn't stop him. We gave him weapons, a stake, and a garlic spray. It's now over to him, isn't it?' Nigel said, trying to placate her. Sue suspected that Laura had started to have feelings for Carl and this was the root of it.

'He will be with her now. He will be bitten and turned. There will be two of them.' Laura replied sadly.

Laura only spoke what the group all feared, but didn't voice. They could see how that would work out. He was weak from not eating. Emotionally fragile from years of her infidelity. She had vampire skills, where she could compel him and the intoxicating mix of being a beautiful succubus too.

23 - Bad Ass

Gary was so thankful to be rescued. First Wee Renee told him about the battle in Melden which had happened after he had left and how Anne had admitted it was a trick, which led them to come over here and help. Next, they told him what had happened over the last couple of days. Now he could understand why he had seen a Priest watching him through the glass of the classroom door. Our Doris moaned about Tina, how she was argumentative and hid their weapons. Even Wee Renee admitted the atmosphere was better without her.

'She hated me because I worked in a pub,' Lauren told him. 'She wouldn't even give me the time of day.'

'It's a good job, I didn't meet her,' Rick said, putting his arm around the lovely Lauren.

'I think she thought we were all a bunch of Jezebels really. Especially Our Doris, for some reason,' Wee Renee said.

'I don't like to speak ill of the dead,' Pat said, 'but I wished I'd have clocked her one up the earhole when she was alive. I'll never be able to let that one go.'

Gary was excited to meet the vigilantes, Joe and his friends. It all gave him new hope, along with his rescue. Laura asked his opinion on the situation with Carl. Gary advised them that for the last two days, Carl spoke about nothing else. He wanted his revenge, and Gary had a feeling he would triumph.

'She will never expect that worm to turn,' he said. 'I'm sure he is sticking a stake in her right now. I am positive that is what Carl is doing.'

'He'll be sticking something in her, I'm sure,' Pat said, but no-one else got what she was trying to say apart from Our Doris, who nudged her, winked, then gave her a thumbs up for effort.

'What is the plan now?' Gary asked.

'Don't you need to rest for a while?' Our Doris asked. 'We can see you are knackered.'

'I'm all right. I feel stronger just being out with you lot, in the daylight and the fresh air. Let's just get on with the plan.'

'We were thinking of going back to the bandroom to get some more of our weapons and take a five minutes breather,' Danny told him.

'That is a brilliant idea,' Gary said enthusiastically, 'because I left my nail gun there, which was damn useful. I kept thinking about it all the time in there. I felt like a lost child. I just don't have any ammo. I will have to try and find some from somewhere.'

'I picked you some up at the hardware shop,' Danny said. 'Thought you would want some. It's on Our Doris's metal sledge.' Gary beamed at Danny, apart from being rescued, this had made his day.

Gary knew Joe as he had been into the hardware store about a hundred times. On the way to the bandroom, they discussed weapons and weapon customisation. This distracted Gary from how many times he stumbled and how breathless he was. He was determined not to hold the group up. They all showed him one by one what they had done with various knives and poles, but when Bob revealed his discovery, he was amazed. Joe assured him that when he got to the bandroom, he would make him a brass neck of his own.

'They're not very comfy if you have a small neck,' Our Doris advised.

'They're not when you have a big one either,' muttered Pat, fiddling with the brass neck under her scarf. It was stuck to her skin with sweat, it felt hot and restrictive. She resigned herself to the fact that it would be chafing. Everything chafed her.

They were quite a party now, noisy and full of hope. Forty humans exactly, a dog and a cat, travelling en masse through the streets of Friarmere.

In the middle of the village, close to the spot that Michael Thompson had stood, just eighteen days ago, a lady waited. It was a happy but total surprise to the group. It was Beryl, an acquaintance of Pat, who they had seen watching them the other day from her upstairs window.

'I'm so glad I've caught you while it is safe, Pat,' Beryl said.

'Hello love, how have you been keeping?' Pat asked.

'Very well, considering. Do you think it will ever end?' Beryl asked.

'Yes, of course. We are weighing the scales on our side every day. Don't be daft,' Wee Renee said.

'Do you want to come with us. You're very welcome. Fight with us. Take a few out yourself. We have weapons and food.' Pat said.

'No, no. I can manage in my flat, and I have food. I won't kid you. I am terrified of them. I would run a mile. It's safer for you and me if I just stay here. If you could check on me every so often though, I would be thankful. Just so I know I am not the only human left in the world.'

'I think we are leaving the village to find help.'

'Are we?' Gary asked.

'Yes,' Pat replied.

'Aye, I don't know if you can depend on us for a while, Beryl love.' Wee Renee informed her sadly.

'We might not all go,' Darren said grumpily but didn't elaborate.

'Have you seen anyone else human, about?' Bob asked.

'Over the last few days I have probably seen about twenty people, in ones and two's running about in the day, after supplies. I wish I could send a message, which them lot wouldn't see so we could have comfort together.'

'We will think of a way. We are the ones who have been firing the nests. It won't be long before *we* start coming across real people, just hang in there.'

'Do you know where any of them live?' Joe asked.

'No, unfortunately. They disappear off the main street, and I don't know where they go.'

'Fair enough. We'll make ourselves more visible in the day,' Craig said.

'Watch out, I think they have a living spy. He is fortyish with glasses.'

'Yeah, we know him. If we find him, he'll get burnt alongside them,' the vigilante named Darren said, grimly.

'I have seen a vampire kiddie running up the street on all fours as well,' Beryl said with tears in her eyes.

'Where do you live anyway?' Craig asked. 'There is only Pat who knows where to find you.'

'Above the posh dress shop, you know,' Beryl said, pointing to the shop. 'The door's round the back.'

'Oh, I know,' Joe said.

'We'll get off, Beryl,' Pat said. 'Lots to do before it gets dark. Keep doing what you are doing, and I'll see you soon, love.' They hugged and went their separate ways, Beryl stood watching them leave waving to the children, who kept waving back. She struck a lonely figure in the middle of the village. They hoped to see her again.

'Do you think there's some food left?' Pat asked the Friarmere Band group.

'I think there will be some food left, but we haven't been there for nearly three weeks. Haven't you learned your lesson with that tripe?' Wee Renee asked. Pat shrugged.

'Well, we certainly have, Pat. We won't be eating anything that could have gone off. At least we can have a drink with the longlife milk, tea, and coffee,' Sue said laughing. Some of them quickly called at the shop again and picked up some tinned meat and items that could not perish easily. They ate some food and filled their pockets as they walked.

It was now just after lunchtime, and they were aware that they would have to find somewhere to stay tonight. This had not even crossed their minds before this. The vampires would be angry after the rescue this morning and the dispatch of three of their own, last night. They would surely check the hardware store and the church tonight. Those two places were out. Even if they stayed in the cellar all night, the vampires could find them and do anything to the shop above them. Burn it, tip caustic acid down the cellar hatch, which was available in the store, or anything. They would be trapped and at the horde's mercy for hours and hours. Bad idea.

Joe thought in desperation that they would probably be better using the church and Wee Renee was confident that the crosses would stop them coming through on the past un-consecrated patch. But most of the others did not consider St Dominic's a possibility since Michael Thompson could smoke them out at any time. Joe seemed quite disheartened already as he was sure that tonight, he would lose his shop.

'There are worse things that could happen at sea,' Our Doris said. Joe replied with a raising of one eyebrow.

Before long they got to the bandroom, which was just as lovely and friendly as they had remembered. All agreed not to stop for long. Just enough for a drink, a quick sit down and bite to eat for the children. This place wasn't safe either. There were a few other weapons here, besides Gary's nail gun. What seemed so right a couple of weeks ago, they now knew to be ineffective, and they had so many superior weapons from Joe's shop. Quite a few instruments had been left here, which were safe, they were pleased to find. They were determined to play them again, one day.

The vampires had not broken in. The door and windows were secure. When the attackers had come to storm the bandroom, they could smell that people weren't in there. Strangely though, there was a set of footprints coming in and out of the bandroom several times. Gary made the very accurate guess that this had been Ernie.

'I think the dead walk where they always did when they were alive. Ernie spent his happiest times here, and I think he has been in the bandroom, remembering us all. Which I suppose isn't too bad. It's better than killing folks.' Gary looked at the boot prints on the carpet again. 'I am sure the person in and out of here is Ernie,' he said again, as much to himself as anyone else. After a little to eat and rest, Gary looked much healthier. Some of the ladies made hot drinks. Here, there were enough mugs for everyone. Tea was much appreciated, and Gary drank four mugs, which he needed.

'You look a different person Gary,' Wee Renee said, passing him another slice of Dundee cake.

'I won't kid you. That tea and cake has put some lead back in my pencil,' Gary informed them.

They had about two hours before it would be dark. After quickly discussing various scenarios, places, situation and the current time limits, they collectively decided what their next move should be. Their new plan was to go over to Moorston, to get right out of Friarmere for a while. Moorston was another village close by, just over into Yorkshire. They had nearly gone to Moorston on their first escape, and if it wasn't for the fact that Freddie's wife, Brenda was over in Melden staying with Our Doris, they might have chosen it. Moorston was to the left of Friarmere and Melden was to the right.

There was a way to get to this village that was quicker, but quite dangerous. They decided it was worth it as it would avoid them going past The Grange and the primary school. The conditions were still treacherous, and they had no idea whether it would snow on top of the huge mass they had over the Moors already. Another problem they had considered was that there would be no den on the way to Moorston. Once they turned left at The Grange, instead of right, it was even bleaker on the way over to Moorston. They didn't know how they would manage. So, they would use this other way. With all its problems too, and it had many, it was a better prospect than over the Moors.

Joe had the idea of an interim place to stay on the way, and this was what they were going to be aiming for this afternoon. They should just about make it by darkness.

Outside the bandroom, they all got their weapons ready. They all had a brass neck. Some had put strips under their coats. Nigel and Rick had had the idea of putting it on their wrists, where a vampire could get to a vein very quickly. This was more uncomfortable than it was worth, so was discarded. All of them including the children were covered from head to foot in either protection, weapons or torches. As they came out of the bandroom and Sue locked the door behind them, Wee Renee stood in front of them all and said she wished she had a camera.

'Why we look a right old mess,' Liz said.

'Yes. But we are totally badass!' Wee Renee replied proudly.

24 - Refuge

Our band of friends, trekked across Friarmere towards the next village, another way. They had decided to go along the old bridle path. There was an entrance onto this directly at the side of the bandroom. That was why it was so perfect. It had not been walked on since the snows had come and were knee-high to the adults and thigh-high to the children. The track was ten feet wide at its narrowest with high tree's either side. What it gave them in one way it took away in another. They were not on the main road, so in some ways felt more vulnerable.

There were no buildings to run and escape into, and there were a lot of trees and foliage that vampires could creep up behind as soon as it was dark. The advantage was that they did not have to climb the steep incline out of the village and it was a quicker route as the crow flies to their refuge tonight and on to their escape route tomorrow. The deepness of the snow cancelled that advantage out, however. It was quiet, and they could hopefully hear and fight any vampires that found them once it was dark. They left obvious fresh footprints in the perfect white path.

This snow was far too deep for the two animals, so Haggis had elected to be pulled on the sledge again, covered in a blanket. Basil, however, had taken a shine to Terry, or Terry's coat, to be more exact. He pestered him to be picked up and then padded the woollen duffel coat as if it was his mother. Finally, he decided that he would curl up in Terry's hood, which caused Terry to roll his eyes and shake his head. Everyone could tell that secretly Terry loved his new little friend, in addition to keeping his neck very warm at the back.

Bob said he knew of another Den just behind a row of trees not far along. But it would provide little shelter and wouldn't be big enough for their large numbers, being smaller than the one they had stayed in previously. There was also the matter of leaving their camping equipment set up there, as they thought that they wouldn't need it again.

Luckily when it was getting close to darkness, they started to see their destination far in the distance. They hoped that there were no vampires or vampire sympathisers stationed somewhere dark to stop any villager from escaping. Gary estimated that at their current pace, which was extremely slow, they would have nearly an hour of walking in the dark, to tonight's stopover.

So very glad to remain undetected and seemingly swerving suspicion, the second it became dark, Adam, Maurice, and Mark ran out of the Reception Class to check what had gone on this morning. They had heard The Master scream and knew he had lost his hostages. But the cry was so torturous, and they couldn't understand why – it ran through every nerve ending of each vampire in the school. Either something else had happened, or The Master was making an awful fuss over two lost men.

They quickly made their way to the side door and were shocked to see that Carl was lying in the snow and had become unconscious through loss of blood, cold and the pain. He had been lying there for several hours and now was close to hypothermia. His body functions were slowing, and they needed to do something and fast. He seemed to be covered everywhere, by greyish green dried squiggles. They were all over the ground too. Adam thought it was crispy seaweed from the takeaway. That was odd.

Adam chanced a quick look inside the door and could see that Kate lay dead just inside it. She was also covered in these curls of crispy seaweed. Her body was mostly dust by now, but still so beautiful even in its grey powdery form. One poke of a finger and she would disintegrate into a heap of dust. It just about held together against the elements. Her evening gown blew every so often brushing a little of her decomposing flesh away gently.

Carl had done what he had come to Friarmere to do. Maurice and Mark managed to get Carl up and put one arm under each shoulder. He started to come around a little, as his body was raised. When Carl realised it was dark and he was outside with three vampires, he was sure this wasn't going to go well for him.

He could do little about it, in his current condition and closed his eyes in resignation. Luckily for him, one of the vampires had visited him earlier and declared that they were three fighting for the good. Gary hadn't believed them. Carl hadn't ever seen the two other vampires before.

'We are going to rescue you. Don't worry we are on your side, as I have said,' Adam informed him. The trio of rescuers could hear stirrings inside the school, but none had exited yet.

'We need to be bloody quick about this,' Mark said.

As fast as they could, Mark and Maurice started to drag Carl across the field and towards the centre of Friarmere.

'What are we going to do with him?' Adam asked.

'He can go back to my house,' Maurice said. 'We didn't plan for this, and there's nowhere else.'

'Look at the state of his leg,' Mark commented.

'Yes, I don't know what we are going to do with that.' Maurice said.

'At least we can take the wood out and stop the bleeding. That woman will know what to do. That old Scottish woman,' Adam said.

'Wee Renee? Yes, she'll know what to do,' Maurice said confidently. They walked very quickly for a couple of minutes, Carl's feet dragging on the ground. 'I've just had a thought,' Maurice said. 'He will need food. He's weak. If he's not fully fit, he won't recuperate.'

'I'll get him something. I can roam free at night with no questions. I have to get food for my er…. well where I get my blood from anyway,' Mark said. The two other men didn't question him. They were just glad to have this bloodsucking vampire in their corner. They both knew it wouldn't do to push it any further.

'Thanks,' Maurice said.

'As soon as he is settled, I will have to get off. I need to get on with that delivery or else they will work it out. We don't want them finding out that we have had something to do with this. The merest sniff of that and they will be at your house, Maurice. I will go to the shop like always and pick up some food, which is usual for me. But I will bring it over to your house after my delivery instead,' Mark said.

'That's a good idea, Mark,' Adam said. 'We all have to be seen acting normally. Me and you will take it in turns looking after him so that they can still see us about,' He informed Maurice.

They hadn't gone much further when they heard the sound of the vampire Brass Band starting up. The first thing they could hear was the bass drum and wondered who was playing it.

'That sounds better than yesterday. They're keeping better time, and whoever it is, they're quicker than Peter was,' Mark said, very interested.

'That's not the important part about it though, is it?' Adam asked. 'What's important is that they are on their way. We have to hurry!' The two vampires had slowed, they were not making much progress with Carl in the snow. He had passed out and was a dead weight.

They were nowhere near Maurice's house, and this street, where Sue and Wee Renee lived was very long and well lit. It stretched nearly from the top of the hill at The Grange, to the bottom and the main street. The vampire band would come out at the top of it soon, and they would be able to see the length of the lane. The three rogue vampires and the human would be quite visible in the streetlights against the white of the snow.

At that moment, who should come out of the door to the left and just ahead of them, but Ernie Cooper?

'Oh shit,' Maurice said, 'we are done for now.'

'Come here,' Ernie said. He started beckoning them to come into his house. 'Bring the lad in here.'

'No way. We're not letting you feed on him,' said Mark. 'We haven't taken him away from them, just so you can get your greasy mitts on him!'

'It's not for that. You've got no choice anyway. You either take your chances with the one of me, or the whole lot will be clapping eyes on you at any second. I can hear they're getting closer, on their way down here. That stupid excuse for a band makes my ears hurt. Come on, before it's too late, bring the lad in here, just until they've gone past,' Ernie reasoned.

They really had no choice but to do it. They started to walk up Ernie's drive then Maurice remembered something suddenly and stopped.

'What about Lynn?'

'She's already out. She walked up the little school footpath to them, you're lucky you missed her. Lynn wouldn't be giving you a choice, I can assure you. She's walking with the band tonight, after hearing it last night. Lynn thinks they sound very acceptable. I think that drinking human blood must mess with your ears because I can still hear every mistake,' Ernie said, shaking his head.

'So can I,' Maurice said. 'Come on, we'll take him in.' Maybe Ernie was on the level. They got Carl up Ernie's drive and into the house. Ernie got an old towel and quickly spread it on his spotless sofa. They placed Carl gently down, all the time the music got closer and closer.

Within two minutes the band were right outside the house, which was very nerve-wracking. Adam thought they would smell the blood because he could, and Ernie was worried that Lynn would nip back in the house for something and it would all be for nothing. At this point, Carl woke and started to groan and make a noise in his pain and confusion. Adam put his hand over Carl's mouth, and Ernie stood above him, a fresh vampire face again, with his finger to his lips saying *Sshhhhhh!* Carl suddenly heard the tuneless Brass Band very close, and it all came rushing back to him. His groans stopped, and he blinked and squeezed his eyes together in fright.

Within another minute the band's noise was beginning to diminish, and the four vampires and their human realised that they had passed. Carl breathed a sigh of relief.

Maurice went outside, peeking over Ernie's hedge to see who was playing the bass drum. When he returned, he told them that The Master, Stuart, and Keith were not with the band.

'Probably out after me and Gary, aren't they?' Carl said flatly. The four vampires said nothing then just to change the subject, Mark decided to speak.

'So who was playing the Bass Drum then?'

'Michael Thompson!'

All agreed that to be fair to Michael, even though they all disliked him, he was doing a better job than Peter had who was an actual percussionist.

'He's killed Kate, you know,' Maurice told Ernie.

Ernie made a shocked noise.

'The Master will want his pound of flesh for that one. She was one of his favourite creations, by all accounts,' Ernie replied.

'Yes, he's in trouble, all right. By the way, how did the crispy seaweed work?' Adam asked, looking at Carl.

Carl thought he had gone back into shock or Adam was talking to someone else but looking at him.

'How does that work? That's something I've never heard of.' Adam was clearly asking him, it was definite. Maybe he was drugged.

'Eh?'

'There was crispy seaweed everywhere. Over you, the floor, Kate……. here's some,' he said, picking a piece of it from Carl's jeans where it was half glued on. He put it into Carl's hands. Carl looked at it. He didn't know what it was. Then he looked at where it had come from. The place on his jeans had a faint black trail up from the hem.

'Oh god,' he dropped it on Ernie's carpet. 'It's not crispy seaweed. It was a blood slug. It came out of Kate's, you know.' He pointed downwards.

'Foo-foo?' Adam asked.

'Flange?' Mark asked.

'Mary?' Maurice asked.

'Lady front bottom?' Ernie asked, all at the same time.

'Yes! First, when she was alive, a couple were wriggling down her legs. Then when she was dead, there were loads, all coming after me. They must have died in the daylight!'

Ernie said nothing but wandered off into the kitchen. He returned in a few moments, holding a sheet of kitchen paper. Ernie picked up the *crispy seaweed*, wrapping the paper around it afterwards.

'Take that with you when you go. Dispose of it elsewhere, please. If Lynn knows about these, she could think I've had a sexy visitor. I don't mind being in trouble for stuff, I've done, but I'm buggered if I am going to get it in the neck for fooling around with a succubus. I'm not having it, I tell you.' Ernie said, looking at the four of them sternly.

When the vampire brass band had gone, and they could hear the music clearly in the distance, the original trio of rescuers thanked Ernie and said they would not forget his help. Adam said he would pass it on to the group of humans when they saw them again and say he should be spared if they could manage it. The kitchen paper square was placed in Carl's jeans pocket, and off they went.

As fast as they could, wishing to be invisible, Maurice, Adam, and Mark began their arduous journey to Maurice's house, aware that Norman, Stuart, and Keith were not out with the band, so could be anywhere tonight. There was one thing for sure, they would be after the return of their hostages and Norman would want to exact revenge on Carl for Kate's dispatch.

The band seemed further in the distance all the time, and they were amazed that they were playing tonight. What was Norman trying to say? That it was business as usual?

When they finally got Carl to Maurice's house and placed him on the sofa. Mark quickly went off to sort out his blood delivery as they would be looking for him, expecting him to be out with his crate, and Maurice and Adam were left with Carl.

'What about you? Won't they miss you loads?' Maurice asked Adam.

'They let me do what I want,' Adam said. 'I'll just have a wander about in front of them later. The Master was only ever interested in me to get Bob back here and look after the kids. Now, Bob's back, I have no kids to look after, he'll not miss me.' Maurice hoped he was right. He took a long look at Carl before speaking.

'Are you ready then lad?'

'What for?'

'Taking the wood out of this leg!'

Mark shut Maurice's front door quietly. He didn't want to attract any other vampires to their hiding place. Snow fell from the gutter as the door shut. He must have closed it harder than he thought.

'Give me some,' a small voice came from above. Mark looked up – a child's face looked down from the roof. Shit. They must have been followed. He looked up and down the street again. It looked like this might be the only one.

'Come down then,' Mark said quietly.

The vampire child slithered down the front of Maurice's terrace house. He wore underpants only. Once pale lemon, they were now heavily stained. The boy stood beside Mark in the snow. Even Mark, another bloodsucker could smell him.

'How many of you are there? There not much to share.' Mark said.

'Just me. Followed you on the roof. Want some. Hungry.'

'Tough,' Mark said, as he turned the boy's neck quickly around. Inside, the boy's head was detached from his body. Outside the skin held together. The blood all secure within. Mark could use that. He folded the boy over in half and put him under his arm. He crossed the road entering the alley – he would use the little footpath tonight.

The group of forty humans and two animals walked the final half a mile to their stopover point. They discussed what they thought happened with Carl.

'I don't know,' said Our Doris, 'but I just feel that she is no longer a threat.'

'I don't know what went on. But something's happened, I feel it too,' agreed Wee Renee. 'I think they probably had a consensual fatal union, with one of them passing.

'Maybe, they died in each other's arms,' Beverly said. It was a romantic notion. That is how someone would write it, but she doubted it had been like that. Laura made a humphhing sound, then spoke.

'The reality is that at least one of them probably ended up in a lot of pain, with blood squirting everywhere,' Laura said.

'You're probably right,' Wee Renee said. 'But it's nice to dream, isn't it? I do hope we see him again. He was a lovely lad.'

'Best foil folder in the west,' Pat said, smiling. 'But who knows what he ended up doing. We can't imagine. With him not being indigenous to Friarmere, he could be up to anything!'

Carl was lying on Maurice's sofa, with newspaper underneath him. Maurice had given him a clean cloth handkerchief to bite down on.

'Are you sure you won't get tempted when the blood comes out of that hole?' Maurice asked Adam.

'Nah, I'll be fine. What about you?'

'Doesn't bother me, at all,' Maurice replied. Carl watched their exchange, his eyes switching from one to the other. He was in no position to do anything about it if they were lying. For all he knew, they would go into a feeding frenzy, and he would wake up as a vampire with no leg. He was comforted by the fact that Maurice had laid out a clean medical dressing, bandage and a measure of whisky on the coffee table at the side of him. He looked into Maurice's eyes. Maurice held his gaze.

'One, two....' Maurice didn't get to three, he pulled the shard of wood out surprisingly after two when Carl wasn't expecting it. There was a moment of extreme pain and then relief. With the speed of two vampires, Carl's leg was dressed and bandaged within one minute. Adam helped him to sit up, and Maurice passed him the whisky smiling. Carl breathed a sigh of relief and Maurice winked back at him, while wrapping the wood in some newspaper.

25 - Match Girl

As darkness finally fell on the bridle path, so did the feeling that all was not well. This was not an uncommon feeling for all of them, and it didn't necessarily mean anything. After all, they had walked in the darkness on the peaks and felt as if they were going to be attacked, but they hadn't been.

They were all involved in various little conversations. Bob was talking to Rick about torching the vampires, with Craig adding macabre details. Terry was filling Joe in with a blow-by-blow account of the battle in Our Doris's house. Joe wished he had been there. Darren who loved kebabs had only just found out that Nigel had a kebab shop in Melden was asking him exactly what was in Donner meat.

Our Doris was talking about lady's fragrance's, with Wee Renee. Gary was filling Pat in about his time in the dark classroom with Carl, Laura listened close by in silence. The rest of them were occupying groups of kids, with the fallback game of I-Spy. Andy had them stumped for a while with C, for Constellation.

'Andy, as if kids are going to guess that. You are making them far too hard,' Liz said.

Lauren made them too easy, so she didn't want a go, as it only lasted ten seconds anyway. The kids found it difficult to think of anything most of the time. Apart from snow, trees, and sky, there wasn't much to see.

'I spy with my little eye, something beginning with G,' the youngest boy there, said.

After guessing a few G words, which were wrong, they gave in, and the boy said, *girl*.

'Hmmm...we should have guessed that, there are lots of them aren't there,' Sally said smiling. 'Do you want another go – you're very clever?'

'Yes. I spy with my little eye, something beginning with T.'

'Oohh, let's think,' Lauren said as some snow fell on her from the trees above. 'Trainers, er…. tree…. tree trunk.' The boy shook his head, he seemed to be getting a little less willing to play. 'I give in, tell me,' Lauren said.

'*Teeth.*'

'Haha, you are right. We all have those.'

'I want another go.'

'How about someone else has a go, you can think of some good ones, for when it is your turn again,' Beverly said.

'No. I spy with my little eye, something beginning with V,' the boy said slowly.

Now they got it.

'Where?' Lauren asked.

'In the tree's above you,' he whispered. Lauren froze rigid. She did not dare turn around to give herself away. Liz and Kathy had heard the last part of the game too and slowly raised their eyes upwards. Two white faces looked down. Both were young girl vampires, who had been following them in trees. Now it was no surprise that they hadn't seen any footprints.

Danny had just noticed that they had stopped behind him and he turned to see what was holding them up. It was usually a child's glove to find, or a nose to wipe. He followed the gaze of Liz and Kathy, into the dark trees. Small clumps of snow fell onto Lauren. Her eyes were wide and staring at the little boy before her. He could see her breath misting out in frantic puffs.

'They're in the trees! They're in the bastard trees!' Danny shouted.

The rest of the party immediately stopped and looked upward at the trees.

'Shit!' Gary said.

'Cool,' said Bob. Rick's impulse was to look for Lauren and saw that, they were in the trees directly above his new girlfriend. He ran towards her, throwing himself over her and the little boy that was with her.

Now that the two child monsters knew they had been rumbled, they hissed down at the heroes below. One of the girls jumped legs akimbo onto the path. She was shoeless, dirty and just wore a simple stained dress, which was torn at the hem and sleeves. Her hair was matted with knots and blood. The child's face was unrecognisable, as it was filthy, bloody and its eyes were glowing amber. She landed down on the snow, like a predator. Legs wide, knees bent and hands raised up, like claws, ready to strike.

'Look how ragged, she is,' Our Doris said.

'She reminds me of that story. The Little Match Girl,' Wee Renee said quietly.

'That always made me cry,' Kathy added.

'There's nowt jolly in that fairy tale,' Pat said sniffing.

'We'd better do it then,' Andy said. No-one made a move. They held their weapons up for protection. This was a new matter to tackle.

'I can't, it's a little kid,' Liz muttered.

'No, it's not,' Nigel said. 'It's a feral monster hiding in a kid's body.'

As if she had heard him, the little girl proved Nigel right, by vaulting over Rick's back towards another child, who stood with Sally. Unbelievably fast and animal-like, she had more in common with Anne's half-breed werewolf vampires than she did with her own kind. These were the two of the lost vampire children that Mrs White had been worrying over. They lived in this area now. The path. The trees. The den that Bob mentioned, now full of bones. This was all theirs.

The other child still watched from the tree. As her friend leapt towards Sally's charge, she clambered into another tree, closer to the action. Red spittle dripped down from her gaping mouth as she prepared herself for her meal. Nigel ran forward. His large kebab knife was already out, glinting and he raised it. He knew every single person was protected by a brass neck, but that child could do so much more damage, than just drinking from a neck artery.

The velocity of the leap, knocked Sally and the little girl beside her, over in the drifts. Sally tried to move backwards in the thick snow, her hands dragging the girl along with her. The vampire child found Sally's boot and started to scrabble up her body. It seemed she had decided that if she killed the big one first, the little one would be easy to eat after.

Nigel reached the three wriggling females and took the vampire child by the hair. She was far too interested in her meal tonight to have noticed him. Nigel was amazed at how incredibly light she was. He raised her head back and brought his knife swiftly down across her neck. He hadn't even had to put much force behind it. The neck was small and thin. And especially soft. The head came away nicely in his hand. The body with its gushing neck stump dropped down, right next to Sally who scrabbled away from it in the snow, holding the living little girl with her. The black issue continued to ooze out. It sank down beneath the snow. The top layers, still a pristine white, now looked grey, as the black pool beneath it spread.

An almighty scream came from Our Doris and Haggis began to bark, jumping off the sledge. The second girl vampire had jumped down from the trees and fallen on Our Doris's back. She struck several times at her neck but didn't make contact. Our Doris couldn't reach her weapons so flapped her arms about. She slipped in the snow, falling forward with the girl on top of her. One of her cowboy boots was now half on and half off her foot, which further hampered her. Haggis grabbed the ragged dress of vampire girl number two and began to pull, growling.

Basil jumped out of his hiding place, which had been Terry's hood on his duffel coat, and leapt onto the head of the attacker, yowling and scratching at the scalp and forehead. The vampire didn't like this at all, and for a moment, stopped trying to bite Our Doris and made attempts to grab hold of the small ginger cat that was successfully tearing wet chunks from her head. The vampire screamed a horrific, weird but weak scream. Our Doris pulled herself away, and Joe was upon this second beast. As it lay on the ground, still trying to grab hold of the cat, the dog still pulling her along every so often by the dress, Joe struck. The axe he held, which they had not seen him use yet, went straight down, through the child's back, pressing her into the snow. He had aimed for the heart and had caught it. His idea was if you didn't have a stake, just chop it to pieces. The vampire made a glugging sound and Joe raised his axe again.

'Wait!' Sue shouted and ran for Basil, whisking him out of the way. Bob picked up Haggis who immediately licked his face. Joe brought his axe down once more. Twice, three times. He stopped then as a second thought, had another couple of goes at her. He was breathing fast and looking down at the creature. Gary approached to see what current state the vampire girl was in. She was now in two parts. Cut straight across at the shoulder blades.

They now had four separate pieces of vampire girl. The children had witnessed every second, so there was no use trying to hide the parts. Wee Renee scanned the trees and bushes for any movement and could see none.

'I think that's it. I think it was just the two Little Match Girls,' she said.

'Let's bugger off before more come,' Pat grunted.

'Yes, their screams will have probably carried a long way. Let's get going. Leave them like that,' Gary said.

The group picked up anything they had dropped and without a word they hastily carried on, every eye trained on the treetops, every ear listening for a giveaway sound.

26 - Mill

When they got to their destination, which was an old abandoned mill, Joe took a crowbar and prised off the padlock that held the two front doors together. Every other entrance was boarded up, and most of the windows were still intact. Immediately on entering it became an awful lot warmer. There was a small foyer on the other side of the doors, and old offices behind this lobby formed a U shape to the door.

The back office was the entrance to the main mill. The lower floor was one huge room, with painted concrete floors and breeze-block walls in cream. For a place this size, and an abandoned building, it was dry, cosy and clean. The whole party were very pleased. The best aspect was that there was plenty of room inside for the children to run around and play safely.

To the left back corner, there was a lift, which thankfully had wooden planks nailed across it. Beside it, there was a staircase with an industrial metal bannister. Once a duck egg blue, the paint had flaked off, showing grey metal underneath, which was surprisingly rust free.

A few of the men surveyed the building upstairs and said that the upper levels had holes in the floor and there were patches of the roof missing on the very top level. Due to this, they were not suitable for the children to play in. The children would be limited to the ground floor. Beverly, Sally, Kathy, Lauren, Sue, and Liz decided to stay on this level to look after them. The floor above was safe too, so some of the adults said they would sleep there. They could see out of the windows and have a better vantage point. All four floors above that were out of bounds.

There was a strange, scary moment when Wee Renee said that it wasn't only vampires that they should be worried about. She said it was dark and they never knew what might be in here roaming around with them. Nigel, Joe, and Gary said, if there was anything, they would just have to deal with it as they were staying put. This place was warm and en route to their destination, with plenty of room for everyone. The snow had been pristine all the way here, no footprints whatsoever and there had been no broken windows on the first few lower levels. Plus, the doors were still padlocked. They trusted Wee Renee, however, so kept alert.

It was decided that there would be a constant watch on the first floor at all times. They were not taking any chances with the children's lives.

Gary had noticed on their way in, that there were piles of old wooden pallets, under a large shelter with a ramshackle roof. They looked dry, and he had the idea that they could make into stakes. Between them they had a few axes, serrated knives and Joe had a crowbar. They could prise the pallets open and make hundreds of stakes. What a great find. They could have a few each and then keep a whole pile of them here for emergencies. Tony kept watch and Terry, Andy, Danny, and Gary ran outside and brought several of the pallets inside the doors, which then they barricaded with five old office desks. The men set to work chopping them up and making them nice and sharp. Soon everyone had plenty of stakes; in fact, there were so many, they started to stockpile them. They were ready to use and would quickly replenish supplies if required. It was also something that kept them busy and their minds off the Little Match Girls.

Joe had chanced it and was on the third floor. He looked across at the village of Friarmere. There were fires there, and he wondered who was lighting them, because as far as he knew, only him and his three men, which were with him there, did it. What was going on? Was there a problem or had his gang of vigilantes started a trend that others were picking up on? He hoped it was the latter. Beryl had confirmed that there were pockets of survivors that he had not found yet. The sight of the fires stuck in his head. He was very intrigued to find out more. He took himself off, to one corner, watching Friarmere constantly and became very quiet.

The ladies started to prepare the evening meals. They had cleared the shop out of naans and tinned beef curry. This was the most requested dish tonight. When they started to eat their evening meal, he made his announcement.

'I won't be carrying on further with the journey. There are enough heroes in this group, to carry on with the mission. I can't leave Friarmere to its own devices,' Joe said firmly, setting his jaw, and they knew there would be no persuading him. Craig and Darren said they would prefer to stay in Friarmere too. Rick said he would decide in the morning, as he looked over towards Lauren.

The hot topic among the ladies was still Carl's current circumstances and how it was like some kind of gothic love affair. They wondered what had gone on, and would have loved to have been a fly on that wall. Wee Renee said that Carl needed to have his justice and that it had become more and more important to him over the past few days. This was not only for recent occurrences but from many years of infidelity.

'It was a very deep wound,' Wee Renee said knowingly. Our Doris thought Carl had this mission as a kind of crutch to get through everything that had happened to them all. Wee Renee agreed with this. She still felt that he was alive and hoped to get a report about it soon. Wee Renee looked over to Terry at this point and caught his eye. She gave a slow nod to him, and he gave a slow nod back. He hoped the messenger visited her, rather than him. *I won't be conversing with a single midge, even if Wee Renee does*, he thought.

After the meal, the adults passed around a few bottles of hard liquor. There was a much more relaxed atmosphere in this building. It had a safe feeling about it, and they wouldn't have minded staying here for a while, but where would that get them?

If ultimately it *was* down to them to get help, they could not wait until the snow had gone. By then there would be so many vampires here, Melden and who knew where else. They could take over the whole world.

Maybe it was a paranoid thought, but it was one that they had to think about. After all a month ago, who would've imagined that even this could happen. There must be about fifty vampires in Friarmere. All coming from a single source, Norman Morgan. He was patient zero. If each one of them made fifty, it wouldn't take long for the world to go down the toilet.

Sue said even though it might sound weird, there had been good points for her about this. They couldn't imagine what she was on about.

'Look at it like this. I've found out so much stuff about myself. I don't need television, jewellery, perfume or the latest coffee machine. All that has been stripped away. I have discovered underneath the plain bog-standard mother that I used to be, is someone who can fight, be brave and is trying to save the world. Me, Sue…. who would have believed it? Plus, the camaraderie that I have felt, the love and support of all you, that I have been part of will never ever leave me. Humans are wonderful, deep down. And I love us. It's not the time for a plague to wipe us from existence. Yes, some of us have made mistakes, some people *are* bad. The child murderer's, the rapist's, the terrorists. But at our essence, we are so worth saving.' Sue was surprised and touched as there was a small round of applause. She hadn't planned that speech, but it had been delivered perfectly.

'Well said,' Wee Renee said. 'I think we can all say what you just so eloquently put into words. Does anyone else have any more positive's that have come out of this?'

'I do,' Pat said. Instantly everyone realised that this would be a very different expression than Sue's. Pat was already smirking, so they wondered what was going to be coming out of her mouth. 'Wait for it. It's controversial.'

'Go on,' Nigel said, putting his hands behind his head and lounging backwards. This was going to be good.

'It's Christmas time, isn't it? What I like about all this shite going down is that it has meant there are no Christmas Parties.'

'Oh no, they're merry and jolly, especially office ones. It's a break from the mundane,' Sally said.

'No, I've been there, bought the tee-shirt. Gutsing dry white wine out of a wine box, from a plastic cup. Talking to people you don't like. Photographing your arse!'

'Don't you mean photocopying?' Kathy asked.

'No. Bald men groping their drunk secretaries. You know, they don't try it if you're not that kind of person. My boss never did,' Pat replied and sniffed.

'Aye, and you used to take your own mistletoe,' Wee Renee said quietly but affectionately. Pat was on a roll now and was moving on to her next piece.

'No. I don't like it. Then you've got your kiddie's ones. Weird Father Christmas's, with cotton wool beards, stinking of last night's whisky. Giving out cheap presents to over-excited kids, which end up in the bin the next day. And you'll wait in a queue for a bloody hour to see the bugger. Then there are the ones you see when you nip out to the shops in the evening for a bottle of brown sauce or some bleach. People visiting our village because they've booked a party in one of the pubs or restaurants. Wondering why they end up Oldham Hospital a day later with pneumonia or amnesia when I've seen them in a black sleeveless chiffon mini dress the night before. No coat, no tights, probably no knickers. Skating around on the ice with their high-heeled diamanté sandals, drunk as monkeys. I'm not missing it one bit!' Pat said.

The other's laughed. Pat painted a vivid picture, and they had seen most aspects of it.

'You've thought about this a lot, haven't you Pat?' Our Doris asked.

'All the time. Especially the photographing of the arses. You're looked down on, Our Doris, if you wear a longline pantie, you know,' she sniffed again, in punctuation.

Lauren found this hilarious but was being polite so said she would go and look out of one of the windows upstairs. Rick said he should probably go with her and they were missing for the next couple of hours.

Pat was silent now, after her rant, and was confident that she had convinced everyone that Christmas Parties were terrible. She opened a large box of wafer-thin mints and began to let them gently melt on her tongue.

'Can you imagine you know, *being* with Pat?' Danny asked Andy and Nigel. Andy mock shivered.

'I mean I love the bones of the woman. She's a fellow horn player, but the only thing worse than fighting her would be having to mate with her!' Andy said. Nigel laughed so hard at this that he had to use the toilet quite badly, which was a struggle, as they had to move the five office desks first. Danny kept watch for him outside.

Terry had been sitting nearby. Andy thought that he had overheard their conversation and carried on. 'Can *you* imagine mating with her, Terry?'

'I can't imagine mating with anyone Andy. I don't think about that kind of thing since I had my vasectomy,' Terry replied sadly. 'I just enjoy the simple things in life now. Repeats of Morecambe and Wise, Horlicks and my duffel coat.'

'Noted. No vasectomy!' Andy nodded.

Pat now announced that she had chilblains and they all expressed sympathy. She also said she was craving tripe again.

'No Pat, we won't be allowing you any more of that, as it doesn't agree with you,' Wee Renee said. No one else would have told Pat she wasn't allowed anything unless they were after a punch in the nose, that is.

'You are right Rene, it doesn't agree with me, but I could still murder some. I fancy a box of milk tray chocolates as well,' Pat said musing.

'Anything else for me lady?' Gary asked.

'No, that'll do.'

'I'd like to watch a really good film,' Gary offered up. 'That's all.'

'A bottle of Baileys,' Our Doris said.

'Gin and Tonic, with lots of ice and lemon,' Sue said.

They went around the group asking what they would like to do or eat right now. This probably wasn't a good idea as people started fancying pizza, burgers and chicken tikka masala. Which in turn made everyone else want them too.

Some of the kids wanted things like Magnum ice creams and popcorn. There wasn't anyone that craved broccoli or anything fresh.

The children were playing with Haggis and Basil. The two little animals all loved the attention, and it did the children the world of good. They needed distractions, and there were few in this world now. No one had asked Wee Renee what she wanted, and she was just about to tell them, but they never got to hear it. Because at that moment they heard wolves howl. It was chilling, but far away. There was no mistaking it. It was the first time that Joe and his three men had heard them. He was totally shocked, and the others were even more so, as they thought they had killed Anne's pack of five wolves. It was clear there was more than one too. There were many wolf howls all at once. This wasn't just a lone survivor.

'So, she had more, and they have ventured out of Melden,' Wee Renee said sadly.

'Yes, it certainly sounds like it. That sound hasn't come all the way from Melden. They are on the Moors,' Liz said.

'After us,' Our Doris said. Haggis had returned to her side. He remembered these beasts and didn't' want to see them again. Or their nasty owner, who smelled of blood. Our Doris stroked him firmly over and over again.

'Probably me and you are on the top of her hunting list, Our Doris. Marked as unfinished business,' Terry said.

'She'll want all of us from that night. For revenge,' Wee Renee said.

The sound was a sign that the horror was far from over. It sent a message to the people that had not heard them, that Norman was not the only threat. For all the success they had had recently with his few vampires, the reality was a far bigger task.

It was a sad ending to what had been a lovely evening. They hoped the wolves could not smell them. Wee Renee assured them that in the end, they were just big dogs, flesh, and blood. Easier to kill than anything supernatural with all their weird super strength and powers. The group had plenty of weapons that would be just as effective on a wolf as on a vampire. The home-made flamethrowers, the nail gun, the spears. They could not be more prepared. However, to hear the beasts and know that Norman also, was pursuing them, chilled them to the bone.

That night the children slept far better than the adults, who kept watch in shifts as usual. They were lucky. No one found their hiding place that night.

The two young men had run out of food a couple of days ago. They had got up late today and by the time they went out, they could hear a Brass Band in the distance. The two of them had retreated to the Park and had hidden between the wall and some bushes. They had decided that now if they saw other humans, they would ask to join them for safety. If this band were human, it sounded like they would have lots of friends. The two youths waited to see the band go pass. They weren't so silly as to give themselves away without confirmation. From a distance as the players had their instruments in position, they just looked like a regular band, if a bit rubbish musically. As they got closer, they could see what a ghastly group they were. One had bulldog clips on her nose, one had an open eye socket. One had tape all around his neck, probably it was keeping his head on, and one was half burned. A bunch of monsters scarily walking through their village unchallenged.

The two youths were starving, quite literally and could not raid any shops. One of them felt he couldn't last until morning. The pain in his stomach was excruciating, and he felt like he could eat a vampire if that was all that was on offer.

'We will have to rob some houses. Got to keep off the main street. That's all there is for it,' the first one, Josh said. He had lost a considerable amount of weight, and his cheekbones were sharp accents on his face.

'We will go down for it after the world is right again,' his friend Ben, who was less hungry looking, said.

'Naah – People have to survive, or *they* win,' Josh said. Ben thought about it, Josh was right.

'Come on then, we have to. But I don't like it.' They walked in the opposite direction to the band, trying to stay against walls or travelling up back alleys, which in itself was dangerous, as they were sure all the monsters weren't in that band. They had noticed that some houses were burnt out.

'Someone else must be raiding house too. That must be what you have to do,' Josh said. 'Burn it afterwards, so no-one finds your fingerprints.'

'That's a bit extreme!'

'These are extreme times. If we burn the place after, no-one will know if it's them or us as well, will they?'

'No, I suppose you're right. But knowing our luck, we will get the blame for all their crimes as well as ours!'

'You're over thinking it, Ben. Have you got a better idea?'

'No.'

'Right then. We're breaking into this house here. Taking all the food, then torching it. End of.'

27 - Marmalade

Anne sat in her house talking to her best and favourite acolyte Sarah. Her foolproof plan with Melden had not quite worked, and she had lost her best pack of wolves. Anne couldn't quite work out how it had gone so wrong for her. She loved Norman so much and couldn't blame him for this. Yes, she had become involved with these humans because of him. But sooner or later she would have encountered them on her mission to turn Melden lupine, so it had just brought it to a head, in her estimation.

There had been mistakes made all along, and she put this down to Len's influence. Sarah had not met Len and wondered how she would recognise him.

'What is he like, Mistress?' Sarah asked. Anne thought for a moment.

'He has the marmalade hair and is a vampire. There is nothing else of significance. That is how you will know him straight away?'

'He has marmalade in his hair?' she asked, wrinkling her nose.

'No, it is marmalade colour. That is the colour that we called it in Switzerland. Do you not know what I mean?'

'Marmalade?' said Sarah musing. 'Do you mean it is an orange colour?

'Yes!' Anne said.

'You mean ginger, then,' Sarah informed her. 'We called it ginger in England.'

'Yes, he has always been, what you would call ginger. It was quite bright when he was younger, but now it has faded. And you know he is very fiery too. It matches his hair.'

'Oh yes,' said Sarah. 'Ginger haired people can be very fiery.'

'He has quite a temper on him, so do not vex him. Apart from that, he will appear very happy to you. He is eccentric all the time and does not like girlfriends, he likes boyfriends.'

'So you are saying that he is a gay fella?' asked Sarah.

'Yes, that is what I think he is. I have never in my life seen him with a lady. He goes to the festival in Manchester. You know, the proud one?' Anne said, her brows furrowed. She knew she wasn't getting it right, but couldn't do any better.

'I think you mean pride,' said Sarah laughing.

'I'm getting everything wrong, aren't I? I think it is losing my children over the last few days. It has upset me so. It is a good job I still have my most devoted Sarah.'

'You have certainly made some losses over the past few days, Mistress,' Sarah said. Anne got angry again and thumped her fist on the table. Sarah wished she had kept her mouth shut.

'Yes, I know. That is because of how Len influences Norman. Len tries to control me, through Norman and I have had enough of him. I know Norman has had enough of him too and would love me to deal harshly with him. I have written extensively about it in my diaries. He won't ask me to deal with Len straight out, that isn't Norman's way, but I know. He won't even talk to me about Len's Lieutenants. Especially one in particular – he hates them so much.' Anne paused for a moment, as if in deep thought.

'So as an older sibling, I will look after my little brother. That's what family's do. If it vexes Norman, it vexes me. I do this all for him, Sarah, all of it. For *him* to sit on the throne. For *him* to be the senior male vampire. For *him* to be happy. It is the end for me. Look at what has happened because of Len. My poor Sophia.'

'Where is he?' Sarah asked.

'Over in Moorston.'

'It's just a small stone's throw, isn't it?' Sarah said.

'Yes.'

'Maybe we could go over and have a chat with him, try and sort things out between you? In the end family is family. Blood is thicker than water.'

'I haven't got on with him for over five hundred years, Sarah. Do you think that you, acting as a counsellor can change that? I do not like walking in on him at it, all the time. I don't walk in on Norman at it with women! But Len cannot help himself. He is at it every night. I am not on about fighting people either. Do you know what I'm saying? Do you know what he is up to?'

'Yes I do,' Sarah said. 'I don't think you have to go into any more detail.'

'He has been coming to this area for years. Especially to the north of England. It has been his favourite place since the swinging sixties, and he has been trying to get Norman and I to move here, for over twenty years. Now with all the problems in Lutry, he has got everything he ever wanted. He has been coming to these villages for such a long time and made three vampires here in the 1980's. These are three lady vampires, and they are his direct Lieutenants. Three powerful vampires now. All *bitches*, Sarah. It has to be said, and I don't say that lightly. He has brought them everywhere with him, since then. Wherever he has gone, they have never been far away, watching his back.'

'Well we are close too,' Sarah said defensively, 'you and me.'

'We don't act like they do. They are all like him, all loving a good time. They go out partying with him into Manchester, and into Leeds. Going out all night dancing, drinking. He doesn't want to think about conquering the world. Doing what he should be doing, as my eldest brother.'

'He does sound very different to you,' Sarah said.

'He has such fun with them, that he is not interested in his family. Norman likes to be alone a lot of the time, which is a natural vampire way, I do not blame him. But it leaves me alone. Why don't they see, I am the only girl too, so feel isolated? I don't like being on my own. I'm not a standard vampire, you know that, but they don't agree with me mixing the wolf blood in with our lovely intoxicating mix. I know I am right, so I can't give in to their demands, just to have company. Can you believe it?'

'Why don't' they see it?' Sarah asked. 'I'm delighted being just like you.'

'I know you are dear Sarah. You are wonderful. I couldn't wish for a better child. However, we have something on our plates now. I have my wolves and my children to avenge, but the group I need to take to task are out of reach, and in Normans lands. I will not tread on his toes, by storming Friarmere, trying to find everyone from Melden. That is for another time. They will keep. I have been sending the other pack out to keep the scent fresh in their noses. They know how close they can get to Friarmere. The minute those murderers step away from Norman's protection, they will be my prey too. Norman knows I have a beef with them. It is clear how much I have lost with Sophia and her lovely pack. They are in Friarmere still, all of them. They were last night anyway. So I have decided to attend to the other thorn in my side, Len.' Sarah nodded. Life was always interesting now she was one of Anne's children.

'I think we should pay a visit to Len. He is not going to receive it well. So we need to prepare. What I would like to do, is to make a lot more of our kind tonight, and if you are agreeable, we can do this together. We can also use David, he is very capable. I am impressed by how well he has adapted as a fresh vampire. Of course, as a human, he was already of that kind – wolfish. And isn't it so ironic that one of my wolves has taken to his side? He is one to watch, Sarah. By that, I mean, he will go far. We don't have many of our sort left. Of us all, we three are easily the finest. But we need to go over to Moorston in force or else no one will listen to us. *Those three females* of his will see us off before we ever get near to my brother.'

'How many do we need to make?'

'As many as we can. If we could make one hundred tonight, I would say let's do that. We will if we can, let's challenge ourselves. Len won't see us straight away Sarah, even en masse. You don't know how he is with me. He will have his friends around him, who he values more than me. They are powerful, experienced vampires for us to overcome. Just wait and see. I have had enough of Len. From tonight, things change.'

Anne picked up the bottle next to her and emptied its contents into her glass. She drank it back like it was water, stood up and slightly wobbled. Sarah joined her, holding her elbow. Anne wiped her mouth on the back of her hand and looked directly into Sarah's eyes.

'Let's go make some more vampires,' she said.

28 - Enriched

Norman, Stuart and Keith had found no trace of the hostages or the human raiders in Friarmere. All their recent haunts were empty. The church, the hardware store, their houses, even the bandroom. The cold winter wind whistled through these places, empty. They must know somewhere else. Somewhere yet to be discovered. They were still here, however. The Master had put a sentry by each bus at the ends of the village and one at the top, near The Grange. The sentry up there was no use in the band anymore. Pat had crushed their fingers, and now they were a mushy dangling mess, with fingertips intact. There would be no repair yet, however. He would instruct Michael when to hold clinic again. Tonight it was more important that they found their prey. It was proving fruitless though, as there were no fresh footprints here and no reek of humans.

He knew they were still in Friarmere and he would find them, even if he had to rip open every door in the village and look behind it.

Norman took pleasure in telling Michael that Kate had been killed. He had advised the others that no-one was to inform the human of his loss. The Master led Michael into the classroom and showed him her remains. This was about three am.

'My lovely Kate. We were star-crossed lovers. Who did this?' Michael asked.

'Her husband. Maybe she was killed because of her dalliances with you. We shall never know,' Norman said with a twinkle in his eye. He was fully aware that Carl had no idea about Kate being Michael's sweetheart.

Michael was so angry. Her husband must have thought nothing of her to do this. This Carl had slain her out of jealousy, because of their love. Michael intended to confront him and deal with him in the matter most fitting to the crime.

The group of rescuers woke that morning feeling very refreshed. In between keeping watch they had had a decent night's sleep. But the sound of the wolves had all terrified the group from Friarmere and Melden. In the end, it was only twice that they had heard them, quite close together, so they did manage to relax.

'Even though this is a new danger to throw into the mix, they are just big dogs, and I won't be losing any sleep another night about it. Flesh and blood can die easily enough,' Joe said resolutely.

'Joe, when you see them, like I did in my shop, close up……. it's hard to dismiss or laugh off. When you see them open their mouths, you know they ain't no dog,' Nigel said grimly.

'They're wily and clever. Bigger than most dogs and when you look at them, you realise they are an actual wild animal, and there is no reasoning with them. They are a force of nature. Don't relax around them,' Beverly said.

Terry asked Our Doris how she felt that morning regarding her past illness and she was thrilled to tell him.

'As time ticks away from when I was infected, and taking the antibiotics, I am sure that I feel actually stronger than I did before. In fact, now I have got over the shock of having it in me, which I can't ever scrub away, I feel that my blood has become enriched by Anne's if there was such a thing. I feel so vitalised. Like I have had an energy transplant!' Our Doris explained. Terry nodded all the time while she spoke. He also felt stronger but hadn't told anyone. She didn't imagine it. Our Doris shouted Liz over, to ask her thoughts.

'Hmm….,' Liz thought hard about it. 'I maybe feel the same as I did before, but not better.

What about you?'

'I was just telling Terry. I feel Anne's blood has enriched mine. I feel at least thirty years younger.'

'What about you, Terry?'

'The same as Our Doris, enriched. Not as much, I think. But very good.' This was news to Our Doris, and she was happy that it wasn't just her flights of fancy. Liz looked at them both and shrugged.

'I'm probably back to where I was I think, which I am happy with.' Liz smiled and went back to packing her bags.

'Maybe it's because she is a vegetarian, or because the virus was different. Or perhaps as she is still so young, she has tons of energy anyway and can't tell.' Our Doris said.

'Or that she was infected way before us and went too long without the antibiotics. I have been wondering, could vampire blood be used for good in medicine?' Terry said.

'It could be that, yes. Liz had been infected weeks before you got to treat her. Whatever, she isn't worse. You got her back Terry. You should be proud of all this. You saved us three, and we know it isn't the end if someone ends up getting infected again. It's a big thing.' Our Doris told him. 'That and the brass necks have been the game changers, Terry.'

Wee Renee was helping Pat pack her bag while she ate some breakfast on the go. In the bottom of her backpack, she saw Pat was hiding something.

'The wee madam!' Wee Renee whispered. 'Pat love, could you come over here, please.' she called. Pat clumped over. Wee Renee opened her backpack so that Pat could see she had found her stash. 'Do you really think you are going to eat all those meat puddings? Pat, think of all our noses, please,' Wee Renee pleaded jokingly.

Joe discussed the merits of using the mill as a base with everyone. They all thought it would be safe and easily defendable. The children could make as much noise as they wanted there too, as it was far enough away from the village. It looked like it had not been discovered by the vampires before or since their arrival.

'The only problem, is now that so many of us have walked down the path, we won't be able to see if we are being followed,' Wee Renee said.

Strangely enough, Michael Thompson had followed the tracks the previous night after he had been out with the band. He couldn't sleep at five o'clock in the morning and just wondered where they had gone, just out of interest.

Michael had followed the tracks from the school, down to the bandroom, then back through the village, via the bridle path. It was harder to track them through the village on the way to the bandroom, but he had quite a few clues that it was them. Clues they didn't realise they were leaving. Pat's large platform snow boots, were distinctive. Our Doris's small pointed cowboy boots were too. One of them wore biker boots with spurs. The fresh tracks in the snow outside the bandroom and the many small children's footprints were a giveaway. They had taken a new direction after this.

Joe hadn't changed his mind about staying to investigate the fires. Two of the vigilante's Craig and Darren said they were joining him. Joe said he was going to liaise with Beryl, from above the dress shop. Try and find other survivors and persuade them to come back to the mill with them. Rick was joining the bigger party as an evident romance had started between himself and Lauren. Joe said he would take the children if they wanted to stay with him, instead of walking all the way to the unknown in Moorston, just to find help. There was also the fact that this place was reasonably warm, big enough to house them, safe and for the moment, undiscovered.

The three men could fetch items over every day. Make it even more into a temporary home. Kathy and Sally put the choice to the group of children collectively. Between them, they wanted to stay with Joe and were happy to stay in the mill. Last night they knew they were safe, something they had not felt for weeks. They didn't want to let that go so quickly. The two sisters said that as long as they promised to behave, that is precisely what they could do. The children had proved over the last few days that they could take instruction, look after themselves and be little trouble.

The children wanted Basil and Haggis to stay with them, but Our Doris and Sue explained that they were their owners and as soon as they had a chance, the animals would run away and try to find them. Which would put them in danger. The two ladies knew that having the cat and dog had been a tonic to the children. But both the animals were only behaving because they had their owners nearby.

It took a long time to split the provisions on the sledges. Mainly because Joe told them to take all food and weapons because he could replace the items anytime and the others felt guilty about this. They said it was like they were taking food out of the children's mouths. Joe insisted and said that they didn't know what they were walking into and how long they would have to last on the contents of the sledges. They couldn't argue with that.

The two mismatched parties said their goodbye's, hugged each other and wished each other well. Joe walked a short way towards Moorston with them. He said, that if they couldn't find them. If they had to move from the mill, for instance, they would leave a note in the till of the hardware store for the explorers to find. Even if the store was trashed, he was sure that the vampires wouldn't be in there robbing money. He would check the till once a day, and they could check too. It would give them each other's whereabouts when they came back.

Joe said the advantage with the vampires now, was that one was ringing a bell and the rest were playing in a brass band, so you always knew where most them were. Besides that, he hadn't been caught yet, even when they were advertising their whereabouts by setting fires.

'Joe, I would like a wee word,' Wee Renee said. 'I know it may be difficult but it is important to me, and I have promised. It is more important to them though.'

'Go on,' Joe said, intrigued.

'I have promised these wee bairn's that Father Christmas will come. I don't think they expect a lot, but they deserve something for being such good kids, don't they? Just a small effort. A little gift each and some chocolate. Could you do that for them and me?'

'Of course, I will. It was at the back of my mind anyway. We wouldn't have let the day pass unmarked. Don't you worry about it, Wee Renee.'

'That's a big weight off my mind, Joe. I won't forget it,' Wee Renee said. As if she had a second thought, she grabbed him firmly and hugged him hard. This was a rare and beautiful thing. Joe knew it too.

He wandered back, and the remaining Friarmere group began their day. Craig was staying with the children, Darren going with Joe into the village. They had one of Bob's sledges to help transport supplies but would be back as quickly as they could.

The three men felt so sorry for the children. Probably none of them had parents left alive and what would happen to them when all this was over. Hopefully, they all had loving relatives. Maybe some parents had lost children, like The Little Match Girls. They could find each other; match up their missing parts somehow.

Michael was surprised to see the direction that they took and had the funny feeling that they would be going over into Moorston, now that they had rescued the two hostages and the children. They weren't using the roads. The main route was blocked, the vampires had seen to that, weeks ago.

They must have gone over the tops. Michael wouldn't tackle it alone, never mind with a group of kids. The local mountain rescue team had had to recover people from that route even in the summer. He thought in these conditions they would be facing certain death.

There were a couple of routes. One was up, where they had gone before, it was the main road upwards. To get to Moorston, they would have to turn left and go across the spine of the Pennines before dropping down. This passed The Grange and the primary school. They hadn't chosen this route. He could see the tracks continuing along the bridle path. The other was up past the quarry, along a very treacherous road. This would take them further away from their destination, and they would have to come back on themselves at the end of this. Still, it was a route to Moorston. It was clear they hadn't decided on this either, as the small route up to the quarry, was in the centre of Friarmere. When he looked up there, he knew no one had ventured up there for weeks. They must know another way.

Michael continued to think as he walked. He looked down at their tracks, which apparently carried flat through and out of the village. Oh no, they couldn't be. Surely other ways were better. Wow, they must be crazy. He knew what they were planning. Michael could not believe they were using the old Standedge Tunnel. The longest and deepest underground railway tunnel in the north. Right through the Pennines built in the early 1800's. There were three train tracks and a canal route, with no towpaths. The fastest way between Yorkshire and Lancashire, by train. But no, there would be no trains there now. They would be safe from that at least.

He wouldn't have gone down there, even before the vampires. He wouldn't be surprised if there were some in there now. Michael was not aware of the whereabouts of every single vampire in Friarmere. He did not know what they would be facing in Moorston, but he got the idea that it wouldn't be something good. After all their struggles, even if they got there, they would find out that Norman had another sibling that lived over there.

Michael hadn't met Len, but Norman seemed to talk about him with affection – very different from his mad sister, who Michael had still not met face to face.

He wasn't close enough to The Master to ask what it was like over in Moorston. It was clear though that a *Morgan* was in charge, so it wouldn't be plain sailing when his old band got there.

After a short walk along the peaceful bridle path, following their tracks, Michael came across a very interesting find. Two of The Master's children and these really were children, dead on the path. Chopped up and dismembered. The Master wouldn't be happy about this if he knew. Two more vampire deaths for this brave group to chalk up!

No, The Master wouldn't be happy at all. Michael was though, very much. He didn't like the vampire children, they freaked him out. And these days, especially after his new career in vampire husbandry, it took a lot to freak him out. It still wasn't quite light. If they hadn't been dismembered, they most certainly would have killed him. They were uncontrollable and never followed The Master's rules, so Michael had been in danger anytime one was close. He kicked one of the girl's heads. A bit of revenge from him. Good riddance. Michael continued to walk on. He thought about the fact that every time The Master or his children had come across Wee Renee's group, they had made a loss. This didn't bode well for the future. Michael Thompson's future specifically.

For now, he didn't want to be on their side, walking through Standedge Tunnel, but at some point, soon, it would be better to be on their side. Because he was confident that in the end – they would win!

His mind drifted back to that tunnel. What if there were more vampire children in there? What if there was another Mrs White? That was another matter to consider, how many vampires might be in that tunnel from Moorston? And were they different, like Anne's offspring? Were there wild and feral children running loose in there? Barefooted and wild, like these two girls, who had never had a Mrs White to take care of them. Were there wolves, like in Melden? Hobgoblins, ghosts or demons? Who knew these days?

Michael shivered, turned around and thought about going back up to The Grange. His life was not perfect, but it was better than living on the streets, off your wits and then wandering into that tunnel. He thought they were either desperate or mad. Then he stopped and laughed. No, he would have to find out, it would bug him too much. *Just don't enter the tunnel, it's as simple as that*, he thought. He continued on his way down the bridle path.

Pat was struggling with her chilblains today, and Wee Renee had been a little worried about her coping with whatever faced them ahead. Pat was limping, and her face was full of pain. Wee Renee had approached Terry and asked him to pretend that he had noticed something was wrong but not to mention that they had spoken. He admitted to knowing nothing about chilblains or how they should be treated medically. Terry very convincingly wandered over and said that she looked a little tired and unwell. Pat openly admitted it was due to her chilblains. He offered her a course of antibiotics, but she refused them, preferring to soldier on. She did take some strong painkillers from him, however. Wee Renee thought that if she still looked the same at lunchtime, she would insist that she had the antibiotics as well.

Gary had a pair of wire cutters and used them to cut open an area on the side of the railway track, by a hedge. Sue insisted that they all remembered where it was, and when this was all over informed the proper authorities, as now the track was unsafe. The short journey down the train track was uneventful. It was clear there had been no live trains down here for a few weeks. The sun was shining, and birds were singing. The air was tingly and minty in their noses. It was a beautiful sparkly day. They got to the tunnel, it's blackness, a stark contrast to their current situation.

29 - Big Willies

The reality was worse than they imagined. The group was faced with the prospect of the tunnel, with all its immense blackness. Yes, it was light outside, it was well known that in the daytime vampires slept, and they had plenty of torches to light the way, but generally, it was a creepy place. They could see the sun creeping in on the first few bricks. These were shiny and wet. There was a lot of moss on the roof. Some of this hung down in little green furry ropes. It swung gently in the wind that blew through the tunnel. Not very welcoming at all. Behind the moss, the whole tunnel was one gaping chasm of doom.

Sally and Kathy voiced their thoughts loudly. The two sisters were sure that it would be full of rats. Sue said Basil would be able to sort that out for them, he was fully experienced in catching all forms of vermin, and this was the first time she had been pleased about that. Our Doris said she didn't know if Haggis had ever encountered a rat, but as he was a terrier he should be a ratter, so he should hold his end up too.

'That's sorted then,' Wee Renee said.

'What if there are thousands though?' Bob asked. 'A whole sea of them.'

'Shut up, Bob,' said Tony. 'People are shitting it enough, without you putting thought's in their heads.' They all laughed, including Bob.

'I for one, won't be holding back with the hairspray and the candle lighter, I am warning you. So, don't get peeed off if you see a flambéed one running past you. I'm not standing for those dirty shits on my boots,' Beverly advised them.

'Nor mine,' Our Doris said. 'These cowboys are vintage!'

'Er, Tony, just a thought, don't fire your gun at all until we are back out,' Sue said.

'Why? What if I need to?' Tony asked, very disgruntled.

'Why? Because you could bring the whole hill on top of us, if it strikes in the wrong place!' Sue said.

'Yes, she's right,' Nigel said.

'Hell, yes,' Terry said. 'That could be the end of us all,'

'Bloody hell, emasculated again!' Tony said.

'You could strike a wee girder, Tony. You must see that,' Wee Renee said.

 The group of friends still looked at the tunnel, they hadn't made another step towards it. Rick pulled Lauren towards him, his arm firmly around her shoulders and Liz grabbed hold of Andy's hand.

'I don't mind telling you, this place gives me the Willies! Big ones!' Wee Renee said ominously.

'I wish someone would give me a Big Willy,' Pat said and started laughing.

'Trust you,' said Wee Renee.

'I don't give a monkey's nuts, Rene. What if there are rats in there? Mice, spiders, bats. What if there are a couple of vampire folk in there? We're big and hairy enough to deal with anything. *They* are in more trouble than us. We couldn't have a better army to scour through that dirty hole. It will probably be a whole lot of fun. Come on you yellow chickens,' Pat said and set off.

She really was nonplussed and seemed confident. Moral was a little higher now, and they started to follow her into the tunnel. The truth was, standing still hurt her chilblains more. They would go in there sooner or later, so what was the point in delaying the inevitable. Just get on with the mangling.

It was incredibly dark inside. Worse than they had thought before. Worse than they imagined just then outside the tunnel. A couple of them put their standard torches on. The darkness seemed to absorb the light from them. It disappeared close before them. Quite ineffective. They kept looking back to the light they had left outside the tunnel. As that got further away, the atmosphere became far tenser.

Switching on their large lamps, which were very bright indeed, helped. Now just shadows were a problem. Andy had a daylight lamp, which did not seem as bright, but it would protect them more. The tunnel felt like it went on a slight incline and then a decline. But Our Doris thought this was an illusion in the dark, as she thought, the railway tunnel had to be flat for the trains.

They could see that other people had been here before this winter, from the graffiti on the walls. The only sound was their footsteps and Haggis's panting. Their eyes became large to enable to see through this ink. Twenty frightened owls in the blackness. Gary was the first to break the silence.

'This is quite an interesting place if we were ever able to enjoy it with a relaxed mind,' he said.

'I don't see how it is,' said Beverly, who had a can of hairspray and a lighter at the ready. 'This is the last place I would say was interesting.'

'Oh no, I can see what Gary means. The engineering, the graffiti, it is a hidden place. Not many sets of eyes have explored down here. It's special and secret,' Terry said.

'I agree with Beverly. It is pretty gross,' Sue said. She had been looking at the ground and noticed how wet it was on under Basil's little white feet. They were getting quite filthy, and it looked like there might be engine oil on the gravel and sleepers. She didn't want him to have to clean that off himself, so she picked him up to protect him, putting him inside her scarf. The others didn't notice, she thought they would just have to put up with the rats if they came. Her priority was Basil.

The friends saw that the last tiny circle of light from the beginning of the tunnel was about to be extinguished.

'Say goodbye to Friarmere,' Andy said, turning to the small bright circle. Everyone looked back to see a figure standing there regarding them silently. The male figure did not wave, but it was obvious that it was Michael Thompson.

'Of all the little shits. How did he find out we are here? Does he have a bungee attached to my arse?' Pat exclaimed. This was a very vivid expletive, and Terry coughed.

'That path was clear before we walked on it and I don't think he has been travelling through the tree's like the kids.' Nigel said.

'Like Tarzan!' Lauren said laughing. 'Can you imagine.'

'He's nothing like Tarzan, don't let him think that. He must have a sixth sense,' Nigel continued.

'He's bold, I'll give him that. Just standing there until we spot him,' Sally commentated.

'That's this route done with. When we want to come back,' said Gary. 'They will be waiting for us.'

'I have sworn that I am going to kill him,' Liz said. 'I tell you, I don't care what thrall he is under and whether he's got vampire blood in him like me. We've all got choices. Don't tell me that he hasn't come to a crossroads every day in his mind because I know I have.' Our Doris and Terry murmured their agreement. No-one else knew that they had urges that they had to fight. That was slightly worrying for the others. Liz continued. 'You reach a fork in the road and take the right way, the clean way, every time, or why else bother in the first place. He has chosen the dirty fork every time.'

'Dirty forker,' Bob muttered sniggering to himself.

'He doesn't have to be here. Norman wouldn't know what he was doing in the daytime. He is just a nasty little shit. He didn't have to show himself if he is spying. But he wanted to be *Mister Big Bollocks!*'

Gary wondered exactly how much Michael could see in the tunnel. They couldn't see this far into it when they were standing where he was. He had somehow followed their tracks, but did he really know how many of them were in the tunnel if the tracks were not clear? If they hadn't walked in individual lines to follow, which they hadn't, he wouldn't know if the kids were just the other side of them. He hoped this was the most obvious conclusion because if Michael realised that only three men defended them all, they would assault the mill and take them all back.

All these deaths, every bit of their time in Friarmere would have been for nothing.

Back to square one.

Setting off again, after Liz's rant, the rest of the group reflected on Michael Thompson and wondered what he was up to too. The tunnel water dripped down on them. It was quiet, foul and wet but luckily, they had yet to see a rat or a bloodsucker. But they did feel as though something was moving at the side of them on occasion. Haggis's ears did not pick up anything, and he walked happily on his lead bedside Our Doris. Sue kept hold of Basil. Along with the problem of the oily sleepers, if rats were running along the side of them, unseen, she did not want him chasing one down a hole, and then they could not get him out. She had learned from bitter experience about this with Basil before. He had been stuck on a neighbour's roof for two days once and embarrassingly they had to call the Fire Brigade out to get him down. He was apt to be very curious and got into places where he shouldn't, so she was keeping hold of him. She stuffed him into her coat when he started to struggle to get down out of her scarf. She zipped the zip up and said *no!* He seemed to understand.

A few of them started to feel quite anxious, and Laura began to feel breathless and have a tight chest. She imagined that all the ground above, was going to fall on top of her and she would be crushed.

'Isn't there a little trick you have, Our Doris?' Wee Renee asked.

'Eh?' Our Doris asked. 'For stopping hill's falling on top of you. No. Whatever gave you that idea. Have I suddenly turned into Arnold Schwarzenegger?'

'I meant, you know, your Spanish trick. That you did when we were cold, over the tops.'

'Penny's dropped. I know what you're talking about,' Our Doris said, putting her finger in the air. She cleared her throat, and her deep voice seemed to come right from her diaphragm. She started to sing her freshly imagined version of Viva Espana very loudly.

Throughout the tunnel, her voice echoed. It sounded strange and lonely. It was as if the tunnel was trying to take it away from her. Remove it from her throat. Squash and kill it. Trying to stop the light and merriment she was trying to offer. One small woman versus a cavernous black tunnel that was trying to spook them. The second party of people from Melden that had been with her that day knew what she was up to. Soon everyone joined in. The tunnel had no power over this many voices. Doing it kept them going for a short while and made them more cheerful.

The lights shimmered around in the dark, the lamps were swinging this way and that with their singing and marching through. Bob was swaying his lamp quite heartily to the song. At one point, Sally said she thought she saw a figure of a woman at the side of them. A transparent woman, but when she looked again, the woman wasn't there.

'Probably a reflection of one of us, in your retina from the lamplight,' Terry said, trying to comfort her.

'It was probably just a spirit to guide us. It will do us no harm. The latter half of this tunnel is within the Melden Triangle. You are all aware of what that means. You've got too used to being in Friarmere, where everything is normal,' Wee Renee said confidently.

'Normal!' Nigel exclaimed.

'Aye, I'll grant you that. Shall we say apart from the obvious? But we don't have an excess of ghosts, wraiths, and beasts, do we? Just the standard amount for a village.'

'Er, how many is that?' Danny asked.

'I haven't counted them exactly. I can't give you a precise figure. Maybe eighty to one hundred!'

'Say what?' Bob asked.

'And that's average?' Tony asked.

'Aye, it is.'

'And the Melden Triangle. How many does that have?' Terry asked.

'You have to understand, it's a bigger area. It might be five times bigger than Friarmere on the whole.'

'So, if it's more on average – it's more than five hundred?' Danny asked astounded.

'Aye.'

'How many?' Andy asked, with an ominous tone in his voice.

'No more than five thousand.' Wee said in a way that was supposed to be comforting. Pat sniffed.

'A bloody bucket load then Rene,' she said. This was the wrong thing to say to most of them. Rats, bats, vampires and five thousand weird supernatural creatures. As if there wasn't enough to worry about.

'There must be a few in here then, going by that then. Wanting to party,' Nigel said and laughed out loud at the thought, albeit nervously.

'What?' Wee Renee snapped, giving him a dirty look. 'It's nothing to laugh about. Mock the spirits at your own peril, Nigel. Not mine!' Pat sniffed and looked at him gimlet-eyed as she always did when anyone questioned Wee Renee's integrity.

'I can tell you tales of ghosts in this tunnel that will make your hair stand on end, and every single one of them is true!' She thundered. Nigel didn't reply, so Wee Renee continued after taking a deep breath. 'The ones currently at the sides of us aren't bad ones so carry on and just pretend you don't see them. The more that you get scared or mock them, the more they will be drawn to you, and the journey will take that bit longer. Now consider this, if the good ones are drawn to you then the bad ones come, the ones that have been murdered or seek revenge,' Wee Renee said this last bit in a quivering voice, 'they will drift along to see what the good ones are looking at. I've seen it happen.'

'Where?' Liz asked, very interested in Wee Renee's answer.

'Skegness, Perth, Stonehenge, Chester, Wilmslow and up above the Reservoir above Friarmere. Is that enough? Oh, and London, naturally.'

'Okay,' Liz replied weakly.

'And Harrogate,' Wee Renee added. 'And the Staffordshire Moorlands.'

'All right, all right, I get it, Wee Renee. I'll just act naturally,' Nigel said.

'Now I feel a whole lot better,' said Sally under her breath to Kathy.

'Likewise. Just keep your eyes on the ground. You know they are going to be there, you've seen them,' Kathy offered. Sally did this, and the first time she forgot and lifted her head, she saw something and knew that this was another one of them up ahead. Sally squeezed her lips tight and breathed through her nose to control herself, keeping her head down. She did not indicate to anyone that she had seen something again. It wasn't worth it. Wee Renee was about ten steps behind them. She never said a word until she reached the place, then said *'greetings'* very clear and loud to the area that Sally had previously seen the spook. That was clear enough to Sally that it wasn't her imagination. She could see ghosts.

Andy kept shining his daylight lamp on either side of the tunnel just in case a vampire was hiding behind a pillar, lying in wait here all along. Sometimes there were little alcoves in the walls for some reason. It would be very easy for one to hide there. He saw nothing. It looked like they were safe. But he wasn't shining it in the right place.

30 - Upside Down

They were three-quarters of the way through the entire length of the tunnel when they came across the hidden vampires. They had not seen them as that they were hanging from Railway Struts above them. This was at the cathedral junction of the tunnel and very high. The lights only illuminated the tunnel's diameter, and it wasn't until they entered the grand junction, and the roof immediately became higher that they realised it was there. By then it was too late.

A female vampire swept down grabbing Sally around the shoulders. She bit down on Sally's neck. The whole act took a maximum of five seconds. The rest of the group started screeching in panic. Their worst fears had been realised.

Pat immediately went for the vampire with the poker. She whacked hard on the back of the vampire's head, grabbing fistfuls of the draping, tattered clothes that the attacker wore. Of course, this vampire had no joy biting down on Sally's neck anyway, and all of them wore their special secret protection, thanks to Bob!

The vampire started screaming she thrashed about in pain holding her mouth, and the back of her head. Black blood coursed down splattering the railway sleepers beneath them. Kathy pulled Sally, who was gasping in fright and pain, away from the thrashing vampire.

About six of the group joined Pat on the attack, while the others looked around for a second creature. They were never that lucky that only one attacked them. They seemed to be pack animals. They all started to beat the beast, who flinched with every blow. She dropped down finally, and it was revealed to be Karen, Colin's wife, known to many of them. Before the invasion of Friarmere, by Norman, she had been a mild-mannered florist. Now the vampire Karen had killed many people, and this had been the ideal place to hide after Colin had been slaughtered two nights ago. How strange that he was the first vampire to try out the mighty brass neck and just by chance, his wife, hidden here underneath a great hill was the second.

Karen had lived here all her life and knew there were very few exits from Friarmere. Someone would come along sooner or later, and they had. They were the very people that Karen wanted to see. For a short while, she thought that some evil god must be watching over her!

The size of the group had surprised Karen, and she had become overwhelmed. When she had swung forward to attack the first person she saw, after hearing the voices, a lovely fresh young woman, she had imagined that there were about three of them. She fancied her chances with that many. Karen had no idea that there were eighteen humans and two animals to tackle. Way too much for one vampire.

Now it was the humans turn to be surprised as three other vampires dropped down to attack them. Andy tried to hit one of them, but this meant that his daylight lamp fell onto the floor and just shone on a railway sleeper at the front of the fighting, which was no use to anyone.

The battle began in earnest, but this meant that lights shot about the tunnel with their actions. This was less than useful as apart from not having them focused on their actions, it also meant that the beam occasionally caught someone in the eye, which blinded them. Their shouts echoed as they struggled to see who they should fight and how many attackers there were. The noise was deafening.

Pat was still pummeling Karen with her poker instead of poking her. It seemed that Pat's default fighting style was beat rather than stab. Nigel rushed forward with one of the stakes they had made from the pallets. He plunged it straight through Karen and out the back, surprised at how soft she was. The vampire dropped to the floor immediately, and now they only had three to deal with. Surprisingly that was a quick dispatch.

One of these vampires was a man and naked which they found quite terrifying. No one recognised him. But he was white, cold and his skin was on the road to transparency. They wondered what his game was. What had possessed him to be like this? How long had he been down here? He had no protection over his heart or anywhere else. He was nevertheless vicious and not worried about his nakedness whatsoever. He seemed to be very agile and evaded them by running up the tunnel walls.

Although many of the vampires could run up walls, having a sticky kind of grip and confusing the laws of gravity, nobody from this band of rescuers had seen them do this. Of course, Norman had been doing it for hundreds of years. Nightly he travelled over the rooftops of Friarmere, hanging by his feet from the gutters, looking through windows, where people thought they were safe with his red eyes. Adam was also another climber, but currently, he was using this ability on the side of the good.

The heroes were so shocked to see this vampire slither naked up the wall that they stood motionless, taking in the sight. Never had they imagined that this was possible.

'Shit!' Rick said. Gary dry swallowed. This told him even more about how far away these creatures had evolved from the humans they had once been.

These tunnels were made for vampires, and they knew them well. The humans were on their territory now. They were many feet underground, basically subterranean even though in reality they were at ground level. The humans were nowhere near any natural light source, in an enclosed space with three supernatural predators. Ones that could crawl up walls.

Our Doris snapped out of her trance and was trying to catch one of them with her sword, but the light kept glinting off it and blinding everyone. However, the light brought them to attention too, and the battle resumed. She was wielding her sword this way and that. It seemed to be catching every beam of light and not in a good way.

'Put the sword down, Our Doris. I can't see bugger all. It's like you are fighting with a disco ball,' Andy shouted. She was most put out about this. Wee Renee's machete was the same. This cast broad patterns of light around the tunnel and was very distracting. Again, this was serving no purpose as the light was not on the vampires, so Wee Renee was not able to strike home with it. They all began to realise that any shiny weapon was a detriment.

Terry who had made a spear out of a dull grey hunting dagger and a brass plumbing rod ran forward at the naked vampire. He got him right in the stomach with force and impaled him into the side-wall of the tunnel, just as he was trying to climb up it again. Beverly walked towards him and lit the hairspray, the light of the fire was constant, and the naked vampire began to feel the heat.

The vampire screamed – this wasn't how he had planned it would go down. He must have been terrified and knew his end was nigh because he started to defecate. Strong brown piss sprayed the wall, while a stream of black diarrhoea sloshed casually onto the tunnel floor. At this point, Wee Renee, sick of being ineffective with her shining machete in the dark ran over to them and prepared to cut off the vampire's head. He spat in her face a second before she did it, which she found thoroughly disgusting. She removed his head from his body with one sweep of her machete.

'Aye take that!' she shrieked. As the head fell and because of his final act, she kicked his head, down the railway tunnel. Wiping the side of her face with her sleeve.

'Aye, you wee naked bastard. I've got yer,' Wee Renee shouted after the head, her Scottish accent becoming thicker.

Laura was spraying garlic spray everywhere. She had noticed that they didn't go where she sprayed, and she was forming a circle around the battle. The whole tunnel stunk of garlic, which was a relief from the smell that the naked vampire had just made.

'That's enough,' said Terry, 'you are going to waste it, Laura. We'll need it more another day.' She got out her drumsticks and went deep into the chaos, trying to slay the remaining two. Bob still kept watch walking backwards and forwards. He was sure that there would be more following these predators. The naked vampire's scream would bring them.

31 - Brass Neck

One of the two remaining vampires ran out at Tony, leaping into the air, teeth ready. The bloodsucker aimed straight for his neck and came across the group's secret weapon. He struck sideways, then immediately drew himself back away from the pain. It seemed like the edge of the brass neck had caught on his cheek, and he pulled, finally disengaging himself from the metal and releasing Tony. Again, the brass neck had saved them. This vampire obviously hadn't been watching Karen's failure earlier.

At this point, a rat ran over Sally's foot, of all people. She screamed, and the others thought that she was being attacked by yet another vampire. They turned towards her in horror, thinking that there was a fifth predator.

'What?' Rick asked.

'Rat!' Sally shouted back so that they knew what it was all about. Haggis ran up and down barking at everyone and adding to the confusion in the tunnel. His barks echoing, along with the human shouting and the screaming vampires. The two attackers that were left were excellent fighters. The first one of them had broken a couple of teeth on Tony's brass neck, and now was holding their mouth. It looked like the side of their face had been ripped slightly askew as well. The other side of their face was perfect, however, and still very lethal. This vampire was not as damaged as the heroes would have liked. They were still in the game.

The other vampire had worked out that this group of humans had something that would stop them being eaten. This one had decided that they would not be getting any dinner unless they could remove those pesky rings around the human's necks. This female was grabbing for the throats of each of them with her long fingers, trying to pull off the thing that would stop the biting.

Pat came behind this one and got to work on the back of her head with a poker. She launched herself at Pat, running past and deftly managing to rip the brass neck off her. The bloodsucker's ragged fingernails catching on Pat's Russian Hat and pulling that away too. The female vampire examined the strip of metal, it was plainly not pleasant for them to touch but didn't do as much damage to the skin as it did to their mouths.

Throwing it to the side of the tunnel, she smiled and then set her sights on Pat again. She now would have at least one meal tonight. She managed to grab Pat by the sleeve of her coat. Danny ran at her with his knife and started to stab her, twice in the side. Danny was a large and powerful man. The blade had been driven into her flesh to the hilt, and two patches of black began to form on her stained orange blouse. He seemed to have dropped the stake that he had had in his back pocket. The vampire decided that it was now time that Danny was relieved of his brass neck too, as he was closer to her than Pat and reached for it, but was only successful in grabbing handfuls of his scarf.

She would not let go and was inches away from him. Her teeth snapped, and once she had removed his protection, she was having him. Danny could smell her breath, which reminded him of shit and fish. She still held Pat by the arm of the coat and Pats big buttons would not give way no matter how much Pat pulled against her. Regrettably now, Pat had no weapons whatsoever. They were either dropped or packed on the sledge. Tony ran towards her, shooting his gun point blank into the arm that clutched for Danny's neck. This did not stop her but made her even angrier, as it had meant she had another black patch on her sleeve this time.

The male vampire with the broken teeth was holding his own against several of the gang. There were two issues. The first was that they couldn't see. He was in a very dark area of the cathedral junction. The tunnel behind him looked like it went off to nowhere and was as black as ink. They were working in about five percent of the light they needed. This vampire had dirty skin and dark clothes. He was virtually impossible to see. The second problem was that, if they did manage to see him, he would run up the walls, like a lizard, right out of their way. He was making a mockery out of them. Twelve people were trying to fight him, using up all their energy to strike and fail constantly. The group felt like they were losing. These two seemed to be unstoppable.

'All run for that one on Pat and Danny,' Gary shouted. About six of them, like a freight train, sprinted across from the climbing vampire to help their friends. They yanked the vampire by the hair, while three of them pulled her backwards. This action at least removed her from Danny. The female refused to let go of Pat, and she twisted to be within half an inch away from ripping Pat's throat out. Four of the men jumped with all their weight onto the vampire, and after this final rugby tackle, she was pushed down onto the floor of the tunnel.

'Get her down, get her head right down,' Gary shouted. Danny put his foot one side of her head, and Andy put it on the other. It was still a struggle, this one was super strong. Nigel and Terry lay on top of the female, trying to keep her as still as possible. Gary got out his nail gun and put it in her mouth, just like he had with Yvonne. He started shooting, his nails going into the railway sleepers. That pinned her down for a while even though she was still releasing a gurgling scream. She made a hideous noise now. Bob shone his torch up every tunnel out of the junction. He was sure more would be slithering along the walls towards them.

'Right, you two, carry on lying on her. We'll be back,' Gary said.

'Shut her up somehow. It's horrible,' Andy said. Terry put his hand over her throat and squeezed. At first, this only stifled the current gurgling scream, but then the pressure forced the nails further into her voice box. This silenced her forever.

Everybody else went to kill the other one who was advancing on Sue, who seemed to be protecting Basil more than herself. The monster had decided to attack now that he had humans trying to actually kill him, rather than evade and play. The male veered quickly one way, then another.

'Wait, I've got an idea, run forward a little. Let him chase you.' Laura said. They wondered what she was talking about and but didn't have a better plan in the heat of the moment, so did as she asked.

They ran forward following Laura who disappeared just around the curve into another part of the tunnel, out of the cathedral junction. This was a part they hadn't entered before. All the group followed, apart from the two holding the female on the floor, who were now left in darkness.

Five of them flanked Pat, as she no longer had a brass neck, along with her beloved Russian Hat. They would retrieve that later. As they ran over to see what Laura was on about, they saw a large circular air vent, cut into the top of the hill, underneath it was a circle that was full of light. Real daylight. The vampire pelted towards them around the corner. As he saw the light, he instantly tried to back off, knowing what they were going to do, but they were already lying in wait. Now they could see by at least eighty percent – the odds were in their favour now. Tony had a large piece of chain. The chain swung out and locked around his neck. For him, it seemed, there was no escape. Tony started dragging him screaming towards the vent. Gary and Andy grabbed the chain to help him. The vampire was inches away, and then the chain began to slip. The vampire smirked, the chain was loose, and he was going to make his escape.

Rick came behind him and with a roundhouse kick booted the monster hard in the back. This sent it flying into the light. He screamed, and flames started to lick his cheeks. All the humans ran forward in a circle to hold the creature under the vent. The exposed skin of his body and hands began to smoke. He could not get out of the light. They surrounded him holding him in there until he collapsed to the floor. His burning provided even more light in the tunnel for them to see each other.

They started to hear footsteps and shouting.

'She's up. She's come loose,' Nigel shouted. 'We can't see to get her back.' The female's running footsteps got closer.

'No problem, let her run over here,' Lauren said, peeking out of the tunnel into the cathedral junction. 'Hey, ugly, over here.' She shone her torch into the black chasm, but the female had already spotted her anyway.

The vampire started to purposely pace towards Lauren who nipped back to safety.

'Get ready, she's coming,' Lauren said. Gary and Tony pulled vampire number one away from under the vent, stamping on the edges of the silent vampire, which were now a crumbly grey, just to make sure he wasn't up for a surprise resurrection.

They stepped back against the wall, so as not to give the game away to this one. She ran around the corner, eight nails sticking out of the back of her head. Her movement was slightly higgledy-piggledy, looking a little drunk. Maybe the nails had damaged her brain, what she had left of it.

She didn't think about the light. Pat and Lauren stood the other side of it. They were much too tempting.

'Come on,' Pat said, pulling down the neck of her cowl-neck sweater, 'I'm ready and waiting, love. Take a big juicy bite of Pat.' The female ran straight through the light towards the two of them. The group all stepped forward, their hands outstretched. At this point, she started to try and run away, but they all began kicking her while she stayed in the centre. She began to burn but was having trouble screaming, as her throat had been firstly damaged by the nails, then finished off by Terry's squeezing. The light now glinted off the nails, visible through her hair at the back. Gary decided he loved that nail gun.

She reached out to them, realising how much danger she was in. It was as if she was reaching for help. Her eyes and the angle of her eyebrows seemed to say *pity me, help me, save me*. The female received none of this and now reached upwards to the daylight for help. She burst into flames with a whoosh, the humans letting go of her instantly. She dropped down like a sack of potatoes and moved no more. They had got them all.

32 - Tunnel

The group hugged each other, and collectively all took in one breath. They had conquered the threat and were now safe for the moment. Nigel and Terry had had to stay where they were, with no lamps and no idea where the others were. When Lauren had flashed her torch at the vampire, they were bewildered and were looking the other way. They didn't know which tunnel the voices came from, the junction played tricks on them. The vampire had night vision and had seen Lauren, even before her torchlight. They hadn't.

Ensuring that they shone their torches above as well as to the sides, they went back to retrieve the two stumbling blind men and Pat's brass neck, hat and poker. The vampire had thrown it a long way, and it took many minutes of searching to find. They wouldn't be leaving without it, however. The brass necks were proving to be essential. This simple strip of copper tape had saved Bob, Sally's and Tony's life for definite.

Searching for the lost items was all eating up their daylight, but finally, Our Doris found the neck and Pat wiped it on her coat and put it back on along with her hat. Pat had dropped her poker when the female vampire had grabbed her, and this was easily found as it lay crossways across one of the train tracks.

The men dragged what was left of the two vampires well off the tracks and into a kind of stairwell. When the trains came back down here, they did not want them being derailed by the rotting carcasses. They then went off to find Karen and put her with the others. The naked vampire no-one wanted to touch, but he was well away from the tracks against a far wall of the junction. For some reason, mainly because the men were dealing with dragging the other vampires away from the tracks, all the women stood looking down at him. Pat shone her torch steadily on his genitals, shaking her head.

'Well, well, well. Just when you think you have seen it all, something like this smacks you in the face!'

They set back off towards Moorston, with their torches shining everywhere, checking and listening. *Surely, they weren't so unlucky as to encounter another horde of them*, Sue thought.

'Okay, I am going to be the one to say it. Why was he naked?' Lauren asked, laughing.

'Perhaps he had been pervy in real life,' Pat commented.

'You did say you wanted a willy, didn't you Pat? If you are good at wishing for stuff, can you wish me and Sue will win the lottery?' Tony asked.

'I think I specified a big one, Tony. Wish not granted,' Pat sniffed.

'I don't see any other reason to be stark bollocks naked in a tunnel, apart from being a perv,' Andy said.

'Yeah, I mean what protection against cold, could the dirty devil have? Apart from that, not being bothered about everyone being able to see your frank and beans. It wasn't even a very big one!' Kathy said. 'I don't know what he was so proud of!' Terry cleared his throat, she had forgotten he was there. 'Sorry, Dad.'

'I don't think he was showing it because he was proud of it. But God knows what goes on in their heads. He probably thought it was ready for action. Who did he want to make sweet love to, that's what I'd like to know? If it was another bloodsucker, then I hope it worked out for him, I say.' Our Doris said. 'He was chancing it getting cut off though, with it blowing in the wind, rather than covered.'

'Who knows whether they can anyway. I mean my Dennis said, when he was on blood pressure tablets, well you know, it restricted the blood flow to the pinkle,' Pat said. Lauren had to hold both of her hands over her mouth to stifle the immediate shriek of laughter she felt welling up.

'What's your point, with the vampire then, love,' Wee Renee asked.

'Their blood's like bloody treacle isn't it? How's it getting a free flow in and out of the er…… member? How is he rising to the occasion? What do you think Terry?'

'What! How should I know? Why ask me?' Terry asked shocked.

'Because you're medical,' Pat said matter-of-factly.

'Oh, I don't know. I don't even know how their blood travels around their body, never mind down there. That's not the area of my expertise.' Terry muttered. He hoped that that was the end of the matter.

'Well it must have blood flow of some kind, or else it would have dropped off,' Pat said.

'I think he probably had lost all sensation in it anyway. Imagine if yours was cold and damp all the time, constantly been dragged against walls and railway sleepers. You've got to admit Terry, it wouldn't do it much good,' Our Doris said.

'Will everyone stop asking my opinion about the potency of vampires! I don't give a hoot!' Terry snapped. They had obviously hit a sore spot. Only Andy knew why – and that was secret. Terry's vasectomy. Before he knew it, he spoke.

'Who likes Morecambe and Wise? Andy asked.

'Shut up Andy, you fool. We're talking about willies!'

'Aye, it's a scary thing, an undressed willy,' Wee Renee said earnestly.

'Not to me, it isn't. Not in the right setting,' Pat said.

'I mean in battle. It's been a fearsome weapon for Scot's on the battlefield for generations. Just think of the wee beastie, swinging free under the kilt, catching a thistle every so often. A whole army of them waving triumphantly towards the enemy. Not knowing the terrors they face, or caring.'

Bob looked at Wee Renee, he didn't think he had heard of anything so terrible in all his life. The thought of his swinging free towards an enemy in battle was horrific. No wonder they defeated their enemies. They must have been brave, hard men. Braver than him. And he considered himself pretty much fearless after what he had done in the last few weeks. But he was keeping that well under wraps.

'Yeah, I hope we don't see a flock of them flying towards us,' Bob said swallowing.

'It's very distracting as well,' Our Doris said. 'I can't put my eyes anywhere else, only there.'

'It's the conkers,' Pat said. 'You've got the lot going on, all in motion,' Pat sniffed.

They all thought this was extremely funny, but would rather not face another naked man or woman.

Somehow, they seemed a bit <u>scarier,</u> as if all forms of normality had gone and they had reduced themselves to mere naked animals without the protection of clothes. Primordial caveman.

'We must be coming near to the end of the tunnel. We have to be,' Sue said. 'Tony, can you carry Basil for a while, give my arms a rest,' Sue said, passing Basil to Tony and fastening his coat around the cat. Tony grumbled incoherently but didn't refuse.

No-one had mentioned that he hadn't been on patrol for rats. It hadn't crossed their minds as there had only been one that had run over Sally's boot, and that had run off on its own.

The group trained their eyes on the darkness in front. They were waiting to see the speck of light that would be the end of this particular ordeal. It must be close now. They had been in here for hours.

'Not long now,' Rick said to Lauren, squeezing her hand as he held it.

'Shhh! Stop! Listen,' Wee Renee hissed.

'What is it?' Gary said. Their breaths caught in their throats, they listened. They all began to hear it.

'Feet!' Wee Renee said. 'Lots of them, running towards us.'

THE END

Until Book 4

Printed in Great Britain
by Amazon